BETTER THAN THIS

ROSE MARZIN

LUCID
DREAMER
PUBLICATIONS

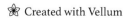 Created with Vellum

For DC, MS and KK

Acknowledgments

Too many people to name have supported the writing of this book. To my friends and family, you know who you are! Thank you for encouraging me, believing in me and putting up with me when all I could talk about was *Better Than This*.

This story would have lacked a great deal without the friendship, insight, patience and delicious cookery of Gunaseeli and Prathiba. ரொம்ப நன்றி!

Thank you to the amazing Jacqueline Abromeit at goodcoverdesign.co.uk for the gorgeous cover design and to queen-estherpublishing.com for initial editing support.

My thanks also go to SS for timely interventions and reassurance and to my wonderful sensitivity readers, who have helped to make this a much better book on several fronts. All blunders are, of course, my own.

Unpaid Pedantry Monkey provided final proofreading and a critical eye throughout. Relentlessly Supportive Owl has offered encouragement, generous criticism and creative advice - I could not have done it without you both!

I have learned from and been inspired by fellow authors and readers on Instagram, Facebook, Goodreads and LinkedIn and by podcasters and bloggers across the bookosphere. You are all amazing.

Most of all, thank YOU for reading this. If you have enjoyed it, please consider telling your friends and leaving a review.

Disclaimer

All characters and places depicted in this story are fictional. Any resemblance to persons living or dead is coincidence.

Please be aware that this story contains some material of an adult nature and is not suitable for readers under the age of 18.

Chapter One

Graffiti leapt brightly from the walls and pools of litter danced like leaves. Taamarai breathed in the fresh morning air. Nowhere looks its best on a damp Saturday morning, but after hours in the musty cab of a U-Haul, it was a relief to be here, to stretch her neck and fill her lungs. The excitement of arriving almost lifted her off the ground. This was it! The street she had been imagining for months, the building she had pictured from Realtor videos and online photos.

Her budget was tight and the area had lit up red when she looked at local crime statistics, but Taamarai hoped she had thought through everything, and the steel door to the apartment block looked comfortingly heavy. Her place was up on the sixth floor, too: her own little castle.

Figuring out which key worked the outside door took a few moments. The other three were to her apartment, a basement storage area and a roof terrace. The Realtor had cracked a slight smile as they said it.

"Welcome to Horton, Ms Calder," they said, with a tone that suggested they usually catered to people moving around a town they never left, not to people moving in. Taamarai was excited to explore. She had never even been to North Carolina until she crossed the state line a few hours earlier. For four months, she had tried her best to find out about this town-like-a-thousand-other-towns but even Horton's own municipal website strained for reasons anybody might want to visit.

At last, the door came open and Taamarai peered inside. A concrete stairwell stretched up out of sight like a dingy Escher print and a narrow passage beside it led to a scratched and dented elevator door. A slight, bracing smell of urine caught her nostrils then wafted away with the breeze from outside.

Gingerly, Taamarai stepped through and was just a second too late to stop the door crashing shut behind her. She cringed with embarrassment in the empty space, chiding herself to close it care-fully in future. Heading for the elevator, she pushed the call button and waited. Nothing happened. Taamarai shoved the button again, listening hopefully for any movement.

"It's broke."

Taamarai span around, startled by a girl, perhaps fourteen years old, who now hung over the stair rail a flight up. Her hair was dyed black and meticulously wild. She wore a large black hoodie, emblazoned with some spiky, illegible band title, and chewed gum with ostentatious ennui.

"You surprised me!" Taamarai felt flustered. "The Realtor said there was an elevator. I guess I didn't think to ask if it worked." She made herself smile, warding off a defeated feeling in the pit of her stomach.

"You're moving in?" The girl frowned curiously.

"Yep. Just arrived."

"Didn't you see when you visited?" Her expression was skeptical and superior all at the same time. She reminded Taamarai of her own youth – not so much the one she had lived but the one she had watched others living, who had seemed cooler and more confident than she was. It made her want to smile, though she feared it would appear condescending. Instead, Taamarai met the girl's eye and gave her a serious, grown-up answer that masked her own insecure sense of play-acting adulthood.

"I've just moved down from Boston. I couldn't afford a trip to come and check things out. Hiring a U-Haul has almost cleaned me out."

This provoked serious thought. "Boston, like Massachusetts? Why?"

Taamarai laughed nervously. "I got accepted on a college course down here, and I got a job as well, working in a restaurant." It wasn't a story by itself. She was too old to be a typical college freshman.

Silence from the girl. Taamarai walked towards the door, where she didn't have to crane directly upwards to talk. "My name's Taamarai. Do you live in this building too?"

"Yeah. I'm Ali." She paused. "*Taamarai?*"

"It means 'lotus flower.' My mother's from India." Taamarai was used to every possible reaction to her name and had spent her life explaining it.

This briefest of decodings was apparently sufficient. Ali nodded, then jogged down the steps, heaved the door open and looked out into the street. "That's your truck? Is it full?"

"Nearly," Taamarai sighed. "My place is on the sixth floor." She tried to stay cheerful. There wasn't much to do but get on with it.

Ali leant against the wall. She chewed her gum noisily a couple of times, then shrugged, her hands deep in her hoodie pocket. "I can help. I mean, if you like."

The girl didn't look like she was joking, but Taamarai worried that she was being set up for something. Darren told her she could be naive about people.

"I couldn't ask you to do that." It seemed a safe answer.

Ali smiled and, for the first time, looked her age, exposing the shyness that lived in every teenager. "I don't mind." She pointed upwards. "I live on the fifth floor. It's a lot of steps."

Taamarai's own smile was warmer this time and more real than before. "I'm not very motivated to argue you out of that offer, Ali. It would be very kind." She paused. "I can at least offer you pizza when we're done!" Ali thought about this, then grinned. A pact was sealed.

Without another word, Ali was out of the door, quick and silent as a cat. Taamarai followed and opened up the back of the U-Haul. It didn't seem so bad from here. It wasn't stacked to the ceiling or anything. But Taamarai knew better. There were a few bags of bedding and clothes, some mismatched pots and pans and plates but the rest.... Ali jumped up into the back, pulled out the first box and let out a surprised "Urf!" She turned to Taamarai, looking comedically betrayed. "What's in here?"

"Slide it over to me?" Taamarai invited. "It's easier to get them down this way." She held her arms out and received the box that Ali obligingly shoved towards her. "Books," she grunted in answer as she took the full weight on her arms.

Ali looked back at the boxes. "Books?"

"Most of them."

Ali seemed bewildered but slid another box gamely to the edge of the truck, hopped down and pulled it out. Clumsily, Taamarai shoved the truck door shut, and together they headed back towards the apartment block. "Off we go, I guess!"

They took to the stairs almost at a run. Soon enough, Taamarai knew they would slow down, but for now, her job had just halved, and it was good to stretch her legs. They made it all the way up without a pause.

"This is me." She put down her box again at the door to 602 and resumed the ritual of sorting keys.

"We're in 502," Ali chirped, with that wonder at the world's little coincidences, which the lucky few never got over as they aged. Ali already looked as if that might not be her fate, but Taamarai enjoyed that she still had it for now.

"I promise not to make too much noise, then," Taamarai joked. Apart from moving books around as she got settled in, she couldn't imagine causing any kind of disturbance.

Ali looked serious though. "That's good. My dad...he works late sometimes. He likes to sleep in."

"What does he do?"

Ali's face clouded over and Taamarai regretted asking.

"Ah, got it!" She exclaimed instead as the right key slid into the lock. "Come on. Let's see what I won!" Taamarai didn't have to feign excitement to draw them both away from the incautious question.

The front door opened into a short hall with room for a small bookshelf. They moved straight down it and deposited their loads gratefully in a large open-plan area that had been marked as a lounge/diner on the Realtor's floor plan. Double glass doors led onto a narrow balcony, monochrome with bird droppings but maybe big enough for some potted plants or a laundry airer. Taamarai immediately liked the space and the light.

Ali seemed perplexed as Taamarai moved gleefully from room to room. The kitchen led straight off the lounge through an arch, and Taamarai let out an involuntary squeak of delight. Everything was faded and tired, but she seemed to have acres of cupboards and sideboards. It was positioned in the exterior corner of the apartment, with two windows facing out across the city at ninety-degrees from one another. Taamarai spun on the spot, imagining gorgeous futures of cookery looking out over Horton's cityscape.

Heading back down the hall towards the front door, Taamarai inspected two bedrooms with adjacent doors. The one closest to the lounge was larger. Worn laminate flooring throughout would clean well enough, she thought. Some throws would freshen up a comfy-looking cream couch and armchair. A small folding table, two mismatched chairs, a bed in the biggest bedroom and a shabby wardrobe comprised the "furnished" part of the Realtor's listing.

"It's just like ours," Ali remarked with unconcealed disappointment, but Taamarai couldn't help grinning as she turned around and around in the living room.

"It's wonderful," she declared in a breathless whisper. "Which is your room, I mean, downstairs?"

"The small one. The other one's Dad's."

It sounded very much like it was just the two of them, but Taamarai didn't ask. Then her thoughts swung inexorably back to her stuff in the truck and her life in this apartment. She had planned it all but it was always different being somewhere. Now, she knew immediately what she wanted to do. "Ali, could you help me move the bed? I think I'm going to sleep in the smaller room, too."

Ali looked confused. "Don't you want the big one? It's just you, right?" she added suspiciously, as if a circus troupe of housemates might be waiting just around the corner.

"It's just me," Taamarai confirmed with a jolt of sadness. "My husband, Darren, can't move down here just yet." It would have been so good to be doing this with him, sharing the work, deciding together how to set everything up.

Ali was watching her intently. "That sucks. Him being away?" It didn't sound like something Ali could really imagine but Taamarai appreciated the effort.

"It does." Taamarai pushed back against the sudden sadness with determined good cheer. "But it'll be fine. He'll visit pretty often." They didn't know when, yet, but he had said it would be soon. "Anyway," – she felt herself brightening up properly – "that means I can choose where I sleep and the small room looks cosier. Besides, the bigger room, that'll be mostly for the books and a table so I can study!"

By the time they had moved the sparse furniture where Taamarai wanted it, it was heading for noon. "How about we grab something for lunch? I saw a mall down the street. Then tackle the rest of the boxes?" She paused. "And you really don't have to help me, Ali. You've already been really kind."

Ali looked around awkwardly. "But I want to. Can I?"

"Of course!" Taamarai smiled reassuringly and was rewarded with a slightly shy curl of a lip. "I just don't want you to feel like you don't have a choice. So, lunch?"

Ali smiled properly. "Yeah. There's this place. They do sand-wiches and stuff. It's better than the mall. I can show you?"

"Great!"

Ali led the way to a small deli wafting a delicious smell into the street. Its specialty seemed to be fresh soft-baked pretzels, and Taamarai picked one stuffed with fresh herb butter, the emerald green of chopped chives bright against the dark dough. As she took the bag, she could feel the pretzel, still warm. It marked the paper with melted butter between her fingers.

They sat eating in the open back of the U-Haul, and Taamarai pictured her belongings unpacked in the apartment, imagined blue lines that she had studied on animated maps as routes to work and college through a real town. Each new discovery added color and texture to the outlines of a fantasy life and she didn't notice how long they had sat in silence.

"How long have you lived here?" Taamarai asked, feeling guilty for her own distraction.

Ali shrugged. "Gabriel Heights? Three years. I mean, we've always been in Horton but...we moved a bit." She looked around. "I guess it's okay."

"Do you go to school nearby?"

"Yeah."

"What's it like?"

Ali shrugged again, that all-purpose gesture of youth. "It's okay." It was clear she didn't want to talk about school, and they had both finished their lunch. "D'you wanna get going?"

"Yeah, let's." Taamarai hopped down and they began the long trek up and down, trying to alternate lighter bags with heavier boxes of books. About an hour in, Taamarai found some of her kitchen things. Up in the apartment, she dragged out mugs and glasses and a kettle and they took a break. By the middle of the afternoon, to Taamarai's relief, they seemed more than halfway there. Without Ali, she would have been working long into the night and paying an extra day's rental on the truck.

They set out again, each with a box of books in their aching arms. Only books were left now.

"I'll race you!" Ali grinned over her shoulder.

Neither of them was good for more than a crawl but it added some fun they both sped up a little. Taamarai quickly fell behind. Ali was incredibly fit. Taamarai wondered if she did sport at the school she didn't want to talk about. As she dragged herself towards the last landing before her own, Taamarai heard voices from what had to be the apartment immediately beneath hers. She stopped, glad of a rest and not wanting to interrupt. She could make out Ali's voice easily.

"She's new. Yeah, right upstairs...didn't know the elevator's bust."

"Doesn't she have any friends who can help?"

The voice was deep, male, peremptory. Taamarai began to move again. The tone made her nervous, and she hated the idea of getting Ali into trouble on her account. Every step made her thighs ache. Taamarai came round the corner, aware that she looked tired, dishevelled and sweaty.

"Hi?" she interjected shyly.

Ali turned around and smiled, as if to say *don't worry*. It had the opposite effect.

Taamarai looked at the man in the doorway. He was barefoot, wearing sweatpants and a loose vest. She saw a tattoo on his chest – something with wings? – but it was half covered by his clothes and Taamarai didn't want to stare. He looked muscular and wiry, older or maybe more weather-beaten than she might have expected with a daughter Ali's age. His hair was cropped short and, like his stubble, was gray. He wore a silver ring in one ear and looked at her through slightly narrowed brown eyes. It was a face carved by a hard life, Taamarai thought – an interesting face, perhaps even a handsome one, if she weren't already worried by his guarded, vaguely hostile expression.

"I'm Taamarai. I'm renting the apartment upstairs." She shifted her box awkwardly and stuck out a hand. He ignored it and after a moment she had to take it back or risk dropping the books on her foot.

"So Ali told me." He looked at them both. "Pretty unprepared – moving in by yourself to a building with no elevator."

Taamarai smiled apologetically. "The Realtor didn't tell me it wasn't working."

"Ali says you just got here. Where from?"

"Boston."

"Hmm. Long drive."

Taamarai just nodded. Her arms suddenly felt very tired. "It's so kind of Ali to help me."

He glanced skeptically at his daughter. "It is." They stood again in silence for a few seconds.

"Um," Taamarai didn't want to seem like she was trying to get away but she wasn't sure how much longer she could hold the box up. "I'm very pleased to meet you, Mr...?"

He looked her up and down with studied impoliteness. "Carl Grigg."

"Mr Grigg," Taamarai nodded. "We've only got a few more boxes to go. Then I need to get the U-Haul to the garage round the block. It's got to be there by six to avoid another day's charge. When I get back, I promised Ali I'd order pizza for us. If that's okay with you? You'd be very welcome, too, of course." Taamarai could feel herself beginning to babble and closed her mouth firmly.

He tilted his head to one side and thought about this, then nodded. "Sure. Why not?" He frowned at Ali, then added with an almost imperceptible raise of an eyebrow, "No harm in meeting our neighbors."

Ali smiled at her father with what might have been relief then sighed and turned back to the stairs. The girl's arms were clearly also beginning to ache. At least she was mortal!

After dumping their boxes, they headed out again and as they got back to the fifth floor, driven now by the thought of a job almost done, Taamarai was surprised to see Carl Grigg, wearing a pair of old sneakers, pulling the door of 502 closed. Without a word, he followed them down and waited for her to open up the U-Haul again. Taamarai had assumed he was going out on business of his own but instead, he gestured to the largest of the boxes left in the truck.

"You...you don't have to. We can manage. It's only a few more." Taamarai felt herself blathering again, freshly embarrassed by her lack of preparation.

"You won't get the truck back by six if you take any more time about it." It sounded like an admonition that wasn't softened in the least when he added, "Just call it being neighborly."

"Thank you." Taamarai bit her lip, grateful, cross and upset. She hadn't asked for help or judgement. For an ungracious moment, tears of anger stung her eyes and she wished everyone would just leave her alone. It was unfair and she knew it. More importantly, between the three of them, they managed to empty the truck in two more trips. Taamarai knew she couldn't have matched the easy strength with which Carl hoisted a final, optimistically over-packed case of books. After their last trip, Taamarai looked around her new home in triumph. Ali sank down onto the deep couch.

Carl glanced around at the two of them and the boxes, then cleared his throat. "You'd best get going. Left at the end of the road'll get you to the garage quickest. And better not dawdle walking back. You may not have noticed, this isn't the nicest area."

Taamarai chafed against the tone of condescension but chose to suppose he was being helpful, still feeling guilty for her earlier ungrateful impulse.

"Of course. And again, thank you." Taamarai hesitated. "Shall I knock on your door on my way back? About pizza?"

"Sure. Why don't you do that?" He clearly didn't believe she would and gestured curtly to Ali to get up and out of the way. Taamarai felt watched as locked up and headed down the stairs. Part of her wanted very much to know what father and daughter would say about her once she was out of earshot. Part of her did not.

Chapter Two

Twenty minutes later, Taamarai was back with a jubilant grin on her face and an air of invincibility. Her legs spasmed in protest as she took the first step then complied and before she knew it, she was staring at the closed door to apartment 502. From inside she could hear music. It felt intrusive to knock, but rude not to after saying she would. Taamarai hesitated, trapped by anxiety. At last, she knocked three times, softly, as if maybe they wouldn't hear and she would have plausible deniability. It was 6:13 p.m.

To her surprise, the music shut off immediately. Footsteps bounded to the door, and Ali grinned radiantly at her above her spiked black choker. "Taamarai! Dad said you wouldn't!" Then Ali blushed and looked awkward before calling out over her shoulder, "Dad, pizza!" She turned back to Taamarai and stood aside in silent invitation.

Taamarai made her way down a hall identical to her own. Through the door of the smaller bedroom, she glimpsed the reassuring, colorful mess of a teenage girl's space. The other door was closed. In the lounge, the feeling of déjà vu was strongest, except that this room seemed even emptier than hers. Three years, Ali said they had been here....

On the table, a mostly empty bottle of whiskey, unwashed coffee cups and a few old magazines lay around. Facing a dusty television set, on a sagging grey couch in the middle of the room, Carl Grigg sat, one leg crossed over his knee, tense despite the relaxed pose.

He turned to face her. "You make it on time?"

"I did, Mr Grigg. Thank you again for your help today." She turned to Ali. It was easier to talk to her. "Do you have a favorite pizza place?"

"JB's." Ali handed Taamarai her phone, the order menu already up. "Me and Dad always get the same."

"What's that?"

"New Yorker." Ali looked shy again, as if this might seem gauche to an out-of-towner, then regained her confidence as Taamarai added a third New Yorker to their slate. Darren couldn't stand anything with dill pickles so it would be nice to indulge. Taamarai flicked through the rest of the menu.

"Do you want some soda and ice cream, too?" She was starving.

Apparently so was Ali, who waited patiently as Taamarai entered her payment details.

"Should be ready in twenty minutes," Taamarai reported, at last.

Ali took her phone back then fixed Taamarai with a look of sudden and anguished concern. "Wait, shouldn't we be up at your place? That's how you do moving-in parties, isn't it? Sitting around on boxes?"

Whatever movie or TV show she had seen, Ali seemed struck by the realization that they were in a moment and doing it wrong.

"Well," Taamarai smiled. She *did* want to be up in her apartment, if only because it was hers, and she wanted to start feeling at home there. She also thought of Carl Grigg, sitting behind her, no doubt keen to stay where he was. "I mean, yeah, but I don't have anything unpacked. Plates, cups...."

"That's okay. We can bring some, right, Dad?" Ali insisted, almost pleading.

Reluctantly, Taamarai turned around. He was staring at her, again through narrowed, evaluating eyes. Then, decisive and smooth, he unwound from the couch and headed to the kitchen. "I guess we will."

Ali headed after him and for a few moments, Taamarai stared around the living room alone, listening to Ali picking out what they would need. The walls were completely bare. She noticed clothes on the floor in one corner, cigarette burns on the table and felt a pang. In such a bleak space, Ali's enthusiasm and cheerfulness seemed tougher somehow.

Father and daughter emerged shortly with a stack of assorted plates and bowls and a handful of cutlery. Upstairs, Taamarai again enjoyed the feeling of opening up her door, learning the particular knack to it. Turning on her light, she walked into the landscape of boxes.

"Please, come in. Make yourselves at home. Let me get you some water."

"Lot of stuff you've got," Carl observed tonelessly.

"It's all books!" Ali murmured softly.

"Well, not quite all books. But mostly," Taamarai added, seeing his eyes glide over the room once again.

"Your husband not coming down too?" he asked, still standing. So Ali had told him that much.

"No, Mr Grigg. Not right away."

"You can call me Carl." It was an instruction rather than an invitation. "Not right away?"

"Yes. It's his work. We don't know exactly when."

He took this in with cold eyes and a neutral "hmm." They all fell silent.

"Food's here!" Ali's phone buzzed in her hand and she passed Taamarai her share of the crockery with a look equally excited and relieved. "I'll get it!" Ali was out of the door in moments, her footsteps loud on the stairs.

Taamarai began laying the table, aware that it was mainly something to do, but the quiet was still awkward. "Your daughter's a lovely young woman," she said at last. "I don't know how I'd have managed today without her."

She shouldn't have left her packing to the last minute or set off so late from Boston the day before. Darren had looked up some great tips on packing up for a house move, but she hadn't had time to follow them. Taamarai was nearly overwhelmed again by the feeling that she was out of her depth. She caught Carl's eye. "I would have done." Her own determination surprised her. "Managed, I mean." She smiled again. "But Ali made it much easier."

Before he could say anything, footsteps echoed in the hall, and Ali wafted in with a stack of boxes, bottles and tubs. Taamarai took the ice cream to the kitchen then they sat together around the table, Taamarai perched on a pair of boxes and the other two on the chairs.

"You said your name was Tamara. Tamara what?" Carl asked between pizza slices.

"Dad!" Ali was mortified in the way only a teenager could be. "It's *Taamarai!*" she declared, as if it were the most normal name in the world, and Taamarai couldn't help smiling.

"It means 'lotus flower,'" Ali added matter-of-factly, then looked unsure of herself. Taamarai realized that Ali probably didn't know what a lotus flower was.

"Yes." Taamarai turned to Carl, determined to help Ali out. "My mother's from South India. Water lilies are sacred flowers in India, so it's a really common name where she's from."

"Taamarai." Carl said the name slowly.

Taamarai gave Ali a reassuring smile and got one of solidarity back in return. Guessing that they'd already clocked her accent, Taamarai added, "My mother came to Britain for university. She met my father and stayed."

"India. That's so cool! And Britain. Have you been to London?" Ali sounded like she was meeting a movie star.

Laughing with happiness, Taamarai finished her mouthful of pizza. The New Yorker really was good – slightly crispy pastrami, caramelized red onions and sliced dill pickles with just a touch of sauerkraut and mustard swirled through the golden cheese. "Yes. I grew up in a city called Blackburn. It's about three hours north of London by train."

Ali had finished most of her pizza and was starting to look less ravenous. Curiosity took over completely. "You said you're going to college here. What for?"

Darren had suggested she keep it vague when people asked. They might not understand. Taamarai knew he was right. But as she thought of something vague to say, her mind skipped right to blank. She was too tired and excited, and reality was too overwhelming in its details. Taamarai squeezed her fists shut under the table, then unclenched them. "It's a catering and cookery course." She glanced around the room at her treasured books, out of sight but here, fortifying her with preserved dreams.

"I did my degree in literature but I've always loved cooking. I decided it was time to do something I different, something I was passionate about, for work."

Ali looked confused and awestruck all at once. "Your degree? Like, at college?"

Taamarai nodded. "Yes. When I was eighteen. That's when I first came to the US. A bit like Amma and my Dad, I guess. I met my husband and stayed." She smiled fondly at the memory, her own love story, just like her parents' happy marriage.

"In Boston?" Ali seemed to be trying to keep up with this alien story of two degrees and foreign climes.

"Yes, but we've moved around a bit since then. We only went back to Massachusetts a few years ago."

"How come?" Ali asked.

"Work, mainly." This time, Taamarai thought her smile must look tired. She certainly felt tired. "I've done this and that. In publishing mainly, and some tutoring. Lots of short-term contracts. Nine months here, a year there. Sometimes I could work from home, but a lot of the time, we'd have to move."

She looked out of the window at the skyline of the city, silhouetted in the sunset. For a moment, it blended in her mind with every other city. So many moves. The stress each time a contract ticked towards its end. Finding somewhere new, sorting out the lease, setting up the bills....

Catching sight of her reflection in the glass, Taamarai looked beyond it, to a high building, probably miles away, with blue and green strips of light around the top. This wasn't any other city or every other city.

Taamarai looked back at Ali and lifted her chin. "But not this time. I'm planning to be here for as long as I can keep cooking." She raised a glass of soda in a mock toast.

"Must've been hard on your husband, you moving like that." Carl had leant back in his chair, holding his glass where it rested on the table, one leg stuck out in front of him. A man who owned space.

"Yes, it has been." Taamarai looked down into her glass. It had been hard for her, too. When she tried to talk about that, though, it never came out right. It had become easier instead just to talk about imagined futures when they were settled and happy, but that stressed Darren out. It was as if they were constantly living in the future, never in the moment, he said. So she had put down those futures. Somehow, though, that hadn't made the present easier to discuss.

Taamarai knew her current plan was a long shot. It likely sounded crazy outside her head. She couldn't help hoping, though. "But once I'm settled here and he can join me, we can think about putting down roots. I'm lucky that Darren's so supportive. He's always got my back, you know?"

Carl eyed her for a while, then looked around skeptically. "Well, I doubt it'll be here." He looked admonishingly at Ali. *Don't expect this one to stick around.*

"Why's that?" Taamarai couldn't help sounding a little hurt.

"I guess you couldn't see online or wherever you found out about this place. Like I said, this ain't exactly the nicest part of town. I'm sure it looked just the right price, but I doubt you'll like the neighborhood." He stared her in the eye. "You'll be moving on soon enough."

Taamarai looked around herself. Maybe he was right. *He* certainly wasn't the sort of neighbor homestyle blogs were full of. She thought of the apartment downstairs with a shiver. On the walk back from the garage, the streets seemed more rundown than she'd expected. Darren had said the same from the photographs. He'd been worried about her. Couldn't she commute just a bit further and be somewhere that looked a bit nicer? Couldn't they just pay a bit more? He'd practically begged her. But it wasn't *their* money. It was *her* money. Joshua's money. And it was *her* decision. Taamarai's spine straightened.

"Maybe you're right, Mr Grigg. Carl." Ali looked suddenly tense. Taamarai guessed that people rarely disagreed openly with her father. "I've got used to moving around, so I never say never. But for now, I'm here to stay, and I've found the place very neighborly so far." She smiled at Ali and the girl smiled back, another tiny cementing of their friendship. "Time for ice cream!" Taamarai broke the awkward silence and headed for the kitchen.

As she got back to the table, Taamarai felt exhausted. The long day and the weeks leading up to it hit her like an avalanche. She sat down and let Ali take over dishing up dessert. Her smile felt listless but it had become quiet again. She rallied one more time. "How about your school, Ali? What subjects do you like?"

Ali was willing to talk about school this time round. Taamarai was glad to have earned that much trust. "It's okay, I guess." Ali thought a bit harder. "I guess I like lit." She smiled shyly at Taamarai and at the boxes of books. "I'm good at math and French, too. My teachers say so."

"A big help that'll be." Carl muttered, then turned to Taamarai, inviting her disagreement and challenging her to do something about it.

She just stared back. "What is it that you do?" She knew she shouldn't ask. In the corner of her eye, she saw Ali freeze.

He paused, clearly choosing his next move. "This and that. Never needed French, that's for sure."

Taamarai couldn't be bothered to fight. "Well, I can't say I've ever needed French, either." She laughed, and he responded with an expression that might have been a shadow of a smile or just disdain. Taamarai couldn't just roll over either. "But life isn't all about what we need." She looked at him this time, seeing if he would push back. He just shrugged and Taamarai, too, was ready to quit.

"Thank you both for coming over. I've still got to make up a bed before I can sleep and I'm exhausted." She grinned over at Ali. "I don't have your energy anymore. I'm not sure I ever did. I hope I'll see you around, though, Ali. And if you ever need some books to borrow," she gestured around, "just come by and see me. And let's do that movie night."

It was a conversation that had carried them through a good few stair runs. They didn't have many films in common but seemed to like some of the same sort of stuff. Mostly, Taamarai hoped her message had been clear: Ali was welcome, Taamarai would be pleased to see her, and she didn't hold her father against her.

Ali grinned back. "How about tomorrow?" Just as quickly, she looked down, exposed by her own enthusiasm. "Or, you know, any time." She scuffed her foot on the floor and hunkered deep inside her oversized clothes.

Taamarai just smiled back, delighted by it all once again. Her unsteady emotions were another warning of impending collapse. It was time to get to bed.

"How about Wednesday? It'll give me some time to get some stuff cleared away so we can sit properly. And to get some food in. Maybe I can cook for us?" She looked at Carl as well because it would be rude not to.

"That'd be real nice." He sounded dismissive.

"Yeah. That sounds cool." Ali at least looked pleased, but she was also getting the hint and gathered up their kitchenware as she spoke. Carl picked up his glass and headed for the door behind his daughter.

"Welcome to the neighborhood, Taamarai." He was careful over her name but got it right, staring intently at her as he said it.

"Goodnight, Carl, Ali."

Taamarai closed the door and turned with a weary smile of satisfaction to her cardboard world. Everything considered, it had been a much better day than she'd expected.

Chapter Three

Streaming morning light woke Taamarai. She would need to get thicker curtains so she could sleep in after late nights at her new job. There was time for that, though. For now, Taamarai felt better rested than she had in months, maybe years.

She rolled over and stretched out. It was strange, waking up by herself. Sometimes she lay in after Darren had gotten up, if she'd slept badly or stayed up working, but this felt different. The sheets on the other side of the bed were crisp and chill as she extended her limbs outwards. The pillow was plump and untouched.

Taamarai missed Darren. It would have been fun picking out curtains and looking for new furniture with him. He hated being woken by the light. She realized how odd it would be having nobody to talk to as she ate breakfast. The enormity of what she was doing loomed around her, but the sunlight pierced it through and as she looked around again, the room already seemed a bit like home. Their home. She would imagine Darren there with her and make it lovely for when he could join her.

After lazing around a little longer, Taamarai got up and wandered to the kitchen in a vest and shorts. She was usually careful about dressing as soon as she got up. After eleven years together, Darren's attraction to her was undiminished and a regular reminder of how good they still were for each other. Working three jobs and keeping house, though, it wasn't always her top priority in the morning and she hated to disappoint him. Getting dressed quickly just helped keep her focussed.

A mirror attached to the back of the bathroom door torpedoed her buoyant mood. Catching sight of herself, Taamarai was drawn to her thick thighs, podgy stomach and saggy arms. She made herself look at the woman in the mirror. Thirty-three, short and overweight. Then she kept on looking. Once, when she was feeling too low to do anything but trawl the internet for stuff about feeling low, she'd read on a blog that it could help.

Taamarai started at her feet, which glinted with silver rings – two each on the second toe of each foot. Darren didn't like them. He worried they would snag on the bed linen. She had insisted though. Her mother wore them. They were the mark of a married woman. Growing up, she had loved seeing them as her mother moved around the house barefoot or went out year-round in sandals. Today they made her smile.

She worked her way up. She didn't like her legs but had to admit that her figure went in and out in all the right places, even if she was carrying too much weight on it. Her skin was smooth and dark, not as dark as her mother's, but almost, with that same velvety softness. Taamarai got as far as her face and looked herself wryly in the eye. "It could be worse," she told herself, with a smile that showed off her teeth. They were okay, too.

As a child and a teenager, she had hated her round, chipmunk cheeks and thick eyebrows. Her hair was a coppery reddish color and always wild without being curly. Her mother had spent hours brushing it when she was little, plaiting it into short braids that never got any longer and came undone by the end of the day. Like a scarecrow, Taamarai had moaned.

Like the goddess Kali, her mother had chided with sparkling eyes and a shake of her finger. Kali, who wasn't afraid of anything, she would whisper as she stroked her daughter's untamable hair. Her mother was Christian, but had told Taamarai and her brothers stories of the temples she had grown up around, and Taamarai felt her mother's fierce love in the memory.

Her hair was still wild, but these days it gave her confidence as well as grief and she could see that she had grown into those chubby cheeks. Her face might always be round but she looked friendly and approachable. Like somebody who could welcome people one day into her own restaurant, she told herself.

After a minute or so, Taamarai shook her head self-consciously. She felt ridiculous but had to admit that she also felt better. Wandering around the apartment again, from one room to the next, the place still smelled unfamiliar, but the morning light was stunning. In the kitchen and living room, sunshine poured through the windows and balcony doors. It was Sunday, and she didn't need to be at her college course or her new job until later that week. She could sense her body and mind relaxing.

Today she would empty boxes and buy groceries. Tomorrow maybe she could find a secondhand furniture shop that made deliveries. In the kitchen, she drank a glass of water, resigned to skipping breakfast. She didn't have any food anyway, but even if she did, she had no idea where her pans or plates were. The sea of boxes seemed daunting again.

It was her fault, of course. Darren had given her loads of useful tips on how to organize and label the boxes but she had been in such a rush, finishing up work ahead of her final paychecks. It was just another thing that hadn't got done quite right. But it had got done, she reminded herself firmly.

From the top of her rucksack, where Taamarai knew she could always find them even if everything else went to hell, she retrieved shampoo, conditioner and a towel. With every step and bend, her muscles ached from the gruelling workout of the day before, but it was a satisfying ache. With a little trepidation, she tested the shower. A good shower could make an apartment. A bad one.... Taamarai's face split into a huge smile as water sprang forcefully from the showerhead and ran hot almost immediately. A good omen.

Fresh out of the shower, Taamarai pulled on some clean clothes and put her hair up in a turban with the towel. As she meandered into the lounge she heard a knock on the door.

"Who is it?" Peering through the spy hole, she saw a shy, slightly smiling face.

"Ali?" Taamarai pulled open the door with relief and surprise. Ali's hair was wet too, hanging around her shoulders. She clutched a bottle of milk and a box of cereal and looked uncertain.

"Yesterday, I didn't know if you'd got any food." She held out her offerings.

"Ali, that's so sweet of you. Thank you!" Taamarai's stomach rumbled.

"There's coffee downstairs, too."

"Oh, that's okay. I...."

"It's okay." Ali looked a little disappointed at the refusal.

Taamarai really did want coffee. "Are you sure?"

Ali smiled properly and nodded. She handed Taamarai the milk and cereal and disappeared, reappearing a few minutes later with a mug of hot coffee, just as Taamarai was digging out her bowls and spoons from a lucky guess among the boxes. Shyly, Ali also held out a crumpled, mostly empty packet of sugar. "I didn't know if you...."

"Thank you. Not with coffee, but this is so thoughtful. Do you want something to eat with me?"

"No," Ali glanced back towards the stairs. "I don't really do breakfast much. But Dad said, you know, that you probably didn't have anything in." Ali said it with a slightly apologetic, conflicted expression. "I know he.... Well, he can be a bit... says I should take care of myself, but he...."

She trailed off and handed Taamarai her coffee with a shrug. He'd still told her to bring the food and coffee.

"It was very kind of him. I'll thank him when I see him."

Ali seemed to want to change the subject, and Taamarai was

just a little stung at the thought of Carl Grigg telling his daughter to take food up to the flake in 602 who couldn't even sort out her own shopping. He probably didn't say flake, but she could imagine his contempt, even if not his exact expression. "What do you do with yourself on Sundays around here?" she asked instead.

Ali shrugged again. "Not much." She looked around. "I could help you unpack?"

"Seriously? You must be bored!"

Ali said nothing and Taamarai became more serious. "I mean, sure, if you want, but only if you promise to quit as soon as it gets boring."

Ali laughed just a bit, buried her hands in her pockets and nodded, then turned as if to go, muttering, "I'll be downstairs when you've had breakfast."

"Ali, stay if you want. I'd like the company." Taamarai gestured to the table and they both sat, Ali gazing at the boxes while Taamarai ate and sipped her coffee. After a while, Taamarai ventured, "Your dad's right. I do need to get some food in. If you really don't have anything you'd rather be doing, maybe you could show me where the local markets are?"

Ali nodded shyly. "I can do that. We need some stuff too. I mostly do the shopping," she added and looked slightly proud of herself.

"It's just you and your dad?" Now it seemed like an obvious thing to ask, where before it might have been intrusive.

Ali nodded, looked at the floor again, and then back up with a defiant glare. "Just the two of us. Mom left. When I was little." She hesitated. "Can't miss what you've never had, Dad says. And I can look after myself."

Taamarai just nodded back. She wasn't about to argue with the girl. Besides, what would she know? Her home had been loving, stable—all the things Ali looked very much like she might be missing. Instead, she said, "You and your dad must be close, then?"

Ali scuffed at the floor with her toe and slumped a bit further into her chair. "Yeah, I guess."

"That's good." Taamarai wasn't sure she could commit to more, and Ali still looked like the subject hadn't changed far enough.

"Maybe I could cook something tonight? If you're helping me out, I mean. Have you ever tried South Indian food?"

Ali looked wary and impressed at the same time. "No. I mean, I don't think so. Can you cook it?"

"Sure." Taamarai considered the real possibilities in front of her. "Well, I can if we can find some fresh vegetables."

"There's some at the mall. But not that much." Ali suddenly looked hopeful. "There's this farmers' market on Sundays I've heard about." Her face fell. "It's a few miles. You have to take the bus." Taamarai's instant enthusiasm for this plan took Ali by surprise and within seconds, they were both interrupting each other happily as they talked plans, buses, vegetables and cookery.

By evening, their chatter had found a comfortable groove. Most of Taamarai's boxes were still packed, but the farmers' market had proved quite the find. Fresh, interesting and not too expensive. Ali had shown Taamarai the local stores and helped her heave several bags of rice, canned goods and spices up the stairs. They had found a thrift store that would drop off six bookshelves, a hall table, two nightstands, three more mismatched chairs for the dining table and a smallish television screen on Wednesday morning, just in time for their film night, which was now a very concrete plan, even if they didn't know what they were going to watch. And Taamarai was pretty sure she could still clear her overdraft before the end of the month. A few times, Taamarai had wondered if Carl knew Ali was with her, but Ali didn't seem worried. Maybe she had texted her father. A stereotype of her age, Ali's phone rarely left her hands.

Throughout the day, Taamarai had felt her own phone vibrate in her pocket, always when her hands were full or when she and Ali were talking about something. It was nearly seven before she had a chance to look and she shrivelled up with instant guilt. Darren had been messaging since nine that morning without a single reply since her good morning text letting him know her plans for the day. She saw four missed calls. His latest message was displayed on the screen.

> Tam, Im worried. Let me no ur ok. I luv u.

Ali saw Taamarai's face change. "You okay?"

Taamarai looked up and tried to smile even though she felt tears in her eyes. "Yeah, everything's fine. Ali, do you mind if I make a call? It's my husband." She looked back at her phone nervously. "I can still make us some dinner. I'll only need half an hour or so?" She knew she was being unfair. Darren deserved more than half an hour. She needed to eat, though. And she had promised Ali she would cook. As so often, she had to let somebody down.

"Oh. Yeah. Sure." Ali looked awkward again, clearly thinking she had outstayed her welcome. "Don't worry about dinner." She was turning to go when Taamarai stopped her with a touch on her arm.

"Please come back, Ali. Darren has just got himself a bit worried. And I really would like to cook with you." The prospect brought a genuine smile back to her face. "It'll be my first time using the kitchen. I'd rather do it with company."

Ali looked anxious but pleased. "You're sure?"

As Taamarai nodded, Ali added cautiously, "And is it okay if I take some back for Dad? I usually cook for us."

"Yes, of course!" Taamarai smiled broadly, her best restauran-teur-in-practice smile. "Or he can come and eat with us if he wants." Taamarai hoped he didn't but also knew that Ali would appreciate the offer. She hadn't talked much about her father over the course of the day, but he was present as much in what she didn't say as what she did. Ali looked delighted, then uncertain.

"It's fine for you to take something for him if he prefers," Taamarai added easily. Maybe that would be best for all of them.

"Thanks." Ali was about to go again when she turned back. "I... I'm glad you moved in." Then she scurried off.

"Me too." It was true and should have been a joyful thought, but as the door closed Taamarai's guilt over Darren consumed her again. She hit the call button and he picked up on the first ring.

"Tam. Thank God! What's happened?"

"Hey. Nothing. I'm sorry. It's been a busy day."

"You could have messaged me."

"I know, I'm sorry. I just got caught up. It was a long day yesterday." Right after Carl and Ali had left the night before, she had rung Darren, only meaning to say goodnight and they had ended up talking for more than an hour.

"And we had a lot to get done. I needed to get some shopping, then I found a furniture shop. And the girl from downstairs, Ali, who I told you about, she's been helping me, so I've been talking to her. I just didn't hear the phone going off." Taamarai felt like she was babbling excuses.

"It's okay, Tam," Darren's voice was soft with forgiveness. "I understand. I know you get caught up in stuff and lose track of things." He paused. "I'm really glad the neighbors are being friendly. Are you sure this girl is okay, though?"

"What do you mean?" Taamarai was mooching around in the kitchen, trying to find where Ali had put her vegetable knife and realized that she must sound like she wasn't listening. "Why wouldn't she be okay?"

Darren hesitated.

"Well, she was around all day yesterday. Then she spends all day with you today. I don't know. It seems a bit much."

"Darren!" For some reason, his suspicions annoyed her. "I'd still be emptying the damn U-Haul without her. God knows what I'd have found to eat last night, or this morning, and I'd have spent all day looking for somewhere to buy fresh vegetables! Darren," Taamarai lightened her tone with some effort. She wasn't being fair. He was just looking out for her. "She's a great kid. Sure, maybe she's a bit bored but...."

Taamarai thought of telling Darren about Carl and the relationship she was beginning to discern between father and daughter. They both liked people-watching and he liked to know who she hung out with. She didn't, though. It didn't seem quite right when he was obviously so worried. Taamarai had known he would be but hadn't realized how bad this would all be for him.

So, instead of talking about all of the new things going on, she told him about the recipe she was cooking. It was one she had made before and she knew he wasn't really interested – Darren wasn't much of a foodie, though he liked what he liked – but he seemed soothed by the normalcy of it. After a while, she said, "Look, Darren, Ali's coming back soon to have dinner with me. I'm going to have to go."

For a moment he didn't say anything and Taamarai felt a physical pain at being so far away. The artificial closeness of chatting while she cooked had shattered in their silence.

"Tam, I'm sorry." He sounded on the verge of tears. "You're all alone there, and it's my fault. I know I'm not good enough for you. I'm so sorry, babe."

"Darren," Taamarai felt her own tears, too. "*I'm* sorry, Darren. I'm sorry I forgot to message you today and that I don't have time this evening. You're the best thing that's ever happened to me. You know that. It's just, I'm tired. That's all. It'll be better when you get here." Taamarai stopped abruptly. She hadn't been going to mention it and wished she hadn't.

"Yeah," he said after a few seconds. "I don't know when that'll be, though, Tam. You know it's difficult."

"I know. I know. I didn't mean it was easy. I know you'll come when you can." She was almost relieved to hear a knock on the door then felt awful for her reaction. "Look, Darren, Ali's here. I'll have to go. I love you."

"I love you too, Tam."

As she headed for the door, Taamarai swiped at her cheeks. She had only cried a little. It wouldn't show. And at the idea of dinner with company, she found herself cheering up. "Hey! Come in." Ali was alone and Taamarai hoped she didn't look too glad.

As soon as the door was closed, Ali halted. "I'm not driving you nuts, am I?"

Taamarai wondered anxiously if Ali had overheard her on the phone before remembering that Darren had questioned why Ali was hanging around so much, not her.

"No, not at all. Why would you think that?" She beckoned Ali in. "Come on, come and be in the kitchen with me. I've got a pot on the stove."

They stood side by side, and Taamarai handed Ali a paring knife and a couple of carrots. "Could you peel these for me?" Once Ali had got herself set up with a plate and begun peeling slowly and clumsily, Taamarai glanced sidelong at her. "Now, what makes you think you're driving me nuts?"

Ali shrugged, her confidence returning. It was clearly now uncool for Taamarai to ask, but she didn't withdraw the question and Ali didn't take long to crack. "Just, Dad said I should stop bugging you. That you must be sick of me already."

Taamarai laughed and carried on stirring various pans. "I'm sure he meant well. He seems like a guy who keeps his own company. How about this, if I get sick of you, I'll let you know? Until then, please assume I enjoy hanging out with you."

She turned properly to face Ali. "I said last night that I'd moved around a lot and that's true, but I've never done anything like this – moving job, turning up somewhere new all on my own. I've always had Darren with me before when we've moved. It's been scary at times, thinking about it. I'm really pleased to have met you, Ali." The thought flittered through Taamarai's head that she had once flown right across the Atlantic on her own with just a suitcase of clothes and a head full of dreams, but that person seemed a faraway memory.

Ali nodded, looked down and seemed very focussed on preparing carrots for a while.

"Are we putting some food away for your dad?" Taamarai asked once everything was nearly ready.

"Oh, um, he said I should stop bugging you, but if you can't tell me to get lost yourself, he doesn't see why he should pass up a free meal." She looked nervous again. "He says he'll come up when we're ready."

"That's great." Taamarai put on her most cheerful expression. It wasn't Ali's fault. She could hear the words in Carl's voice and sensed that Ali was trusting her just a little further by repeating what he'd actually said instead of something friendly and polite that maybe somebody else's dad might have said in the same situation.

Half an hour later, they sat back around her table, Taamarai again perched on a stack of boxes. Carl had brought two beers up with him, and she accepted one gratefully. He, in turn, had been surprisingly complimentary, in a gruff way, about the coconut rice and dal with light carrot *poriyal*. He hadn't said much else except to ask about their adventures. Just enough to set Ali off with a potted and slightly helter-skelter recounting.

"Six bookcases?" he finally asked.

"It should be enough." Taamarai smiled. "It'll be good to get them all out again. It didn't make sense having books all over the place when we were moving so much, so most of them have been in boxes for the last few years." She'd gotten them out in each new apartment until Darren told her gently that it was okay. She didn't need to. It only made it harder packing up again.

"Sure." Carl took a slow swig of beer and seemed to be weighing something up. Before he could ask whatever it was, though, Ali jumped in.

"What are they all about?" She looked mystified.

At this, Taamarai let herself laugh right out loud. "That's the thing about books. They can be about absolutely anything." She became a little more serious, caressing the boxes with her eye. "Everything. A lot of them are recipe books, but...." Suddenly she stood up and opened the nearest one, lifting out a motley assortment of poetry books and battered novels. One of her college boxes.

"There. Try this one." She put a tatty paperback into Ali's hand. "You can have it. It looks like that because I've read it so often. I'll be interested to know if you enjoy it." Ali stared at the book reverently.

Taamarai was about to get up when Carl asked, "Nothing for me?"

He was holding his empty beer bottle in one hand, eying the scene a little suspiciously. Taamarai couldn't tell if he was joking or spoiling for a fight but felt certain it was one or the other. He'd seemed to grow more uncomfortable throughout the meal and she felt her nerves jangling. The only thing to do was smile.

"What do you like to read?"

"What makes you think I do?" He glared back at her.

She kept her smile on. "If you didn't, why would you want a book?"

He let out a dry sound, possibly a chuckle. "I like useful books. Something practical I can do something with."

Taamarai remembered his comments the night before about learning French and felt certain he was thinking about them too. She was even more sure he was trying to antagonize her, and her anxiety gave way abruptly to weary annoyance. After her miserable chat with Darren, this could have been just a simple, fun dinner.

"Like propping up a table or starting a fire?" she asked, a little sharply, and felt the temperature drop.

His eyes narrowed and his voice became very soft. "I'm no idiot. Whatever you think."

Taamarai stared back. Only their second meeting, and she was already getting tired of the sudden jagged edges, that feeling of walking along a cliff-edge in the fog. She glanced around and saw that Ali was frozen, evidently waiting for something to kick off and wanting it not to. When Taamarai replied, her own tone was several degrees cooler than it had been. "You don't know what I think about very much at all. If either of us is making assumptions, I don't think it's me."

Before he could say anything else, she turned and dragged a box from the corner of the room, forcing a look of cheerfulness back onto her face and wondering exactly what impulse was moving her. It wasn't a plan, at least not a conscious one. She rummaged among the hardbacks, grateful that she could remember packing this particular box. A distinctive orange sticker clung to one corner. Near the bottom, she found what she was looking for and turned around on her knees with a mock bow. "Here you are."

Carl took the large volume from her with an outstretched arm, as if keeping it, and her, as far from him as possible. Carefully, he flicked it open. *"Poems of the Great War?"* He looked momentarily stalled. Whatever he'd expected – maybe a children's book or a guide to home decorating, some attempt to belittle or pander – it clearly hadn't been this.

Still kneeling beside the box, Taamarai looked steadily at him. "I wouldn't presume to know what use you might have for anything, Mr Grigg. But the men who wrote those words, they were in the middle of losing everything, even their lives. But they still wrote. I think they found their words useful and hoped they might be to other people."

He frowned and turned over another page. "Who's Joshua?" He didn't look at her this time, just stared at the paper. Ali was watching with eyes slightly too wide, unsure how any of this played out.

"My brother."

"He give this to you?"

"Yes, a long time ago." Sometimes it seemed like a lifetime ago. Sometimes it felt like yesterday.

"Won't he mind? You giving it me like this?" He sounded caught off-guard by the whole conversation, and if there was an edge to the question, Taamarai couldn't see it. Besides, what could she do except tell the truth?

"No. He won't."

"How can you be so sure?"

"Because he's dead."

He looked up then. "How?"

"Afghanistan."

"I can't take this." He snapped the book shut and held it back out to her. She didn't reach for it.

"Yes, you can. When he gave it to me, it had a use. It helped him to say goodbye. Now, when I read it, I just feel angry. It can't be useful to me anymore. Maybe it can to you."

He looked shaken, suddenly sober and poised, unsure how he had just been outplayed, but he took the book back almost casually, as if he wasn't holding it at all. "I told you to call me Carl." He turned to Ali. "We'd better get going. Let our neighbor get some sleep. Say thank you for dinner and your gift, Ali."

"Thank you." Ali held up the novel and then, with awkward spontaneity, hugged Taamarai briefly around the shoulders before stepping back and hunching into herself again.

"You're welcome, Ali. Tell me what you think of it." She turned to Carl. "And I told you my name is *Taamarai*. Goodnight, Carl. Thank you both for your company."

As Taamarai closed the door this time, she felt sadness but also relief. She had been carrying the book around for so long. This felt like some strange intervention. Her brother, helping out again, as he always had.

Chapter Four

Spaghetti with canned mackerel and spicy vegetables: quick, easy and cheap. Taamarai's first paycheck had come in and mostly gone back out on rent and stuff for college. Between class four days a week (plus assignments) and shifts in the restaurant Friday to Sunday and alternate Wednesdays, her favorite fifteen-minute economy meals were becoming staples.

It was good to be cooking for people again, though. Ali was getting over her amazement that Taamarai could apparently conjure food out of thin air and canned goods but remained impressed. Carl's methodical demolition of anything Taamarai put in front of him or sent down was a quieter source of appreciation but still satisfying. Every meal stoked the embers of the love that had drawn her out here to Horton and her college course in the first place.

Tonight, the three of them sat together around her table. The shelves had arrived and the apartment looked warm and cozy. Books, posters and rugs filled everywhere with color. Darren didn't like too much clutter and Taamarai knew she was overdoing it, but dragging her things out of boxes had felt like reuniting with old friends. Ali had helped her to put up the posters one evening, along with new blackout curtains for her bedroom and blinds in the kitchen for when the evening light lanced across the city in blinding shafts of gold.

Darren had observed, when she had been in the apartment for nearly three weeks, that Ali seemed to come by quite often. Taamarai couldn't argue. Three times that first week and three or four times a week after that, Taamarai ended up inviting her to stay for dinner, and Carl joined them about half those times. At first, her heart would sink when Ali said he was coming upstairs. It was less comfortable. She had to admit that he mostly didn't cause any trouble, though. Taamarai kept her own conversation light and cheerful, and neither of them mentioned the book of poems.

There was plenty else to talk about between Taamarai's job and course and the everyday melodramas of Ali's school, which she seemed more and more happy to chat about as it became clear that Taamarai really did want to know. Sometimes Carl brought a pack of cards. Ali was getting more used to this social ritual, too. She seemed less nervous when he joined the conversation or Taamarai disagreed with him. For her part, Taamarai was becoming surer that she *did* want to know what, if anything, the pair said about her when she wasn't there.

When he arrived that night, Carl had brought a six-pack. "It's Thursday," he'd offered by way of explanation. Taamarai enjoyed the cold beer while she cooked and, as she sat down, was surprised to find Carl's beer bottle thrust in her direction.

"Cheers." He didn't smile. He rarely did, but she was beginning to recognize shades of expression, the tilt of an eyebrow, the set of his jaw. The gesture was friendly.

"Cheers."

They clinked bottles.

"And thanks." He nodded at the food. Taamarai smiled in acknowledgement. "Public holiday on Monday," he remarked as they started eating. "So, what does a fancy college lady do in a town like this on her first day off?" It was her first real day off, Taamarai realized. Things were so busy she hadn't even seen it coming.

Taamarai looked him squarely in the eye and smiled. "I wouldn't know. I can ask one of my fancy professor ladies tomorrow, if you like?" She was learning how to avoid those jagged edges. "But this poor student thought she might head over to the Schiff Library."

Her poverty was a running joke. To begin with, Carl had needled at Taamarai about her slumming it in Gabriel Heights – her with all her books and college education. As he saw her getting by on a part-time kitchen-hand's salary, the jibes had become gentler. Here they all were, after all, and here she was, cooking dinner for them nearly half the week. Polite would be a stretch, but he could manage not to be hostile and sometimes, apparently in spite of himself, couldn't help being curious. Now he raised an inquisitive eyebrow. "The Schiff Library?"

It had been front and center on the city website when Taamarai was researching her move – the only thing Horton could find to boast about. And from Taamarai's point of view, it couldn't be better. "It's free and has one of the best collections of first-edition nineteenth-century American fiction in the world." She grinned as if nothing more needed to be said.

"Huh. What's it doing here?" Carl's skepticism bordered on indignation and Taamarai supposed she could understand. It was a bit random.

"Schiff was a book collector." She had read up on him months ago in what seemed like another life. "He wrote to a lot of authors, too, so lots of the copies are signed. He'd inherited his family business making hair oil, and they did really well. When he died, he offered his house to the city as a library and museum. An endowment keeps it open and free for the public, and he insisted that all of his books and paintings have to be on display all the time."

As soon as she finished, Taamarai felt awkward. She overtalked, spilling details out of her head that people didn't need or want. Darren had joked about it with her so many times but she couldn't seem to stop. Hesitantly, she looked up. Carl's face was unreadable.

She looked at Ali, who after a few moments sigh and murmured wistfully, "Sounds cool."

Taamarai saw her silent question, hiding with all the subtlety of a circus clown at a funeral.

"Why don't you come with me?" Taamarai asked gently. "You could show me some of downtown on the way."

"Really?" Ali immediately looked over at her father. "I mean, you don't wanna go on your own?"

"*I'm* sure Taamarai would rather go on her own." He looked over at Taamarai as he spoke, expecting confirmation.

"No, not really." Taamarai gave him a friendly smile and held his stare. She had no intention of letting him speak for her. "I'm just going for a look around. It'd be great to have some company."

"Dad! Come on! We never go anywhere!" Ali whined, then realized exactly what she'd done – invited and accused him all at once. Without intending to, she might have upset both of the adults in the room at a single stroke. Taamarai's heart hurt for the girl, for her nervousness and uncertainty. Jumping in seemed the only choice.

"That's a great idea." Taamarai beamed at Carl. "And I'd be glad to go with Ali if you're busy." He had all of his options available and looked aggrieved at having nothing he could plausibly be cross about. Taamarai got up to clear the plates just so her smugness wouldn't wind him up even more.

Next morning, the three of them stood in a persistent but light drizzle, waiting for the bus. It was already a few minutes late, and Taamarai felt like it was her fault. "I'm sorry. The schedule said ten past."

"They're always late." Ali sounded excited about going on an adventure. Carl said nothing, and Taamarai interpreted his silence as accusation. She should have prepared better, checked the forecast, brought them all umbrellas. Part of her knew she was being irrational but that only helped a bit. As she glanced nervously along the block, a bus hove into view, and Taamarai breathed out with relief.

When it pulled up, Carl murmured behind her, without apparent sarcasm, maybe even something like encouragement, "Like Ali said, they're always late." His voice rumbled beside her ear, and Taamarai felt it as an unsettling prickle down her spine. He stood back and waited for her to board, and Taamarai fumbled her change awkwardly, reacting to all the things Carl hadn't said, and didn't even seem to want to say. If she'd asked about the buses being late, they wouldn't have had to stand in the rain. Why hadn't she looked up other ways to get there? Taamarai found herself hunting Carl's words for criticism but couldn't find it. The feeling was strange.

On the mostly-empty bus, Taamarai picked a window seat, relieved that things seemed to be working out. Ali flopped down next to her, and they spent the journey watching the city go by. Carl said nothing from his seat behind them. When they disembarked, it took Taamarai a moment to get her bearings. Darren teased that she could get lost in a parking lot. She missed his confidence at so many things she wasn't good at and the jokes they shared that softened her own sense of inadequacy.

The website said the library was right by the bus stand! Taamarai was mumbling an apology when the neoclassical façade appeared, instantly recognizable from the pictures online.

At the door, they had to deposit their bags and walk through a scanner. Both Ali and Carl evidently expected somebody to stop them, but when Taamarai went forward, they followed. Taamarai cast her eyes around hungrily and made straight for a glass display case with some of the stars of the collection. In the middle of it sat a signed copy of Nathaniel Hawthorne's *The Scarlet Letter* beside a note from the elderly author to the then-young and earnest Daniel Schiff.

Finding her own excitement at last, Taamarai drew Ali over and after a few minutes, realized she was babbling about descriptions of East Coast woodlands without even checking if Ali had heard of the novel or knew what happened in it.

"I'm sorry. It's been so long since I've been in a really great library. Darren was a math major so they aren't really his thing. I guess I'm over-excited!"

Ali grinned from ear to ear and said nothing, gazing at the book with curious eyes.

Around them, a few other visitors turned and stared. In jeans, a tight t-shirt and a loose, slightly shabby sports jacket, Carl looked older than he did in a vest and sweatpants, and a little less out of place, but together with Ali in her teenage black, they both looked very different from the rest of the library's sparse attendees. As Carl stared pointedly back at a young couple – clearly art students – Taamarai began to wonder again if this had been a stupid idea.

Her mother, sari-clad and impenetrably elegant, had taken Taamarai and her brothers to galleries and museums all their lives. The tiled walls and echoing parquet floors of her hometown's city museum had been a second home to Taamarai. Only when she was older and began to travel to places on her own, did she realize how hard her mother had worked for that comfort – to armor them against other people. The looks, a whisper, "us" and "you", the hints, however polite, that they didn't fit in places like this. To give them the wonder for old and beautiful things that belonged to anybody who chose to find it.

Now she had put Ali and Carl in the same situation, but she was not her mother. Before Taamarai could suggest maybe doing something else after all and running away, though, Ali peeled off, apparently unconcerned by looks from passers-by, and headed for a case of miniature paintings. Carl turned his back on the students.

"How much is this stuff worth?" He seemed awed and perplexed all at once, and Taamarai was caught off-guard by his clear sincerity. She heard an elderly couple nearby utter a low tutting sound. She shut them out of her mind, willing Carl to do the same and feeling a sudden surprising solidarity with her neighbor.

"It's an interesting question. It depends, really." Taamarai pointed to the signed copy of Hawthorne. He listened intently as she outlined the legal and illegal market for collectibles. Taamarai stared at the book lovingly.

"It's amazing, seeing Hawthorne's signature like that, knowing he actually touched that copy, like there's only a smear of ink between your hand and his."

She reached out until her fingers hovered close to the glass, not close enough to worry a guard or set off an alarm, but as if the object might come to meet her halfway and she might shake hands with the author across the gulf of time. Taamarai fell silent and, after a few seconds, turned to find Carl staring sidelong at her. Standing so close, his height was freshly surprising and her eye was caught by the strong line of his jaw, always just a little rough with stubble. Taamarai felt her face flush. Darren loved it, he said – it was so *her* – when she got emotional about stuff like this, but it was a bit weird.

Before she could apologize, Carl tilted his head and asked, "Would you take it if you could?"

It wasn't a flippant question or a criminal one. Taamarai felt sure of that. Finally, she did turn to look at him, and her smile was small and real.

"No." She tried to put her thought into words. "I mean, it's a book. I've got a copy of *The Scarlet Letter* at home and if I open it, the words will all be the same. Hawthorne can talk to me and to a million people, and we'll all hear the same thing and think something slightly different. It's special, seeing this one. His handwriting. But it's right for it to be here, where anybody can come and see it, just like anybody can read the story."

Carl seemed to search for some hidden joke or concealed ridicule, then just nodded. He looked back at the book. "I read it once. Didn't get much out of it."

Just in time, Taamarai checked her impulse to ask when and why. Her surprise might insult him, and the question would seem like prying. It would be easy to say instead that Hawthorne wasn't for everyone. It was a safe answer, but it wasn't what she really thought.

"I didn't the first time, either. There's magic in books, to show us things we're scared to think, but it isn't always the right time when we pick them up."

The last time she had read *The Scarlet Letter*, the closeness of the town, the watching eyes and claustrophobia had crushed her in the dark, using a torch to read when she was sure Darren was asleep. He worried about how tired her work made her and it disturbed him if she stayed up while he was asleep. Still, she hadn't been able to stop turning the pages, and he hadn't woken up.

As the quiet became absolute, Taamarai looked up again to find Carl still looking at the book or perhaps at her reflection in the glass. It was impossible to tell. Taamarai sidestepped to the next cabinet, relieved that they could talk more equally as she knew little or nothing about the objects either. They each noticed different things and as Carl continued to question and comment, Taamarai felt more and more comfortable that he was having a good time. Ali stayed a few cases ahead of them as they made their slow way from room to room and kept returning to the cabinet of miniature paintings.

It was more than four hours before they left the library, stepping into a brighter, drier day than they had left. They grabbed hot dogs and went to sit beside the river, looking out over the gray water.

"Those pictures," Ali said at last. "Like, people carried them, when they were away. Because they didn't have photos or phones or anything." She seemed to be processing this rather than asking a question.

"They had letters," Taamarai said.

"Yeah." Ali thought about this too. "But didn't they take weeks to get somewhere?"

"I guess information travelled slower then," Taamarai mused.

"That would've been so weird. Not knowing if somebody was okay for weeks and weeks. Like, you think they're fine then it turns out they've been sick or...." She trailed off, the word unsaid. "For weeks and weeks and you didn't even know."

They sat quietly together. Taamarai half-expected Carl to tell Ali that this should all have been obvious before now, or that people survived for centuries without smartphones, but he seemed lost in his own reflections, staring into the moving river. She was surprised that she wanted to know what he was thinking about.

"That was cool. I never knew it was there," Ali murmured after a while.

"It's a great collection." Taamarai was delighted. "I can't wait to show Darren when he gets here." He wouldn't enjoy it as much as they had but at least she had something to show him in Horton and it would be great to spend time together. Taamarai couldn't help feeling bad that she had barely thought of him as they wandered round.

"Yeah. He coming for a visit, then?" Carl's question was offhand, but he cast her a pointed look, breaking out of his silent reverie. She had mentioned Darren visiting quite a few times at their dinners without there ever being a specific plan.

"I don't know. He's got a lot going on at the moment. It's a bit difficult." Taamarai stared out at the river herself, wanting to have a better answer and sad that she didn't.

Carl didn't press his question, and after a while, Ali filled the gap, but to Taamarai it felt like a reserve hung over the rest of the afternoon. They took the bus back in tired quiet and at the door to 502, Ali hugged Taamarai tighter than usual.

"This has been the most amazing day ever!"

Taamarai laughed and was about to agree when she felt her phone vibrating in her pocket. How many messages had she missed for Darren to be calling her so early? He would be worried about her. Her gut tightened with remorseful anxiety and she was already heading for the final flight of stairs when she was startled by Carl extending his hand.

"Yeah, thanks. Can't say I've had a day like it." His face was closed.

As she took his hand, Taamarai realized that, for all his help unloading the U-Haul, through their dinners and card games and their day at the library, they had never actually touched. His hand-shake was brief, a squeeze from a hard, calloused palm. Taamarai felt the strength of his grip and the warmth of his skin and was self-conscious without being sure why. His eyes never left hers, but Taamarai looked away. Then she headed for the stairs, already reaching for her phone. As she expected, Darren answered imme-diately.

"Babe, you're okay! I've been messaging you all day."

"Darren, I'm so sorry."

By the time she got to her front door, Taamarai felt sick to her stomach, full of regret at her stupid plan for the day and consumed by guilt – guilt for taking Carl and Ali somewhere they might have felt uncomfortable, for leaving Darren hanging. Most of all, she felt guilty at how the chaos of her life had eaten up the time for her passions. She felt the dullness that had crept over her in the passing years.

As he always did, Darren reassured her that it would be okay, that she would be okay. He was glad she'd had a good day and he was sure it was fine. Her neighbors didn't really have any right to complain about the day – they hadn't, she interjected tearfully. It was just that she felt so bad. With all the time she spent with them, Darren continued, and all the cooking she did for them, they could put up with an afternoon in a library. Taamarai found herself nodding and feeling bad on behalf of Carl and Ali too.

They talked until nearly two in the morning. Darren was finding it tough, her being away. It was harder for him, with nothing to do all day but dwell on it. As he had picked her up earlier in the conversation, so it became her turn to reassure him until they could both turn out the lights, full of "I love yous" and how good it would be to see each other again. Whenever that might be.

Chapter Five

"Here. We need to add three cloves of garlic."

Taamarai leaned over and threw it into the pan. Ali kept stirring, stopping the fresh thyme and garlic from sticking. After three months of cooking with Taamarai, she was becoming more confident in the kitchen and offered to cook herself on nights when Taamarai had a college deadline or picked up an extra shift at the restaurant.

"Is this one you made up?" Ali asked.

"No, this is how Amma makes it. With a couple of twists. I've been cooking it all my life."

When she first arrived in the US her lemon, thyme and garlic pasta had been an instant hit with her college friends. It was quick, cheap and could be scaled up from Taamarai and her roommate to a whole floor party. She'd cooked it less recently. Darren didn't like lemon, or nuts and when they moved in together, he admitted that even the smell of it made him feel sick. It wasn't his fault, but she had missed it.

Now the scent of garlic and thyme and freshly squeezed lemon juice filled the room with memories of old friends and carefree college days. She turned curiously to Ali, so young and full of the possibilities of the future.

"Do you know what you want to do when you grow up?"

Ali shrugged and looked away. Taamarai laughed. "That's fine. You don't need to know. And anyway, plans can always change. I just wondered."

For a while, they cooked, each thinking their own thoughts. Taamarai put on pasta and threw fresh spinach and roughly chopped walnuts into Ali's pan. Then Ali asked, "Like your plans changed?" Taamarai turned to her and Ali flushed with embarrassment. "I mean, like, I just thought, you didn't plan to go back to college again, right?"

Taamarai had never thought about it so bluntly. "I guess not."

"We don't have to talk about it," Ali said hurriedly. She was getting more comfortable sharing things with Taamarai, but still worried about overstepping. As Taamarai had begun to realize, Ali didn't have much contact with adults other than her father. She didn't expect teachers at school to think much of her. At home, the few business associates of Carl's, whom Taamarai occasionally passed on the stairs, looked best avoided and Ali appeared long ago to have decided the same.

"No, it's fine. I don't mind." Taamarai wanted to keep the channels open and besides, it was a fair question. She tried to consider it from a perspective that might make sense to Ali. "I was shy, quiet, when I was growing up. I always preferred being in the library, and I never felt confident or sporty, like you."

Ali snorted, but Taamarai didn't invite her to deprecate herself further. It turned out that Ali's stupendous fitness was built on a lot of running. Taamarai guessed, though Ali never said, that, apart from working off the excess energy of youth, it distracted her from worrying when her father was out doing whatever it was he did.

After a while, Taamarai tentatively asked if Ali might show her a running route nearby, and now they went together a couple of times a week. Ali didn't seem to mind how slowly Taamarai ran and never laughed. On her part, Taamarai had nudged Ali towards the school athletics club. After a month or so of competitive practice Ali was having to confront the fact that she might be quite good.

Taamarai drifted back through her memories. "It seemed obvious that I'd go to university. Most people at my school did. I loved reading books, so literature was a simple choice. I knew I wanted to have a bit more of an adventure. When I got a scholarship to come to the US, it was a no-brainer."

Taamarai couldn't help smiling at the memory – how exciting everything had seemed the first time she stepped off the bus in the States. "It was so much fun. I made a bunch of new friends. And that's where I met Darren." Their story was one she had told so many times.

"He was doing mathematics. We met in the canteen one day at the start of my second year. I bumped into him and spilled my drink all over him." She'd been trying to catch the attention of a friend. Whenever she dropped something he still joked affectionately that if she wasn't so clumsy, they might never have met.

"His house was off campus, so I invited him back to mine and lent him an old jumper. When he came to give it back to me the next week, he sort of stayed over and never really left." Taamarai smiled fondly. "After that, we were together all the time. We got married a couple of weeks after graduation. We needed to so I could stay in the US, but we wanted to, anyway."

Taamarai's thumb slipped unconsciously up to touch her wedding ring. Over the years it had become tighter and tighter until she had begun taking it off at night. Now it was getting looser as she ran and ate properly and didn't seem to have so much time to worry about her weight.

"I'd always thought I wanted to be a writer." Taamarai felt embarrassed and looked away, but if she wasn't going to let Ali talk herself down, she guessed she shouldn't do it, either.

"I used to write all the time. I got a few stories published. But we needed money. It takes time to get established, and it isn't a great income. Darren was right – we couldn't rely on it. He really struggled to find a job, too. It was a tough time. So I started working in publishing. That was fun, I guess. I met some great people and I was really good at it." Taamarai felt the sentence settle. It was true, no matter that it hadn't worked out. But that had been hard to see when she was in the middle of it, failing to land secure jobs or make the rent.

"But publishing doesn't pay much either, and I had to move a lot. Darren found it really hard. He had his friends. He'd grown up in Boston. He loves watching the football every week. So I tried to get jobs around there, but it's expensive. In the end, I was working three or four jobs at a time, and we were still struggling." Taamarai felt her chest tighten in reflexive memory.

She turned and smiled at Ali, trying to make it right, or at least not a downer of a story. She knew she had a tendency to be negative. "Like I said, it was fun. I learned a lot, but I couldn't keep it up. I was managing to save a little bit and wondering if I could maybe do some evening courses, you know, retraining. Then my brother, Joshua, he left me some money." Ali didn't ask, and Taamarai moved on quickly.

"Darren doesn't think it's the right decision, me coming out here." It had been one of their few proper arguments. "I mean, he supports me, obviously, but he worries that I'm taking a big risk. I guess he's right. It's quitting all my old business networks and I've got no experience in catering really, but this was something I knew I had to do. Something had to change." Taamarai looked back down at her hands. "I guess it doesn't make sense."

"It does." Ali sounded surprisingly serious. After a while, she said, "I don't think many kids from my school go to college."

Taamarai shrugged. "Somehow, I doubt you're many of the kids from your school." She paused. "Anyway, it's up to you." She stopped again and reached out to squeeze Ali's hand. "It *is* up to you." They shared a smile. "And this is nearly done!"

Taking over the pan from Ali, Taamarai poured lemon juice over the pasta before adding a flourish of salt and a hefty dose of black pepper. "Is your dad coming up for dinner?"

"Yeah. Should I get him?"

Taamarai nodded and began dishing up as Ali disappeared. On her own, Taamarai sighed. She missed Darren desperately. She just wanted a hug, a kiss. All they seemed to do these days was have long video calls that didn't go anywhere. Taamarai had started not mentioning how often Ali and Carl came over, or how much fun she was having at work and college. It seemed like rubbing it in when Darren was so lonely and down.

Her phone vibrated, and Taamarai was about to reach for it when she heard the door open and Ali move the chairs at the table. Ali came through to help carry the plates, and Carl grabbed them glasses of water. Both of them looked completely at home in her kitchen.

"What's tonight?" Carl asked. It was always hard to tell whether he cared but he always asked.

"Tam says it's an old recipe of her mom's. It's got nuts and garlic and spinach in it."

Ali sounded authoritative and awestruck in equal measure and Taamarai tried not to react to the shortened form of her name. Ali had heard it plenty of times when she answered the phone with Darren but had never used it before. Apparently Carl noticed her face change, though. As they all sat down, he turned directly to face her.

"You mind Ali calling you Tam like that?"

Taamarai's cheeks burned, and she looked down at her plate. She sensed Ali crumple next to her. "I'm sorry. It's what Darren calls you and...." And he's the person you love most. Taamarai flinched at Ali's hurt.

"No! No, it's fine. Ali, you've done nothing wrong." She shot Carl a resentful look and got back something between a frown and a smirk. Just as Ali stood up to run for the bathroom or her own room downstairs, Taamarai took her hand. She wanted to say that they could talk about it later, when Carl wasn't there, but couldn't take the rejected look on Ali's face.

"Ali, look at me, please."

Ali's eyes were a little red and glittered with tears, but she sat back down, looking sidelong at Taamarai with a guarded, betrayed expression.

"Ali, Darren's always called me Tam. I don't know why. I guess he thought my name was complicated. Anyway, he made it sort of my pet name. All of my uni friends picked it up and Darren's family, too."

She looked down, wondering to herself why it hadn't felt good just now when she'd been used to it for so many years. She wanted to think it through, figure it out, but Ali was tense and Taamarai owed her something. She didn't have time to filter it first.

"Nobody else ever called me Tam. Never. All the time I was growing up, even when kids made fun of me, I loved my name. It was mine and it was special." She smiled at Ali, who at least looked like she was listening.

"When Darren called me Tam, we were young and I'd never had a boyfriend before. It was...nice." She hesitated. "It still is." Without knowing why, she flicked her eyes to Carl and saw his own narrow, watching her. "But, well, I've never really *been* Tam, Ali. It never felt right."

She squeezed Ali's hand and Ali didn't take hers away, though she didn't squeeze back.

"When I met you, do you remember asking me my name?"

Ali's head tipped forward the tiniest degree.

"I almost said Tam. It's what everyone in Boston calls me. But I didn't. I'd just arrived." Taamarai examined the memory again. "I don't know. It was a chance to be somebody new, or somebody I'd always been. I told you my name and," she looked up at Ali with a smile full of affection, "you didn't even blink or think it was weird or anything."

Taamarai felt tears in her own eyes. Her first impulse was to swipe them away, but she just breathed in deeply, willing them to stay back but also glad for Ali to see them. "Ali, every time you call me Taamarai, it makes me happy. It makes me feel like a person I used to be, somebody I liked more than the person I'd been for a really long time. And like the sort of person I want to be, who somebody like you could meet for the first time and think was cool enough to hang out with." She grinned, and Ali at last gave her a small, shy smile in return.

"I'd rather you didn't call me Tam, but it's not because you're not special to me." Taamarai wanted to turn away or close her eyes, feeling exposed by it all, but she didn't.

"Ali, you're my best friend."

The truth of that saddened Taamarai a little. She had had lots of friends once. But she had this one now, and this time Ali did squeeze her hand back. "That's why I love it when you use my name. Do you understand?"

Ali clung to her fingers and, after a moment, nodded, then swiped a tear off her cheek and slouched back in her seat in a semblance of normality.

They ate quietly after that, joking lightly about nothing in particular, finding their way back to somewhere comfortable. Carl stayed quiet and, to Taamarai's surprise, after they had eaten, he joined her in the kitchen, drying dishes as she washed them. Ali had stuck headphones in and was flicking through her phone on the sofa.

"Quite the speech." Carl sounded slightly mocking, but Taamarai didn't react to that anymore. It was just how he kept distance from people. She was still angry at him, though.

"You didn't have to bring it up." Taamarai remembered him at the table, setting up a show and then sitting back to watch. She hated feeling that she and Ali were both just performing monkeys.

"And she'd be calling you Tam, and you'd hate it. Would you have said anything if I hadn't?"

"Probably not." Taamarai conceded it without malice, and when she looked at him, he wore a slight, sardonic smile that made his eyes sparkle with something mischievous but strangely warm.

Taamarai had to make an effort not to smile back. "That still wasn't the best way to handle it."

"Probably not."

She let her smile show a little.

"You ever tell your husband?"

"What?"

"That you don't like it."

Taamarai looked down at her hands. They were puffy from the water, making her ring tight again. "No. And anyway, I'm not sure I don't. I mean, it's what he always calls me." She looked over, but Carl only lifted an eyebrow; she hadn't sounded like she weans't sure talking to Ali.

Between the two of them, the washing up didn't take long, and he put down the towel and leant back against the sideboard. Taamarai watched without meaning to. The way he moved fascinated her – casual yet controlled. As he'd become more comfortable around her, she had realized he wasn't actually tense all the time. It was toned muscles under loose clothes and a sureness that made him always seem ready. He met her eye now and said, almost gently, "You don't like something, Taamarai, most times ain't nobody gonna say nothing but you."

"I guess that's true." She wiped her hands dry on her jeans. "Thanks, I suppose."

He nodded, then walked out of the kitchen, hooking a deck of cards out of his pocket and onto the table. Taamarai hung back for a moment and looked around, feeling foolish. The fact that he wasn't wrong made it worse.

Chapter Six

It was a Thursday evening – as close as Taamarai got to a weekend. She worked Fridays to Sundays and most of her college classes were piled into the first half of the week. Normally it was a chance to unwind, but this evening her shoulders were tight and it was an effort to make cheerful conversation.

She had come downstairs and cooked with Ali, wanting the company but not knowing what to do with it. Carl wasn't there and arrived when they were nearly done. He had a bruise on his jaw that she and Ali both chose not to notice and he chose not to explain. He, too, looked irritable and distant.

As they ate, Ali entertained valiantly with an account of the selection process for her first running competition. The unsurprising climax was that she'd made the school's first team. Taamarai was genuinely delighted and Carl seemed sincere in his brief praise. Ali sat visibly taller and for a while things felt better.

When they were done, Ali cleared the table and then dragged out some homework. Good grades were a condition of her place in the athletics squad. Carl sat back and cast his eyes about as if searching for something hidden. What he found was Taamarai, about to get up and head upstairs.

"What time's Darren getting here tomorrow?"

Her back stiffened. He couldn't know, yet he always seemed to pick on the thing that hurt. Taamarai placed her palms flat on the table, ready to stand and leave as soon as Carl had the answer to his question.

"He's not coming after all. He's not feeling well."

"Huh," was all she got in reply. It was the perfect opportunity to go, but Taamarai glared at Carl instead. She was angry. She wanted somebody to argue with and it couldn't be Darren. Her fingertips clenched the tabletop. Carl held her stare. His smirk was so brief it almost wasn't there. He'd be able to deny it ever was, though somehow she knew he wouldn't.

White hot rage filled her lungs. Taamarai clamped her lips shut. She closed her eyes and when she opened them again, the anger was gone. In the cavity it left behind lurked a childlike desire to cry. Not here. Not with Carl watching her, his face serious again. Maybe even curious? At last, he said, "That's a shame. With you paying for his tickets and all."

Taamarai couldn't remember exactly how that detail had come up. A few weeks ago, Carl had asked some other question that somebody with better manners wouldn't have. He'd known then, too, what to ask that she would rather have kept hidden, especially from herself. She'd ended up explaining that she was short of money because of paying Darren's bus fare. Carl had looked contemptuous. "I thought Darren was working up in Boston. Isn't that why he's still there?"

Taamarai had got up to clear the table as she answered, her voice breezy and jovial as a 1950s washing powder commercial.

"Sort of. He did have a job but it didn't work out. They put him in an awful new department, and he just hated it. He's been looking for something but there isn't much going."

Carl hadn't asked her any more questions. He'd just looked like a man who had won this round and decided to cash in. For now. Tonight, he'd apparently found the moment he was waiting for. Time to play again. Taamarai pursed her lips and waited.

"I've been thinking," Carl mused. "If your husband doesn't have a job, why don't he come here and look for work? You're always saying how he misses you and you can't wait to see him again."

Taamarai sank back in her chair. She knew what Darren would say. He didn't want to leave his friends. It was cheaper for them both, him living with his parents. She was out so much working they would hardly see each other anyway.

"He...." The usual words blocked her throat. Her tongue felt thick. "He was going to have a look for something on this trip. Until he got sick. He thinks it's a cold."

"He must be real sick not to be able to sit on a bus."

"It's three buses." The words jumped out of her, straight from Darren's mouth on the phone that morning, when she had said nearly the same thing to him. Carl just stared at her.

"He says he's been sleeping badly. He's tired and he pulled his back doing some jobs for his mom." They sounded like excuses. She knew they did because they had to her, too.

Not for the first time in one of these conversations with Carl, Taamarai didn't know why she couldn't just walk away or change the subject or lie, like she did to everybody else. She'd told her parents that Darren had come down with a really bad flu bug. He could hardly get out of bed. At work, she already knew she would say the same when they asked. She hadn't even thought of it as lying until lately. It was just what partners did, covering for each other. Saving face.

With a shrug, Carl got up to get himself a beer. He brought one over for Taamarai and she took it, even though she was still about to leave. "Guess you can't get your money back now?"

Taamarai glared at him but still ended up saying the things she normally kept in her head. "If he'd told me yesterday, I could've got half back, but he left it until after the bus had already gone."

"How long is it now? Since you moved?" Carl's voice was flat and remorseless.

Ali glanced up from her homework and frowned at her father, but he nodded to her books and she bent her head again, trying to look like she was writing instead of following the strangely tense conversation.

Taamarai sipped her beer while she pretended to work it out. She knew exactly. "Fourteen weeks this weekend."

"Long time."

Anger flared again. Of course it was a long time! Tears stung her eyes and she squeezed them back. She had been so looking forward to Darren getting here, to hugging him, showing him the apartment, introducing him to Ali. And Carl, she supposed. In her head, they all got on. It would have been great.

"It's fine. We'll make something work before Christmas. He says maybe I could go back up there next weekend or later this month."

"Sure. You could cover the bus fare *and* lose a weekend's pay."

Meeting Carl's eye, Taamarai let her anger show. What was she supposed to do? She couldn't change what Darren had done. He just looked at her and took another swig of his beer, shoulders relaxed, refusing to give her a shred of anger back.

"I guess with Darren not working, you paying for everything, it's easy for him to forget how hard it is."

Taamarai couldn't think of anything safe to say. It was fourteen weeks since she had seen Darren but it was another anniversary too. She might have pretended to forget about it if Carl hadn't brought up Darren's work. Now it loomed in front of her. A full year – it had been a full year that day since Darren quit his job. She'd just started talking about her plans for college, maybe them moving away when suddenly it became them moving in with his parents because they couldn't afford anything else. She finished her beer in silence then tapped Ali on the shoulder. "Night, Ali. I'm heading upstairs."

Ali put down her pen, stood up and moved around the table to hug Taamarai tightly. Taamarai squelched her tears down again as she hugged Ali back. She wondered how she would have coped with the last three and a half months if she really had been on her own. "Sleep well," she murmured, then headed for the door.

"Night, Carl." She didn't look at him as she went past.

The stairs were exhausting, and her legs felt heavy. In her apartment, Taamarai sank back against the door and finally, the tears she had been holding onto all day flooded out. She slid down to sit on the floor, hugged her knees and sobbed. It wasn't this weekend. Not really. Not just the weekend. It was everything. Everything that she didn't want to see but let Carl keep poking at anyway.

Darren hadn't come because he didn't want to. He hadn't told her until it was too late because that way there was nothing to argue about and because Carl was right – he didn't know how many hours she had worked for those tickets.

Taamarai wasn't sure who she was angrier at: Darren, herself, or Carl. She wrapped her arms around her knees and choked on her tears, ashamed to sob out loud even on her own. Her phone began to vibrate. It was Darren. He'd want to tell her how much better he was feeling. That it had been the right decision not to travel. That she shouldn't cry. That he loved her and they'd see each other soon. She let it ring.

Chapter Seven

The wind whistled outside the windows to her apartment. Taamarai liked it. It felt like living in her own eyrie high above the city. As Fall had drawn on, the patchwork greens of Horton's streets and parks had turned to fiery orange beneath her, then fallen away. Now it was usually dark by the time the three of them sat down to dinner.

Taamarai put a box of chocolates on the table when they finished. Ali and Carl took one each. Carl reached for the box again and, instead of taking a second, inspected a gift tag on the lid. Taamarai's heart sank a little. She already knew what it said and kicked herself for not acting on her first instinct when the chocolates arrived to rip the tag off and throw it away.

Happy birthday babe. Luv u 4eva. Darren xxx

"Your birthday?" was all Carl asked.

Ali reached for the box too. Taamarai cringed inside. "Is it today?" Ali asked eagerly.

Taamarai shook her head. "Couple of weeks ago." She glanced at Carl, who didn't say *when Darren was meant to be visiting?* though she felt sure he was thinking it.

"You didn't say!" Ali looked affronted.

Taamarai shrugged. "It's no big deal. I never make very much of it."

Ali's face betrayed a sudden intense sympathy, then she grinned. "You could've eaten the chocolates by yourself."

"They only arrived today and chocolates are better for sharing." Taamarai was making herself smile and hoping it didn't show.

"Darren don't know when your birthday is?" Carl took another and held it up appraisingly. If he was thinking that it was an impersonal kind of gift or a thoughtless one for a woman who worried about her weight, he didn't say those things either. They were all things Taamarai had thought to herself, though, and seemed to hear in Carl's voice.

"Of course he does." Taamarai's voice jingled with fondness and good cheer. "He phoned me for ages on the day. It was just that he'd planned to bring them when he came to visit. Then he had to find time to post them."

"Huh." Carl ate his chocolate. Maybe that was all the response it deserved, a small, disloyal part of Taamarai thought.

"Anyway, when's your birthday, Ali?" Taamarai asked to change the subject.

Ali froze, blushed, then looked away. "Um, tomorrow."

"Ali?!" It was Taamarai's turn to look aghast, and Carl appeared diverted rather than annoyed by the absurdity of it all. It didn't last long.

"Carl?!"

"What?" He glared at Taamarai, surprised to be suddenly in the spotlight.

"You could have said something! Have you got any plans?" Taamarai demanded then hesitated. "I mean, I could have baked you a cake." She looked apologetically at Ali and then accusingly back at Carl.

"Do I have plans?" He raised a skeptical eyebrow. "What plans am I gonna have? And what plans would we have that didn't include you?"

Taamarai didn't quite know what to say, but her face split into a smile, then a grin.

"Tomorrow?" she checked.

Ali nodded and looked confused.

Taamarai pursed her lips. "Honestly, I had a pretty lousy birthday. When Darren cancelled his trip, I was going to tell you guys and do a dinner or something, but then Darren said he wanted to spend the evening with me on the phone, so...." She shrugged, not wanting to dwell on the memory or invite any questions from Carl. "So, why don't we celebrate both our birthdays tomorrow instead? Together?"

Ali's face lit up.

"I guess you don't have plans, so that's okay for you, too, Carl?" Taamarai grinned at him, enjoying batting one back at him for once.

Carl could only shrug awkwardly. He felt pinned. Whatever. Why did he feel like he should have done something?

The following night, Carl and Ali sat together at the table in 502. Carl had done his bit, on Ali's orders, to tidy up, and Taamarai had brought down a colorful cloth that covered the old cigarette burns on the table. As soon as Ali got in from school, she and Taamarai had cooked together. The remains of burritos and chips surrounded an empty bowl smeared with guacamole. They still had a little room, though.

Looking down the hall to the front door, they waited expectantly. It opened and Taamarai walked in backwards. With a flourish, she turned and booted the door closed, the image of a chef in command. How she'd managed to get it down the stairs like that Carl had no idea, but on a purple and orange cake sat fourteen lit candles, and a fizzing sparkler made fifteen.

Carefully, she put the cake down on the table and then sat,

watching Ali blow out the candles in a single breath, just as the sparkler burned down.

"You didn't wait for us to sing." Before the words were out of his mouth, Carl wondered where they had come from. Ali and Taamarai both looked at him in astonishment, then burst out laughing.

"You can sing if you like!" Ali declared the challenge and then stared at him expectantly.

"On my own?" he grumbled evasively.

Taamarai, who was giggling too much to drink her beer, managed, "Me too. On three?"

Carl felt embarrassingly committed and unsure what idiot impulse had led him there. The rendition was tuneless and terrible, as they always were, but Ali laughed through it all, then got up and leant on both of their shoulders, apparently with nothing to say.

"Now can we eat the damn cake?" Carl finally muttered.

Inside were layers of orange and purple sponge and cream cheese frosting. He glanced at Taamarai. The only time she could have baked the cake was last night after they'd left her place. It was plated up in minutes and gone almost as quickly.

Carl saw Taamarai reach for her pocket, no doubt feeling the vibration of her phone. He frowned but then she put her hands back on the table. "I guess I left my phone upstairs." He waited for her to spoil the moment and rush to get it, but she didn't.

"So, Ali, what does the birthday girl want to do for the evening?" Taamarai asked instead.

"You not gonna get it? You know, in case Darren's trying to call?" Carl wasn't sure why he asked, why he always had to shove Taamarai into the place that made her cringe and apologize and look anxious. To his surprise, though, she just smiled back.

"Nope. He knows it's Ali's birthday. He says happy birthday, by the way." Taamarai didn't quite look like she meant it and even invoking Darren's good wishes seemed to bring the energy down. "Anyway," Taamarai continued brightly, "I'll call him when I get back upstairs. So, what'll it be, Ali?"

Ali gazed around the table in slight mystification. "This is so much fun." She looked at both of them. "Thanks."

"Hey, nothing to do with me." Carl leaned back and held his hands out. "Oh, except...." He stood up and came back to the table with an unwrapped box. "I got you this." He passed it to Ali offhandedly.

Ali seemed surprised by the gift and Taamarai felt a stab of something. Despair or hope? She couldn't tell. She looked at Carl and saw uncertainty in his eyes and in the set of his shoulders. Maybe most people wouldn't notice the way it softened the lines of his face just a fraction.

"New headphones? Dad, that's cool!"

"Yeah, well. The other ones, I can hear that shit you play nearly as loud as you." He sat down and didn't visibly react when Ali got up and kissed him on the top of the head.

"Thanks, Dad."

Ali walked around the table and hugged Taamarai tightly around her shoulders. "And thanks. When did you even make this?" Ali gestured at the remains of the cake. Taamarai just shrugged and smiled. When she was seated again, Ali contemplated her options. "What about a movie?"

"What movie?" Carl tried and failed to sound even a bit excited. He could suddenly imagine himself sitting through ninety minutes of giggling girls in some excruciating high school fantasyland.

Ali stared at him as if this were a stupid question. "We can stream anything we like. Literally anything."

"Like what?" He frowned again.

"Dad?! Whatever. Anything!" She looked at Taamarai, who was just laughing into her beer, then back at her father. "Like, what's your favorite movie ever?"

"What?"

"Your favorite movie. Come on?" Ali sounded like she had never thought to ask the question before and now wouldn't back down without an answer. Carl looked like he had never thought about it either.

"I dunno." He cradled his beer almost defensively against his chest. Taamarai laughed again, then caught him looking at her. He narrowed his eyes, but she just smiled through.

"Dad!" Ali prodded him.

"Okay, okay. *The Godfather*, I guess."

"The what?" Ali was mystified.

"*The Godfather*? It's a great film!" Carl looked offended.

"It's an awesome film," Taamarai umpired. "If you haven't seen it, Ali...."

Ali rolled her eyes mockingly at them both but was already reaching for her phone. "Yeah, sure." She peered at the screen. "*The...Godfather*? Right?"

"Yeah." Carl wasn't quite sure what was happening around him. Ali got the TV set up, Taamarai turned down the lights and produced popcorn from somewhere. He was dragged over to the couch and parked in the middle of it. Ali plonked down beside him and waited for Taamarai to come back with more beers and Coke. Then, Taamarai lowered herself carefully onto the sofa, in Carl's usual spot in the corner.

As soon as the music began, Carl felt the tides of memory tug at him. He'd almost forgotten about the film until tonight, though once he'd known every line. A lifetime ago. They had played it one night in the juvenile detention centre. In retrospect, it probably hadn't been a great choice. When he got out, he rented a copy and watched it over and over, never knowing if he was dreaming of being a gangster or a movie director.

Ali fidgeted for a few minutes, getting comfortable and wolfing down most of the popcorn. Then she became very still. Carl sat back, crossing one foot over his knee. His arms felt trapped, and he stretched them out across the back of the couch. There was no way not to reach out towards Taamarai's shoulder, but it was his couch. Anyway, she was squeezed into a ball in the way she sat that always annoyed him, like she was trying not to exist. He glanced over but her eyes were fixed firmly on the screen.

About half an hour later, she reached across for a handful of popcorn. The bowl had come to rest in the space between them. Ali reached across him at the same time, and Taamarai handed the popcorn over to her. Carl knew that in some other moment, he'd have been offended to be so invisible but they weren't ignoring him. They just weren't scared of him. Taamarai uncurled her legs and resettled. She looked more normal now, less compressed and, as she leant back, her head touched his arm.

Taamarai felt it too and turned quickly to check that it really wasn't the back of the couch. She glanced over, her face lit white from the screen on one side and in darkness on the other. When he didn't move his arm away, she simply turned back and rested her head against it. Her knee began to relax as the film sucked her in, falling to touch his thigh. Carl froze.

On his other side, Ali was loafing adolescently against him, a thing that he was sure had never happened before. He was surprised that he didn't want to jump up and shake off the claustrophobic press of bodies. Instead, he looked sidelong at Taamarai, who was still apparently fixated on the film. Her hands were in her lap, like a schoolgirl. It didn't look uncomfortable but it didn't quite look natural, either.

Carl realized in a flash that that was because, if this had been the scene it almost looked like, her hand would be resting on his leg or touching his arm. The claustrophobia crept in then, a panic that was just reaching his throat when Taamarai's hand moved, apparently dropping unconsciously. It landed exactly where it should, just on his knee, and stayed there. The blockage in his throat disappeared like morning mist, and everything felt disconcertingly, momentarily right.

As the movie ended, Ali turned to them both with a look of revelation.

"That was so good! I never knew you liked movies, Dad." On the basis of one film, a world of respect for her father's taste appeared before her.

Taamarai laughed, coiling back into the corner of the couch. Carl looked over but couldn't catch her eye.

"When did you...?" Ali came to a screaming stop, realizing that she was about to cross a line. The silence was crushing for a few seconds before Taamarai stepped in.

"Ali, everyone's seen *The Godfather*. It's a classic!" She got up and turned the lights on. The unreal time was over but its perfume lingered. Taamarai watched Ali off to bed, giving her a birthday hug and a kiss on the cheek.

"Happy birthday," Carl said as Taamarai was preparing to leave. He knew he sounded sarcastic, but Taamarai no longer reacted to the tones that made most people flinch or bristle.

"Thank you. It's been fun." Taamarai looked ready to head out but didn't. "I'd forgotten how good a film it is."

Carl just stared at her. He didn't want to talk about the film. He didn't know what he did want to talk about. He just knew he didn't want her to stop talking. Taamarai looked like something was stuck just behind her lips too. The silence dragged on.

"Well, I'd best head off. Goodnight, Carl."

"Yeah, night." He watched her to the door then made his way to the couch, sinking down into the still warm cushions. The apartment felt different, and his heart was beating just a little too fast.

Chapter Eight

Taamarai propped her phone expertly against a can of chickpeas. She had promised Ali and Carl brunch and this was a rare chance to phone her parents while she cooked. It always made her feel extra homey, as if they were sitting just out of sight in the kitchen behind her.

"Hello?" Her mother never looked at who was calling before she answered her phone, so she always sounded surprised to hear from her.

"*Vanakkam*, Amma."

"Taamarai! *Vanakkam!*" Taamarai sensed her mother's voice warm in a way that was impossible to define or ignore. "*Eppadi irukkayaa? Saaptayaa?*" *How are you? Have you eaten?* "It's Taamarai!" That was to her Dad, whom she could hear coming into the room.

Her mother peered into her phone camera, evidently trying to get a view of where in the apartment Taamarai was standing.

"I'm good." Taamarai's smile sounded in her voice. "And I'm just making brunch for me and Carl and Ali. Baked chickpeas and egg with flatbreads." They switched into English without thinking, so that her father could join in if he liked or just sit and listen to them chat.

"How did Ali's birthday go?"

By now, her parents knew Taamarai's downstairs neighbors as well as if they had met them and were keen to know how the cake, which Taamarai had cooked on the phone to them two days earlier, had been received.

"It was great! We made burritos together, then had the cake and watched *The Godfather*. It was Carl's choice. I think Ali really liked watching something he knew. It was fun." Taamarai felt a sudden quiver of something unsaid.

It had been wonderful. But it was nothing she was willing even to think about too much, let alone talk over with her mother. She had lain awake that night wondering why she hadn't stayed put in the corner of the couch, hoping that Carl hadn't noticed.

Since then her brain had fizzed with memories and flashes of sensation: of her hand resting on his leg, the shape of his face in the screen's glow when he hadn't noticed her looking at him. She had stolen her glances, taking in the clean lines of his profile and the flickering shadows of exposed emotions.

Now she moved on quickly, but her cheeks were warm. "What about you? How was Aunty Sue's party?"

Her mother filled her in on who had been there, who hadn't, how her nieces and nephews were growing, Taamarai chopped vegetables and enjoyed sharing the threads of connection that made her still feel part of her big, boisterous family. Later she would share the pictures her mother promised to send with Ali, who seemed to love this vicarious family life nearly as much as Taamarai, laughing over old stories about strangers who weren't completely strangers any longer, helping Taamarai to decide what gifts or cards to send ahead of birthdays.

"Have you thought about Christmas?" As the conversation changed topic, her mother's tone turned careful.

Taamarai felt a familiar tightness in her chest. They had had this conversation in years gone by. Her parents would offer to pay for her flight back, even though it would be a strain for them. Taamarai wouldn't accept. Not unless she could afford it herself. It wouldn't really be about the money, though, for any of them.

Darren had spent one Christmas with her family, back when they were first together. He had hated being away from home, the unfamiliar routines. Taamarai had tried to cheer him up, give him breaks from her family, make things as normal for him as she could but was left bruised by her constant anxiety and his unhappiness.

Her family had tried their best, too, and didn't make a fuss when Darren stayed upstairs for meals or played on his computer while they all sat around talking or cooking. They still noticed though, stoking Taamarai's embarrassment.

Since then, Taamarai hadn't been home for Christmas. Her mother, who understood being so far away from her own family, and the pressure it created, never wanted Taamarai to feel she was letting anybody down. Taamarai felt like she was, though, and wanted so badly to see them all. It made the holiday bittersweet.

This time, though, there was a different answer, and Taamarai reached for it with relief.

"Actually...." She hesitated. She hadn't told Darren yet but her mother had as much reason to know as he did. "I think I'll be spending Christmas here."

There was a pause filled with unspoken disappointment and Taamarai rushed on.

"I mean *here*, in Horton." Taamarai couldn't stop herself grinning at the big reveal. "I've been promoted at work!"

There was another slight pause on the line, then her mother's face lit up with excitement. "Promoted? Already? Oh, *chellam*! To what?"

"Assistant chef!" Taamarai could feel her heart pounding as she said it. Assistant, junior, under-qualified. They could have put anything they liked in front of the title. It didn't matter. In a week's time, she would officially be a chef.

"Taamarai, that's wonderful! Well done."

"Yes, well done, sweetheart," her father's voice added from off screen.

"Thanks." Taamarai was buoyed up higher by her parents' delight. "So, yeah - it looks like I won't be going anywhere over Christmas. They've said they'll need me every day, including Christmas Day, and I can't really say no."

"No, of course not!" Work, dreams, goals. Those were things they had taught Taamarai to value growing up, and sometimes they required sacrifices. Then came the quiet on the line. "What about Darren? What does he think?"

Taamarai hesitated, too. "I haven't told him yet. You're the first ones to get the news. I'm sure he'll be fine about it, though. He'll understand."

She already feared he wouldn't. Taamarai was dreading giving him the news but also felt she was being unfair to him. In any case, that was between them. And it was easier for her parents to think that everything was fine. She never wanted to worry them. Her mother didn't sound convinced. In fact, Taamarai was surprised by the worry in her voice.

"Are you sure?"

"Of course! Amma, he'll be fine. And I'll make sure we do something special for his birthday in February. Maybe I'll get a bus back up to Massachusetts for a couple of days." Darren had admitted that week that he wouldn't be able to come and see her before Christmas after all, but she didn't tell her parents. It was just something else they might worry about and she didn't like to think that they might judge Darren unfairly because of something she said.

"Oh, that sounds nice." Her mother paused again. "How long did you say it takes?"

"About two days. It's twelve hour's drive, but there's a couple of awkward bus changes. It's way cheaper than flying, though." Taamarai had made longer journeys, as had her mother.

They chatted on, and Taamarai found herself slowing down her cookery, keeping her parents on the line a bit longer. Since moving to Horton, it felt so good to talk like this, without making sure that everything they all said wouldn't be misunderstood if Darren, or in the last six months before she moved, his parents, overheard. She knew Carl and Ali wouldn't mind the wait. And it put off the call to share her good news with Darren.

Chapter Nine

It was a very different kind of Christmas, but it was Christmas nonetheless. Taamarai woke up and, for a few minutes, resisted getting out of bed. She was warm and could see ice on the window pane between her curtains. But she was eager to get on with the day, too. Taamarai loved Christmas and had decided that, despite the strangeness of waking alone, far from husband and family, this would be a good one. And that, as she knew from many years' experience, meant plenty to do.

Back in Boston, she would organize their movement between Darren's parents and grandparents. Then Darren had decided it would be lovely to spend part of the day by themselves, so she had fitted in a special breakfast together. And she always tried to check in with her parents. There never seemed to be much free time. Darren's family liked to keep a tight schedule, so Taamarai ended up calling her parents two or three times, for five or ten minutes each, knowing that it made them feel like an afterthought.

Today, Taamarai had worked her schedule out in advance and was determined to stick to it. First, she would phone her parents for a real chat and get to see her elder brother and his family as well. Then she had made her and Darren's special breakfast. It was a heavy one that would hold her through the busy day. Darren would do the same, and they would eat together on a video call.

On her way downstairs she would drop into 502 to see that everything was ready and head over to the restaurant. Her boss had said they should be done by five, so back home with time for a second quick call with Darren while she changed out of her work clothes, then Christmas dinner in the evening with Ali and Carl. Taamarai pulled on her clothes in the cold air, smiling at the prospect.

Taamarai wandered into the living room, where she had gotten herself a plastic Christmas tree. It was small and a bit threadbare, but she had enjoyed every second of putting it up and covering it with glittery nonsense. Taamarai couldn't shake the feeling that she was still letting everybody down, not giving anybody enough of herself, but at least it felt like she was trying her best.

The call with her parents was a wonderful start. It might all work out. They were cheerful and well into their day. The grand-children had torn a trail of chaos through the house, which her father was cheerfully cleaning up. Taamarai opened the presents they'd sent: a book of recipes in her mother's distinctive, left-leaning handwriting; a scarf and gloves against the chill outside; and some of her favorite British chocolates. They opened the things she had sent, too, and Taamarai was pleased she had taken the time in November to choose just the right gifts. It had been many years since she'd managed.

Her face still lit up with love and Christmas cheer, she scrolled through to Darren's number next. Taamarai suppressed an involuntary reluctance. It was just doing two calls back-to-back. That was all. She moved to the kitchen and began setting up the elements of their breakfast, carefully prepared the day before.

When Darren picked up on the first ring, she knew it hadn't just been making two calls so close together. "Hey! Merry Christmas!" She grinned broadly, showing off her Santa hat, ready for work.

"Yeah. Merry Christmas." His voice was tired and flattened by half-concealed resentment. "You look like you're having a good time."

"I've just spoken to my parents. It was good to see everyone." Taamarai felt guilty for her smile.

"I guess they would get to see you first."

"Darren!" Taamarai flinched and tried not to sound hurt. "You know I have to call them first. With the time difference, it's the only chance I'll get."

"Yeah, I know that." His voice softened and he cracked a small smile. "You could have texted me, though."

"Yeah." Taamarai wouldn't even have thought twice about it once. "I should have. I'm sorry. I just, well, we're having breakfast together now, and I didn't want to wake you." That was true. He seemed to sleep so badly these days and was always tired. Sure enough:

"I didn't really sleep."

"Oh. I'm sorry." She tried to plaster her smile back on, feeling it wobble over tears. "Have you got breakfast ready? Let's...."

"I'm sorry, babe. I couldn't face it." He cut her off with a shrug. "I mean, it's like, what's the point? It's special because we do it together."

"But we can be together." Taamarai felt her face starting to crumple. They had talked about this. It was the best way for them to be together on the day. "We agreed this would be nice."

"You said it would be. I always said it wouldn't be as good without you here. You always make breakfast." He looked bereft. "Mom offered, but she'd just get it wrong."

"But you know how to make it." Taamarai was pleading with him. She knew he didn't like her being away but they had talked through every detail, over and over again. She had explained why she couldn't come back to Boston. He had said he understood. He had promised her it would be okay.

"I know," he muttered, now. "But it's not the same. I know you thought it would be a great plan but it's like rubbing in that you're not here. Our first Christmas apart since we got married."

Taamarai's guilt lanced through her but anger followed it, shocking and fierce. "That isn't just because of me!" She could feel tears in her eyes. "You know how important this job is. You could've come out here. I've got the flat all decorated. We could've had a lovely Christmas together."

Darren looked shocked too. "Oh, come on, Tam. That's not fair! You'll be out half the day."

"It's five hours, Darren, six at most."

"Yeah! And what would I do? Sit around on my own on Christmas Day? How is that okay?"

"Darren," Taamarai felt her anger draining away. They had talked about all of this. They had had a plan. Instead, she saw another Christmas vanishing into the tainted memory of things she should have done differently. She made her case one more time, but her heart wasn't in it. "You could've called your family or watched a movie."

He didn't say anything for a long time and when he did, his tone was resigned and sad. "Look, Tam. I'm sorry. I'm here and it's Christmas, and I just wanted to wake up in the morning next to the love of my life, have a romantic breakfast together like we always do and then spend the day with my family." He stared at her through the screen and tried to smile. "I get that this job is important to you. I'm not saying I don't. I'm just feeling a bit lonely and upset. That's all." His eyes suddenly reddened and filled with tears, and Taamarai felt the bottom fall out of her.

"I'm sorry, Darren." She wished she could reach through the screen and hug him or be on a plane that instant to make it right, but she'd made her decision and had to live with it. "I'm sorry. I shouldn't have said what I did. I wish I could be with you too." She felt tears sliding down her cheeks.

Darren was crying a little now, too. He never bawled, but the tears ran down his cheeks, and he wiped them angrily. "I'm sorry, too. That I can't be the husband you deserve so you didn't have to be away working."

It seemed like there was nothing Taamarai could say that didn't damn her further. "Darren, you're a great husband. This isn't your fault. I'm here because this is important to me. But I should have come home for Christmas. I'm sorry."

He nodded slowly, blinking back his tears. "It's okay, Tam. I know you did what you thought was right." He sniffled. "And you know I love you."

"I love you, too." Taamarai tried to smile. They carried on talking as Darren calmed down. It would be okay. It would be good to see his grandmother and his mom had got him all of his favorite Christmas treats. And yes, he'd got her present to him. He'd open it after lunch. He hoped she liked his later. He gave her a boyish, slightly furtive grin.

Taamarai glanced at her phone. "Look, Darren, I've got to get going. I can't be late to the restaurant."

"Oh, yeah. Okay." He looked disappointed again, and Taamarai missed him so much. It had been so long, and she should never have agreed to working over Christmas, even if they had withdrawn her promotion.

"Look, Darren, I promise, I won't do this again. Not another Christmas apart."

"You promise?"

"Yeah, I promise."

He smiled wanly. "You'd better go, then. Mom says 'cus we can't have our special breakfast together, she'll make me one of my favorites that she does."

"Look, I'm really sorry, Darren. I'll make it up to you. I love you. Have a great day, and I'll call you when I get back from work."

"Yeah, okay. I love you too, Tam." He gave her a last, desolate look, then dragged on a brave smile and hung up.

Taamarai wiped her eyes and hugged herself for a few moments, as the pain subsided. She didn't have long. Quickly, Taamarai dragged on her coat and headed down the stairs with five minutes spare to check everything was in hand at 502. She knocked softly at the door. It was still early.

"Merry Christmas!" Ali pulled her in through the door and gave her a huge bear hug. "Are those new?" She admired Taamarai's scarf and gloves from her parents and led her over to the kitchen.

"Look, it's all ready!"

In the kitchen, chopped vegetables covered the surfaces, and a small but thickly glazed ham sat in the oven. They'd prepared it the night before, and Ali had instructions written down beside the cooker. "I've got alarms on my phone for everything." Ali looked happy as a clam. "And I haven't opened my presents! Not until you're back."

"You didn't have to do that." Taamarai felt her smile returning.

"I know," Ali said simply and hugged her again. "This is awesome. Like, a proper Christmas ham and stuff!" Taamarai didn't dare ask what a usual Christmas *chez* Grigg looked like but when she had asked Ali what they should cook, Ali had promptly raided a montage of movie memories from which they had built a detailed and luxurious menu. Over the weeks before the holiday, they looked up recipes together, went shopping for treacle and canned pineapples, and tried out sample glazes on potatoes and bacon.

"You been crying?"

Taamarai turned to find Carl leaning in the kitchen doorway in sweatpants and a vest, looking closely at her past Ali's head, noticing the last thing she wanted him to.

"Oh, yeah." Taamarai reached up and scrubbed at her face a bit more. "I just got carried away talking to Amma and Dad." She laughed for Ali's benefit. "It was really great to see them. And my nephews and nieces. The whole family was there." She ratcheted up her excitement word by word back to that first call of the day, hoping to carry her audience along.

"Mm." Carl didn't move. "You had breakfast?"

Her resolve wavered again. How did he always know? And why did he always have to ask?

"No."

She hadn't had the heart to cook or eat while Darren sat there on the call looking so miserable. Now, she felt trapped and wished she'd never told Carl and Ali about her breakfast plans.

Carl looked entirely unsurprised. "Darren not in the mood?"

"He hadn't slept well. He said he wasn't really feeling that good, and by the time we were done talking, I hadn't realized the time. Anyway, it doesn't matter. I'm not that hungry."

She had noticed the time. Terrible as she had felt, she had also worried on the call with Darren about how she would get through her shift on an empty stomach. She was starving and it was Christmas Day. There probably wouldn't even be anywhere open on the way where she could grab something.

"Sure." Carl turned around and walked off. Taamarai felt again like she might cry and was determined not to in front of Ali, who still looked exuberant. Then to her surprise, Carl reappeared. He handed her a paper bag without a smile. "Merry Christmas."

Taamarai opened it and saw inside two mince pies and a couple of flatbreads, the sort Ali used for her lunch, stuffed with hummus and lettuce. She looked up and met his eyes, narrowed again, gauging something. Her, maybe. Drawing her in as they always seemed to.

"Thank you."

She mouthed it and knew she needed to get gone, only partly not to be late. She hugged Ali and made for the door. Out on the street, Taamarai walked as she ate, staring around the weirdly quiet city. As she passed people, they wished her a Merry Christmas, and she returned the salutation, feeling her equilibrium return. Yes, it was a Merry Christmas, or it still could be.

Chapter Ten

Her shift flew by and Taamarai's boss gave her a lift back to Gabriel Heights, which was especially kind as the buses weren't running. And, she had two bags of goodies, shared out between the staff when the cleaning was done. Taamarai took the steps at a run. She'd feel tired soon, but not yet.

At 502, she knocked on the door. Ali popped her head out, sweaty of face and hair in authentic disarray. Triumphantly, she declared, "Everything is perfect!" Then she disappeared again.

In her own apartment, Taamarai peeled off her restaurant clothes. She always liked to dress up on Christmas and had laid out an outfit the night before. Darren had talked about her calling him while she got dressed. Maybe they could even have a bit of phone sex, he'd half-joked. Taamarai wondered where he planned to do that. His grandmother's bathroom? Anyway, there certainly wasn't time. She jumped into the shower, got dressed and only called him with five minutes to spare and her hair to brush.

"Hey, babe." Darren looked better than earlier. In fact, he looked extremely cheerful.

"Hey. How are you feeling?"

"I'm good! It's been fun here. Mom made me toast soldiers for breakfast, then Nanna got me these great frozen potato snacks that I used to have when I was a kid. We've just had dinner. Mom's ham is the best! They forgot the ice cream sauce but Mom's gone to the store to get some, then we'll be having dessert. And I got some great presents. Mom and Dad got me the new Sweeper game and Nanna got me a season ticket for next year."

Taamarai held her face in place. He was meant to be coming out to live with her in the new year. At least, that was what she thought they had agreed. He had said soon. So what was he going to do with a season ticket? She didn't want to be disappointed now, though. "That's great."

"Yeah, it's been pretty good. I mean, it would have been better with you here."

"I wish I could be there." Taamarai couldn't help a flatness in her voice. She was just tired.

"Well, next year. Like you promised."

She stopped brushing her hair. Taamarai remembered promising no more Christmases apart. She searched back over what she had said. Had that been what she meant, Christmases forever in Boston? Wouldn't they be together in Horton next year? She just smiled.

"Well, I've got to go. And we'll see each other in the New Year." She knew immediately it was the wrong thing to say.

"Yeah. I mean, I've got the tickets now, so I'll need to check when the games are. It might be easier for you to come up. That would be awesome. We could go to a game together."

Taamarai's disappointment became a flare of resentment and she squashed it. Not today. "Yeah. Anyway, I've got to go. Carl and Ali will be up any minute. I'll call you again in the evening, before bed."

"Yeah. Don't be too late, Tam. You need your sleep, doing all this work."

"I'm fine." Taamarai reached for the call end button, already hearing steps on the stairs outside. "I love you."

She wasn't sure if he heard it before she rang off and felt bad until Ali tumbled through the door and the rush began. Carl, looking like he'd been press-ganged, carried a stack of steaming oven dishes, his hands wrapped in a towel. Ali carried the ham. It took another two trips to bring everything up while Taamarai set out her offerings from the restaurant and things that she'd prepared with Ali over the week before.

At last, the door closed behind their final trip up and down the stairs. Ali balanced a small stack of presents in her hands. Carl had a six-pack. He checked the door was locked, as he always did, then wandered into the lounge and looked around properly. It was exactly the same as their apartment but like walking through a mirror into a different world.

Taamarai's colorful posters and bright bookshelves glimmered with fairy lights. She had turned the main light off, and in the corner, beside the balcony, a Christmas tree sparkled. Up close, he knew the decorations were cheap or secondhand, but in the low light he had to admit she'd done a good job. Ali was laying boxes under the tree, trying to stack them decoratively.

In the middle of the living room, the table was laid with more cutlery than anybody could ever need. Wine glasses awaited a couple of very nice bottles donated by the restaurant and fizzy grape juice for Ali. Taamarai came out of the kitchen, her usual long skirt and t-shirt or sweater and leggings swapped for a dark red wrap-around dress, belted at the waist with tinsel. A black beaded necklace looked a bit too glitzy but seasonal. She wore her hair down and small silver earrings. Nothing fancy, yet somehow unfamiliar.

"You look nice." He was too surprised not to say it and immediately regretted it but didn't stop looking.

"Thanks." Taamarai glanced away and crossed her hands over her stomach. He knew she did it when she was worried she looked fat.

"Amma says you have to dress up for Christmas." She glanced at his t-shirt and comfortable trousers and quickly tried to backpedal. "I mean, in our family. It's just our tradition."

Ali, wearing freshly washed baggy cargo pants and her favorite band t-shirt, laughed. "This *is* Dad dressed up."

Carl turned sharply towards her, but Ali didn't even notice and was already heading to the kitchen.

Taamarai smiled at him instead. "Thank you," she said again.

"What for?" It didn't seem like it was about the dress.

Taamarai looked around as if it were obvious. "For letting me share your Christmas. I mean," she looked around again, "I don't think I'd have bothered getting the place decorated on my own, and I really appreciate you both waiting to have Christmas dinner with me. It feels like a proper Christmas instead of a day at work."

Carl folded his arms. She'd made a real effort, so why couldn't he just say that? Instead, he said, "I don't know what Christmas is usually like for you and your folks, but this is more trouble than we usually take." With that ambivalent comment he headed for the fridge to dispose of his beers before getting out of the way as Ali and Taamarai coalesced into a single frenetic whirlwind. He just watched and, with nothing broken and no screaming, in a few minutes, they deposited paté and crusty bread on the table, poured drinks, lit candles and insisted on the pulling of crackers and the donning of silly paper hats.

"So, how was the restaurant?" Carl asked as they began eating.

Taamarai regaled them with the saga of the day. They already knew most of the regulars from her accounts, and it had the feeling of a festive instalment in a running drama. Their chat was easy, and with a half-bottle of wine inside him, Carl felt as contented and relaxed as he had for a very long time. Ali looked almost comatose from fine food and excitement and when they cleared away the main course, Taamarai discreetly slipped out to the kitchen.

When she came back, it was with a flaming pudding on a plate, a recipe he had watched her and Ali make weeks before. Then it had seemed needlessly elaborate and distinctly unappetizing as they mixed dark beer and sweet spices and what looked like little maggots but which Taamarai had assured him were actually granules of fat from around a cow's kidneys. As he took a mouthful, though, he had to admit it was delicious and not like anything store-bought or institutional he'd ever eaten.

Taamarai beamed. "Is it okay?"

He and Ali nodded and grunted their assent. "Good. I haven't made one since coming to the US. I didn't want to mess it up."

"How come?" Ali asked. She clearly couldn't understand why anybody wouldn't want this every Christmas.

Taamarai dug into her own pudding with her spoon. "Darren doesn't really like it, so I don't bother. It would only be me eating it, after all."

Carl felt his lip curl at her words. He could have predicted the answer before she said it. There was so much that Darren didn't like and the result always seemed to be that Taamarai did without. He was glad when Ali changed the subject back to how the pudding was made, whether everyone in Britain made them this way, whether they could make one again next year....

They settled into an after-dinner lull, stuffed and warm and comfortable. Eventually, Taamarai began to clear the table. Ali got up to help but quickly lapsed onto the couch, and Carl stepped in.

"You'll get your dress dirty," he observed as she leant towards the sink.

"Oh, that doesn't matter." Taamarai seemed to be floating just above the ground. He had never seen her quite so happy. "I hardly ever wear it anyway."

He didn't want to hear her say that Darren didn't like the color or thought it didn't really suit her figure. Which it did, very evidently from where he was standing.

"You should. Looks good on you."

"Thanks." She smiled.

Carl began washing up, at least enough that they had plates for leftovers and could move in the kitchen. Taamarai was already sorting the food. When everywhere looked a bit clearer, she gestured with a half-empty bottle of wine. "Do you want another glass?"

"Sure. Why not?" Carl knew why not but held his glass out

anyway. He wasn't really properly drunk, nowhere near how he sometimes got on a Friday night, or had until these last few months. He rarely drank wine, though, and it was affecting his head. Taamarai poured their refills.

"Shouldn't we toast?" he asked.

That. That was exactly why he shouldn't. That wasn't a question he asked. She smiled again, a little uncertain, then came over and gently touched the rim of her glass to his.

"To what?"

Carl stared past the wine in their glasses and met her eye. His mouth felt dry. To what?

"It's good. You. This. Christmas."

Taamarai nodded as if what he'd just said made perfect sense. "To Christmas, and friends." Was that what he'd said? Or meant? They drank carefully and, before Carl could consider his own words any further, Taamarai headed for the living room.

"I think it's time for presents."

Ali agreed and rummaged enthusiastically under the tree, handing each of them their offerings before collapsing back onto the couch. Taamarai looked at the small stack in front of her. Darren's gift was still in its brown paper, the address label peeling slightly. It was a large box, and Taamarai was curious. Even if the breakfast date hadn't worked out, she was interested to know what he had gotten her, especially after talking it up for most of the last month.

Beside it were two smaller packages, one wrapped and the other in a plastic bag. "I got you that one," Ali said with a nervous grin. "And Dad got you that one." She pointed towards the bag. "I said I could wrap it for him, but...."

She trailed off and shrugged. *Why?* he'd asked. It would be what it was just the same. He'd seemed embarrassed at having bothered at all and muttered about it just being some old bit of junk, so she'd left it.

Taamarai laughed gently. "Well, I'm suitably excited, and," she held up the bag, "I can't see what it is, so I'll call that wrapped." She looked at the gifts again. She should leave Darren's till last. That was what you were meant to do with the special present. But some protective impulse protested. Something that had been disappointed too many times?

Justifying herself out loud, Taamarai pointed at Darren's gift. "This one first, since Darren isn't here. Then definitely this one!" She picked up Ali's gift and looked at it delightedly before laying it aside.

She already knew the weight of Darren's gift and that it rattled when she shook it, as if there were a couple of things inside. Taamarai peeled open the packaging and felt an ache in a familiar spot: *told you so.* A cereal box. It was an old practical joke in his family to make gifts harder to guess.

She'd enjoyed the gag well enough now and then. When there were presents stacked everywhere, it could make things exciting. When something perfect was hiding inside, it could be wonderful, she supposed. She glanced up and found Carl staring across at her.

"Aren't you going to open yours?" She pointed to the two gifts lying in front of him, one from her and one from Ali. Ali was making her way through a slightly larger stack from friends at school.

"I'll wait." He didn't look away and Taamarai felt that he knew he was being cruel. She peeled the end of the box open and was glad an instant later for not just emptying it out to see what was inside. She pulled out a DVD. She didn't have a DVD player but maybe Darren had forgotten.

"*High School Sweethearts.*" They'd seen it at the cinema the year before with friends. It was okay. Taamarai felt a smile squeeze up and across her face like scar tissue, hard and false.

"What is it?" Ali asked eagerly.

Taamarai held it up. "This is so sweet of Darren. We saw this movie just before I left. It was a really lovely afternoon." She could already feel the history of the event becoming what she made it, transforming the gift into something thoughtful. "And hidden in the box so I wouldn't know what it was." She laughed, high and jangling, then caught Carl's eye and stopped.

"That all that's in there?" He nodded to the box. Taamarai pretended to check.

"Yep, that's all." As she looked down, her knuckles were pale, crushing the cardboard. "I'm just going to get some water." She still had the box in her hand and Carl didn't say anything.

In the kitchen, Taamarai sagged onto the sideboard. She only had a few moments. Quickly, she slid her hand into the box and drew out the brightly colored sex toy that Darren had also included. Hardly wanting to touch it, Taamarai looked around in a panic then threw it into the bottom of a corner cupboard. She would retrieve it later, but in the meantime there was no reason Ali might go looking there for anything.

A confused feeling of humiliation and a deep, wounding sadness bubbled up in her chest. For a moment, Taamarai thought she might not be able to draw breath. It was a compliment, Darren would tell her. A sign of how much he was missing her. A tear spilled onto her cheek before she could stop it, and she turned to the sink as a shadow approached the door.

"Thought I'd grab some water, too." Carl sounded like that was all he was there for. Nothing in the world else. No triumphant sneer or well-observed intrusion. "Ali," he called out, "Go grab some Christmas music or something."

"Sure. Wait, my phone's downstairs." A miracle in itself.

"Well, go get it then!" The peremptory tone always sounded so harsh to Taamarai but Ali had assured her it was really okay. Now, Taamarai was glad of it, or what it meant. Ali would be gone for a few minutes. He waited until the door to the apartment closed.

"You okay?"

Taamarai suddenly felt like lashing out. Of course she wasn't okay. That was why he was asking. Why did he have to ask?

Carl had seen something change in Taamarai's face. He wasn't sure he wanted to know what was in the box, but it had cut her to the quick, and he knew that the friendly thing would be to leave her alone, distract Ali and let her deal with it. So why wasn't he doing that? *To friends.* That had been their toast. Her toast. Friends didn't make a point of sticking the knife in.

When she didn't answer or turn around, he stepped into the kitchen. Taamarai was almost hanging off the sink, looking limp and tired, but when he reached out and touched her shoulder, she was stiff as a piece of wire. He didn't need to see her face to know, with bitter certainty, that for the second time that day, Darren had made her cry. It didn't matter whether she could admit that to herself or to him. She jumped at his touch and moved away, then reached out to get herself a glass of water and one for him.

"I'm fine. Just...." Taamarai stacked her words against tears she wouldn't let fall. "Just felt a bit.... I missed...." She still hadn't turned around fully. "I don't want to spoil things for Ali."

This seemed an irrelevance to Carl. "Ali's gotta know it ain't all reindeer and snowflakes."

Now she did turn and her tearful eyes blazed fire. "I think she's pretty clear about that, Carl." She looked at him defiantly and some part of him cheered with silent approval. "But she deserves to know that sometimes it is."

Her face was on the verge of crumbling again. Taamarai felt a gulf of loneliness between her and the world. She ached to see her parents, her brother, her nieces and nephews, her friends, most of whom she had lost contact with years ago.

But there were new friends, too. Maybe Carl wasn't even trying to torment her. Maybe he was trying to be kind. As the despair threatened to overwhelm her, as it had done so many times before, alone in the dark, trying not to wake Darren with her crying, she straightened her back and swiped at her eyes. "If Ali asks anything, I just missed my parents."

"Sure." He heard the subtext, too. *If Ali doesn't ask anything, leave it alone.* They both heard her footsteps on the stairs. Without a sideways glance, Taamarai headed past him towards the lounge. Carl watched her go and felt confused and angry. By the time he got through to the lounge, Ali was playing a jolly Christmas jingle on her phone. He was about to tell her to turn it off when he remembered that he'd asked for it.

"You haven't opened your other presents yet." Ali bounced over to Taamarai then sat on the floor, watching expectantly.

"No, I wanted to wait for you." Taamarai hoped she looked fine. Maybe a bit tired. Still, Ali scooted over on her knees and rested her head for a moment on Taamarai's shoulder, then sat back down and nudged her gift over with one foot.

"Well, what about yours?" Taamarai asked with a threadbare grin. To her relief, both Ali and Carl set about opening their presents, too. Ali chose her gift from Taamarai, Carl his gift from Ali.

As Taamarai peeled back the wrapping paper, she found a small cardboard box. She pried it open to find tissue paper pressed around something. Nestled in it was a small copper-colored spice grinder, the sort sold at Turkish markets, made from pressed metal with a rotary handle. Taamarai felt a very different kind of tear in her eye. She had pointed them out to Ali in a corner shop downtown once, but she hadn't told Ali how badly she had always wanted one. Darren thought they looked tacky so she'd paid more for an electric one that she rarely used.

"Ali, it's perfect!" Taamarai leant across the small circle and hugged Ali tight, interrupting Ali's careful unrolling of a large poster painting of a cityscape. It was by a local graffiti artist. Horton's skyline marched away black under a shimmering pink sunset.

"Wow!" Ali just gazed at it.

"There's a frame for it behind the couch," Taamarai added with a smile. "I didn't have enough wrapping paper to cover it!"

Ali bounded over to find out more and Taamarai looked to where Carl sat, staring down at a small box. He seemed lost in thought.

"Hey, Dad?" Ali leaned over him, still grappling with the large plastic picture frame. "Oh, I made that in class," she remarked casually. "Look inside!" As if the best bit weren't the lovingly shaped and painted wood. He opened it, and Taamarai wanted to see but held back so as not to crowd the moment. When Carl said nothing, Ali added, "It's not one of the expensive ones, but I remember you said he was your favorite." She sounded suddenly unsure.

Carl silently lifted a baseball card out of the box. He didn't remember ever talking to Ali about his old card collection. It was never that much of a collection, really, but in a childhood with few fond memories, it had been special for a while. He didn't remember telling her that Frank Robinson was his favorite either, but he must have because how else could she have known? Ali touched him on the shoulder as she came to sit down again.

"Thanks." It was all he could manage. It was all that was needed as he met Ali's eye. He placed the card carefully back in the box and set it in front of him and her face transformed into a warm, loving smile.

"So, what did you get me?" Ali picked up the final package in front of her and pulled it open eagerly. It was a largish box and quite heavy.

"Oh, Dad!"

As the wrapping paper came off, her eyes lit up. She'd been talking about the running shoes for months, a sleek black design endorsed by three of the Olympic middle-distance team. Ali knelt up and put her arms around Carl's neck. "Dad, you're awesome." All he could do was squeeze her hand and say nothing.

Ali was now set up for some time, what with sorting out the frame for her picture and trying on her new sneakers, but the ritual was not complete. "So it's just you two now." She picked up the gifts that lay in front of them and shoved them forward with excited impatience.

"You didn't have to." Taamarai held up the gift Carl had got her. She hadn't imagined that he would and had told herself that she was only getting something for him because it would be rude not to after inviting him over for Christmas. And it had been right there in the shop. And she had thought of Carl and couldn't resist the reckless impulse any more than she could ignore a feeling that it wasn't quite neighborly.

"Neither did you."

Unceremoniously, he pulled the wrapping paper off his gift and turned the volume over in his hand. It was old and battered. A proper bookshop find. *The Scarlet Letter*. He opened the cover. "For when the time is right! Merry Christmas, Taamarai." Carl looked at her and nodded. He wasn't sure what to say that wouldn't spoil things. It seemed to be his specialty. To his surprise, she smiled and seemed to accept the silence.

Then Taamarai opened the small plastic bag. She reached in, found her fingers wouldn't fit, and turned it over carefully to let something fall out onto her palm. It was a thin silver chain. On the end of it hung a star, trailing its own tail. A shooting star the size of a fingernail. Taamarai cradled it in her hand, taken off guard by the unexpected loveliness of it.

"It's beautiful."

Carl shrugged and looked awkward. "Was just there. I guess it seemed like something you'd like."

She reached up and unfastened the black necklace she'd been wearing.

"Hey, that looks good," he interjected, but Taamarai smiled and let it fall away.

"It's pretty enough, but I've never really liked it. It never really fit." She looked at the floral beaded black necklace, then set it aside and reached behind her head to fasten the silver chain. The shooting star fell right between her collarbones. "How does it look?"

"Looks good," he murmured. Carl hadn't really known what he was thinking when he picked up the necklace. It had just been there in the pawn shop next to his favorite bar. From the dust on it when he asked to take a look, it had been there for a while, but he'd never seen it before, and once he had, he couldn't unsee it. That had been a month ago, just after Ali's birthday. He hadn't gotten it for Christmas or planned it as a gift. He'd just bought it and it had sat on the chest of drawers in his room. Then it was Christmas Day, and Ali had proudly gathered up their gifts and bet that Taamarai would have got something for each of them, and it had made sense to grab it and bring it upstairs.

"Thank you." Taamarai leaned over and touched his hand just for a moment. Carl's eye was caught by the star again, so that he didn't meet her eye. Then Taamarai was up, bustling to the kitchen and coming back with water for everybody and leftover nibbles from dinner.

Ali suggested a movie to finish the evening and searched up a suitably atrocious Christmas comedy. Once again, Carl found himself placed in the middle, and Ali made no pretense of not leaning cozily against him. He lifted his other arm to rest along the back of the couch and, instead of trying to disappear into a singularity in the corner of the universe, Taamarai, too, settled down beside him, not leaning, but close enough that her crossed legs touched his, and if he looked out of the corner of his eye, he could see her face silhouetted beside him.

By the time the movie ended, he had his arm around her shoulders, and Taamarai was almost asleep on his side. Ali was equally limp and lethargic. As the credits rolled, Carl didn't want them to end. The long day had caught up with them all, and he felt a strange, comfortable lassitude. The credits did end, though.

Carl stayed where he was, hardly moving, until Taamarai seemed to spring awake. She stood, suddenly full of bustle again, heading for the kitchen, the table, clearing away plates, and never looking at him. After a few minutes, she came back and bent down with a smile to shake Ali's shoulder. "Come on. Time for bed."

Ali looked around blearily, a sleepy smile in her eyes and lifting the corners of her mouth. She dragged herself off the couch.

"Night." She yawned enormously. "Merry Christmas, Taamarai. Thanks for my picture."

Taamarai hugged her. "You're very welcome. I'll come down, and we can hang it tomorrow? And thank you for my present. I've always wanted one. It's beautiful." She kissed Ali's cheek and stroked a wayward wave of her hair. Then Ali turned around. She looked like she might head for the door but instead reached for Carl and hugged him close.

"This has been the best Christmas ever, Dad. Thank you." Taken by surprise, he hugged her back with one arm, then watched as she headed for the door. She was moving like a zombie and would probably be in bed before he got down the stairs.

Carl turned back to Taamarai and felt awkward. "Thanks," he muttered.

Taamarai gave him an embarrassed smile. "Ali did most of it. But," she touched the shooting star at her throat, "thank you."

Carl looked at her hard and felt suddenly cross.

"Don't do that. Ali's done a great job but you put this all together." He waved his arm around the apartment. "Ask Ali what a regular Christmas with me looks like." He looked away and was about to stalk off to 502 but he turned back again. "Merry Christmas."

A wave of her hair hung down, covering the necklace. He reached out and pushed it away, finding it easier somehow to talk to the star. "Whatever it was...." He pulled his hand back, and felt her gaze fixed on him. "Whatever he said, whatever was in that box, you did good today. Today was a good day, and you did that. I hope you had a good day, too." Carl felt he had a lot more to say but no more words.

Taamarai nodded slowly. "I have had a good day." She seemed to consider this for some time. "The best Christmas I can remember for...a really long time." She held his eye for an agony of silence, then her phone rang. Maybe it had earlier but in the quiet there was no ignoring it. She looked around guiltily. "What time is it?" Past midnight.

"I'm sorry. I've got to go. Goodnight, Carl." She reached out and, just before he could turn, took his hand in something like a handshake. She squeezed his fingers then let go, heading for the kitchen to take the call, knowing he would let himself out.

"Goodnight, Taamarai." Just as he pulled the door closed, Carl heard her say, "Hey, I'm sorry. I lost track of the time. I know. I'm really sorry."

He headed for the stairs with an unfamiliar feeling in his chest. When he got to 502, Ali was indeed already in bed, and he had *The Scarlet Letter* in his hand, though he didn't remember picking it up. He set the book down on the table with the box that Ali had made for him, and headed for bed but despite the food and the wine, sleep came slowly.

Chapter Eleven

It was past noon on a Friday and Carl had just got up. A big job had finished and an open bar the night before had been part of the deal. Now, his hangover dulled the sickening sensation of stress leaving his body.

For a month, he'd been watching shadows while Jackie got a new club off the ground. His job was to make sure that everything went smoothly with Jackie's many competitors in town. Nobody had caused trouble. Jackie had been pleased and wanted to show his thanks. Last night had also been meant as a sweetener – capable men were hard to find, worth keeping on retainer.

Carl remembered the offer. Other parts of the night were blurry, but he knew that he'd said what he always did. He didn't work with anyone or for anyone. Period. He did fixed jobs, took what he was owed, and owed nobody. All the men who'd ever hired him lived their whole lives as he had for the last month. That was their choice, and they expected to live rich for it.

Once he'd wanted to be one of them, maybe. It was hard to remember. But then Ali had come along, and slowly, Carl had made his peace with what it meant to have lines he wouldn't cross and to be a part of nobody's feuds. Among other things, it meant that jobs like this latest one – fixed term and well paid – were hard to refuse, even if he knew when he started them that he'd be right back here, his head pounding and his fingertips itching with excess adrenaline.

The first ill-timed knock on the door had been Taamarai. She'd worked an unexpected late shift last night at the restaurant. When she woke, it was to sour milk in the refrigerator. At the door to 502, she'd gestured apologetically with a full coffee cup, and the smell made him gag. He let her in and slouched back to the couch. She knew where everything was and made her own way to the kitchen in blessed silence.

Minutes later, a key turned in the front door then the door slammed back with the force of a hurricane. Heavy, hurried footsteps followed, and Ali stormed into the kitchen, ostentatiously ignoring both him and Taamarai. She dropped her bag noisily and grabbed a glass of water, which he could hear sloshing onto the floor as she stomped back past them and slammed her bedroom door behind her.

Taamarai appeared in the lounge seconds later and looked inquiringly at him. Then she seemed to realize that she'd done it and flinched back in case she had overstepped a mark. The gesture usually annoyed him, but today he couldn't be bothered to care. Carl just shrugged, pulled out his phone, and tried to concentrate on the sports news. He hoped everything would settle down and stay quiet, but as Taamarai headed for Ali's door and knocked gently, he knew it wouldn't.

"Hey, Ali. Ali, what's up?"

He could hear Taamarai calling softly and, even from out here, could make out the spiky, static sound of music blaring from Ali's headphones in return.

"Ali, can I come in?" Taamarai asked quietly.

Carl rose in frustration and reached the door just as Taamarai put out a hand to open it. He landed three heavy bangs on the wood, shaking it in its frame.

"Ali, get out here. Now!" Carl saw Taamarai step away, looking

nervous and annoyed. Well, he was annoyed too! Her scrabbling at
the door was nearly as aggravating as the sudden arrival of a
problem Ali didn't want to talk about.

"Now!" he yelled again and slammed his hand once more onto
the door. Ali emerged moments later, her headphones still playing
where they hung round her neck. "And turn that shit off." Ali glowered but pulled her phone out and turned off the music.

"Well?" he asked angrily.

"Well what?" Ali retorted, pushing her jaw forward pugna-
ciously.

He could feel his temper bubbling. "Don't you give me that!
What are you doing back here in the middle of a school day acting
like the world just crapped on your parade?" If she was playing
hooky, he didn't really care, but he couldn't handle the perfor-
mance she was bringing with her.

Ali stepped forward, clearly trying to wind him up. "They
suspended me! Now can I go back to my room?"

"What the hell did you do?" He stepped forward too, not sure
what he was planning to do, when he felt a movement beside him.
He turned and stopped dead. Taamarai was looking at him coldly.
She came closer, and suddenly he felt crowded and criticized. He
stepped back.

"They suspended you? What for?" Taamarai seemed deeply
concerned but also calm and full of sympathy. It had probably
never happened to her, Carl thought. He fought the urge to head
for his own room and leave Taamarai to find out what it could be
like on the other side of Ali's temper. To his surprise, though, Ali let
Taamarai take her by the arm and steer her back out to the lounge,
where Taamarai sat with her on the couch.

"Tell me what happened," Taamarai instructed softly.

Ali looked up defiantly. "I hit a boy." She laughed maliciously.
"Sent him to hospital."

Taamarai looked aghast and glanced up at Carl. He shrugged
back. If she wanted to do it her way, that was her business. He only
wandered back here to watch as it all went to hell, he told himself.

Taamarai turned back to Ali, still quiet. "Okay. Why? Were you arguing? Had he done something?"

"What do you think?" Ali set her chin, her eyes blazing with anger and wounded pride. Carl had no trouble recognizing himself in the expression. There was some other hurt in her look, though. It was something more childlike that stirred a worry he had never known what to do with except try and toughen her up against the inevitable pain of the world. He was about to tell Ali to mind her tongue when Taamarai spoke again, apparently now counting him out of the conversation at his own request. Her voice carried an unfamiliar authority.

"I think that you're angry and scared. And you should be. He might be in hospital, but a suspension could do you more damage in the long run. I think whatever you did, you must have had your reasons, and even if they weren't very good reasons, it won't change the fact that I'm on your side, just like your dad." She glanced his way again but this time it was clear to Carl that she wasn't asking him for anything, only commanding his acquiescence or his silence.

"And I think that we can only start trying to deal with the situation once we know what it is, so what happened? I'm going to make us some tea, and you can have a think about where to start." Taamarai left Ali sitting on the couch, looking like the world had just gone slightly sideways.

A few minutes later, Taamarai came back with two cups of tea and a fresh glass of water for Carl, which she handed to him where he stood. Carl suppressed an irate temptation to refuse it and sat down at the table, reaching for a pack of painkillers. Taamarai sat beside Ali, handed her a mug of tea, and ignored him again and Carl felt judged. He heard her silent questions. *Why wasn't he doing something, saying something?* And it made him even more morose and bellicose about the whole damn thing.

It wasn't that Carl didn't care; it was just that it wasn't much of a surprise. Getting suspended was most of what *he'd* done at school, when he'd bothered to show up. His education that mattered was all from prison. At least there, classes were an alternative to the boredom. Whatever the fight had been about, he supposed he was pleased Ali ended it on her terms, but he didn't think that was what Taamarai would want to hear.

Ali sipped her tea for a while, and Carl wondered if she would clam up. When she began to speak, she was clearly on the verge of tears but still full of anger.

"He's in the class above. On the football team." She looked down at her tea. "I guess I liked him. I thought I did. Since I've been on the running team. He...he'd hang out with me after training meets. I dunno. We'd talk." She looked up at Taamarai, studiously avoiding catching Carl's eye, where he knew she would see the scorn he couldn't hide. Hadn't he raised her better than that? Taamarai, however, just reached out and took her hand.

"Okay. Then what?"

Ali blushed scarlet and looked at her hands. "A few days ago after practice, he sort of...." She looked mortified. "We were kissing. Just kissing. But then he told everyone that it wasn't just that, that I'd...." She looked up. "I didn't hit him for that. I swear!" It seemed to matter deeply to her.

"But then, he was crowding me. And these guys who hang out with him and all these other kids were watching. He was laughing and saying stuff. Like, how I was that trashy I'd do it right there, that we'd, you know, on the sports field. He was pulling at my top. That's when...."

She finally looked at Carl with a defiant jerk of her chin. "I broke his nose and a couple of his ribs, I think." Taamarai's eyes widened in astonishment as Carl nodded, more than a little proudly.

"Too right. Not that he'd have got ideas if you hadn't been fooling around in the first place."

"Carl!" Taamarai's rebuke was sharp and short, and he felt it. She looked away from him, still speaking low and steady. "Whatever you'd been doing after practice doesn't justify what you say he did today, Ali."

"What I *say*?" Ali's anger flared again.

"Yes, what you say." Taamarai was firm. "I believe you, but to fix it at school, it would help if you have any proof, anybody who you think would be willing to say they saw it too."

"What do you mean, fix it?" Ali looked hopeful and confused all at the same time.

Taamarai, in turn, was businesslike. "This is your first suspension in senior school, right?" Ali just nodded. "Most colleges and employers won't look any earlier than that or pay much attention if they do. You were acting in self-defense, so the least we can have them do is clear your record and bring you back into class. We should try to get the boy moved out of your classes too."

"He won't come near me again!"

"I don't dispute that. But he tried to molest you in a school corridor. That's not okay. And what about the other girls?"

Ali looked like she'd been slapped and, for the first time, that deeper vulnerability surfaced. Carl saw the change. It was one thing to be brave about some boy making a fuss and getting his ass kicked. It was another for a grown woman she respected to talk about what had happened as something serious, adult, and fundamentally wrong.

Taamarai reached out and drew Ali into a close, long hug, holding her as Ali suddenly began to cry. Carl felt that helpless fear again. He was about to snap at Ali to stop whining and be glad nothing worse happened when he caught Taamarai's eye over Ali's shoulder, and the words wouldn't come.

They stayed like that for some time, apparently none of them sure what to do next. Then a strange expression passed across Taamarai's face. She checked her watch and turned to him with a look of determination. "Come on. If we leave now, we can get to school before the day is out and try to get this sorted." She stood up and gently disengaged from Ali. "It's probably best if you stay here, but can you write down everything that happened? Email it to me? We won't be gone long. Carl?"

Taamarai was gesturing to the door, and his first reaction was to tell her to go to hell, but instead, he found himself pulling on a pair of shoes and a jacket. In the bathroom, he brushed his teeth and rubbed a wet cloth over his face. He still felt dreadful and probably looked it, but Taamarai either didn't notice, didn't care or knew that saying anything would only make things worse.

At the bus stop, they only had a few seconds to wait. For most of the journey, Taamarai tapped at her phone and muttered to herself. She exclaimed once, when a mail from Ali arrived, then sat reading it at speed. As they approached the school building, Taamarai undid her plait and ran her fingers through her hair so that it sprang out around her face, wild and bold. It didn't look smart, but he saw her stand a little straighter. At the reception, they were stopped by a security guard.

"Good afternoon. We're here to see Principal Morris." Taamarai took the lead and Carl just stood by, an extra in a movie that wasn't about him. The guard asked some more questions and, to Carl's surprise, a few minutes later, they were ushered upstairs.

Principal Morris was a tall woman in her fifties, stern faced and sharply dressed. He had met her a couple of times before and always felt like he was being evaluated. She greeted them cautiously and addressed Carl.

"Thank you for coming in. I've been informed about the incident. It's good to see parents taking disciplinary issues seriously." *And unusual in your case*, he sensed in her reprimanding tone. She reached out to shake his hand, then paused. "Good afternoon, Miss?"

Taamarai stuck out her hand, shaking the other woman's firmly. "Ms Calder."

"You aren't Alison Grigg's mother?" That much was apparent from Taamarai's age and appearance, and Taamarai only shook her head. "Well, I'm afraid that, in that case, I'll have to ask you to wait outside. I can only discuss a case with parents."

Carl could feel a rude and angry comment building in his throat. He hadn't wanted to come, didn't know what to say, and in his limited experience, he only made things worse. He'd be damned if he was going to sit in a room and listen to this woman berate him for his parenting and insult his daughter. Then Taamarai said the last thing he expected. "Of course, Principal Morris, but I'm Ali's stepmother. I'm sure that's covered by school policy."

The woman's eyes widened in shock. Carl felt evaluated yet again and clearly found wanting.

"Ms Calder, are you sure?" It wasn't a considered question, and Principal Morris knew that it was both rude and inappropriate the moment it was spoken, but she could hardly take it back. "I'm sure Alison never said anything about her father marrying," she added lamely.

Carl hoped his own surprise wasn't apparent as he felt Taamarai's hand slip into his. She squeezed once, a silent plea to play along, before saying, "Ali is a very private young woman." She kept hold of his hand as Principal Morris stood aside and beckoned them into her office.

From there, the meeting passed Carl in a blur. They sat down, and the principal tried her best to sound disciplinarian and firm, but she had already lost too much authority, and Taamarai didn't give her a moment to find it again. He watched as Taamarai methodically, politely, inexorably ploughed her way through the defenses that the other woman threw up.

Consulting her phone like a lawyer in a court case, Taamarai cited school board regulations. She quoted Ali's email, which listed complaints to class teachers and the school guidance counsellor about bullying and sexual harassment, though Carl was sure Ali had never used those words, and finally she played the woman a video that Ali had forwarded of the confrontation in the hall. Apparently, several students had been filming.

Long before Ali landed her first punch, Carl saw Principal Morris's face fall as it became clear that the boy had indeed been behaving in a manner unbecoming of the laws of the state, let alone the honor code of the school football team. Brushing a hand through her unruly hair, Taamarai turned squarely to Mrs Morris and took a surprisingly conciliatory tone.

"Principal Morris, I know that you are doing a difficult job in impossible circumstances. Ali speaks very highly of her teachers and of this school, and I know that she appreciates all of your efforts to stand up for your students." Carl kept his face inscrutable.

"Clearly," Taamarai continued, "there has been a very unfortunate misunderstanding. We're not interested in making your life difficult or in damaging the reputation of the school, but Ali is a brilliant and determined girl who, I'm sure you will agree, deserves to feel safe and protected and has the right to defend herself if she is not?" The principal only nodded mutely.

"I hope that this can be resolved appropriately," Taamarai continued pitilessly. "Obviously, the young man in question should not be allowed back to school, at least not before he has attended suitable counseling. Any reference to suspension or misbehavior regarding this incident will, naturally, be removed from Ali's record, and I hope that the school will see the necessity of providing her with some additional tuition to support her in completing her examinations this year, in light of the ongoing disruption and trauma associated with this situation?" She looked up in the same way that she had at him earlier when he had followed her out of the house without a word. Carl was not at all surprised to see Principal Morris nod again.

"That's wonderful," Taamarai said with a generous smile. "Thank you for being so understanding and supportive." Her tone became troubled. "We should get going now. Ali is very upset. We were reluctant to leave her at home alone, but her education matters so much to her. I was worried about the stress this might cause her if we didn't resolve it before the weekend." She rose, and Carl stood too. "I'll put in writing everything we've discussed and send you a copy to confirm, and Ali will be back in class on Monday first thing. I can put you in touch with our lawyer if any further questions arise."

"Of course, Ms...?"

"Calder."

"Ms Calder. And my apologies to Alison for the misunderstand-ing." Principal Morris's voice was weak and quiet.

Within minutes, they were back out on the street, heading for the bus stop. Taamarai seemed to be shrinking to the woman he knew who lived in the apartment upstairs, played cards with them after dinner or came by when her milk ran out, who always seemed on the verge of apologizing for something and who he had never heard raise her voice to anyone. She looked a little anxious now, like she couldn't quite believe what she had done either, and only as they rounded the final corner to the bus stop did she think to let go of his hand. Carl had noticed her holding it but only now real-ized that he could have let go, too.

They journeyed back in a different silence from earlier. This was more consciously the silence of two people who didn't know how to share whatever was going on in their heads. When they got in, Ali was still sitting on the couch, looking expectant and afraid.

Taamarai didn't beat about the bush. "The school stuff is going to be fine." Taamarai grinned shyly and hugged Ali as she explained what the principal had agreed to. To Carl's surprise, Ali didn't even complain about the extra tuition but instead squeezed Taamarai more tightly and whispered a thank you.

Ali looked awed. "But how did you know? That they'd agree and stuff?"

Carl was glad she asked. He didn't know how either, but he had definitely wondered.

Looking mortified and a little pleased with herself all at once, Taamarai shrugged and stared down at her hands. "It wasn't that big a deal. I've worked in schools now and then. When there wasn't enough editing work, I'd do cover teaching. I didn't really enjoy it but I know a bit about how the disciplinary stuff works." She looked up and giggled shyly. "And I used to watch a lot of court-room dramas. All day, sometimes, when I was working from home on publishing jobs."

Ali gave her a disbelieving look and then burst out laughing, both of them exhaling the stress of the last few hours. At last, Taamarai took Ali off to the kitchen, and he heard both of them calming down over the rituals of cooking.

Still sitting at the table, Carl took a while to register that he was looking at his own hand. He went to the bathroom and found himself staring at his reflection instead. He felt sorry for Principal Morris, though not a bit sorry at what had happened. Taamarai had been bluffing.... He decided he was more, not less, impressed by that. Carefully, he shaved, drank some more water and showered. By the time he was done, the apartment smelled like dinner was ready.

Afterwards, Taamarai hung around a little longer than usual. She normally left for work with plenty of time to spare but tonight she waited until Ali headed for her bedroom. Ali said she had homework to do but looked drained by the whole experience and like she would be asleep as soon as her door closed.

As soon as Ali was safely in her room, Taamarai got up, looking hurried and nervous again and evidently getting ready to leave. Carl got up too, determined that she wouldn't before he'd said what he needed to, no matter how much easier it would be to keep quiet.

"I didn't think you had it in you." He kept his voice light.

"What?" She paused just inside the kitchen and looked over at him in guilty uncertainty.

"The way you were with the principal."

Taamarai glanced away in embarrassment. "Yeah, I'm sorry about that. I had to do something and I thought, well, I know what they need to hear. I'm sorry for lying, though. I didn't think about them not letting me come into the meeting, and then I didn't know what else to do." She turned away again, fiddling with things in the sink and checking her phone for the time. Carl stepped close, close enough that he could be sure Ali wouldn't overhear through the thin walls.

"I never could've fought for my girl like that!" His voice was fierce. "You hear? Hell, she'd've been expelled for good if they'd let me do the talking." His tone softened. "I guess I should've known, the way you are with me."

They rarely argued, not as such. Carl had the good grace not to be an ass when somebody was cooking for him, and Taamarai would usually back off and change the subject if she saw a disagreement coming, but not always. A few times, she'd made him work for his opinion, mostly causing him to shift his ground as he did. Now, he smiled slightly, and Taamarai echoed the expression, faintly but warmly.

"Still, I never thought I'd see you go after something like that." Determined and stubborn and nothing like he'd ever seen before, he thought, but couldn't find the words to say.

Taamarai looked down. "Ali's a wonderful young woman." She looked back up again. "She doesn't talk much. About you, I mean. Not to me, maybe not to anybody. But I know how hard you've fought for her, too. So does she." To his surprise, she reached out and touched his arm. "The most important thing is that she knows she isn't alone and she can make all the choices she wants."

Carl nodded slowly. "You didn't have to. That's all. And I'm glad you did." With a grin, trying to back off from his own sense of exposure but somehow ploughing forward into even more dangerous territory, he added, "The look on the principal's face when you said you were Ali's stepmother!"

This time Taamarai smiled properly but only seemed to share the joke so far. Carl felt disappointed, then foolish. What did he expect?

Taamarai glanced over his shoulder towards the door. "I should head out. I've got a late shift tonight. And I should call Darren before that." She looked momentarily guilty, probably for not sounding more enthusiastic about that phone call, he thought.

"Thank you, for letting me fight for her with you." She met his eye and seemed frozen, as still and unsure as Carl felt. His heart thumped heavily. Then she stepped away and was back to her normal self. "Do you mind if I cook lunch for us all on Sunday? It'll be good to catch up with Ali and see how she's feeling before she goes back to school."

Assuming his agreement, Taamarai went to step through the kitchen doorway, but Carl was in the way. He should move. He knew that. She didn't seem to notice. Why should she? They spent enough time in each other's apartments, in each other's space. Taamarai moved past him so close that Carl could feel her body brush against his. He reached out and held her arm.

"That'd be good."

She looked up at him and Carl noticed her eyes, dark brown and flecked with gold, as if he were seeing them for the first time. Then she gave him the tiniest nod and went on her way.

Carl watched her go, heard the front door close and headed to the refrigerator to grab a soda. Standing with the door open, caught mid-routine, he wondered what Darren – the husband he'd never met but who was somehow always just around the corner – must feel like walking into rooms with a woman like that by his side and not having to worry about somebody finding out the truth. The fridge motor began to hum more loudly, bringing Carl back to the moment without any kind of answer.

He picked up a second soda bottle and put the thought out of his head as he walked over to Ali's room. He knocked gently and then opened the door.

"Hey. You want a drink?"

He held out the bottle and came in when she reached out for it. As he expected, she was already snuggled under her blankets with the curtains drawn. "How you doing?" Ali gave him a crooked smile, hesitated, then hopped out of bed, walked over and wrapped her arms around him in a brief but fervent hug. Stepping back, she smiled more confidently.

"I'm glad you taught me to fight back."

Chapter Twelve

Darren had arrived in Horton late and tired. His flight via New York had been delayed by four hours. He had wanted to take a direct flight, straight from Boston to North Carolina, but that had been two hundred dollars more and Taamarai simply hadn't been able to afford it. Now she felt that he was right: the extra money would have been worth it to save all the disruption.

He was quiet in the taxi from the airport and held her hand limply. Back at Gabriel Heights, he huffed his suitcase up the stairs despite Taamarai's offers to help. He insisted that she hadn't warned him how many stairs there were though she knew they had talked about it. She had offered to ship his stuff instead, but he hadn't liked the idea.

Inside the apartment, Darren sat in the living room while she brought him tea and a slice of the cake that she had baked. It was a bit dry and not his favorite kind, but he ate it anyway and looked around with tired eyes. Taamarai could feel herself tensing. She had shown him around the apartment in their video calls, but it felt different seeing his critical gaze over everything.

He got up, wandered around and dumped his bag in the

bedroom, his rucksack in the hall. Taamarai immediately wanted to clear up, and then she felt guilty.

"I'd have put the bed in the other room. It's bigger."

She had explained her choice of bedroom when she moved in, and he hadn't seemed to notice or care. "I know it's bigger," she repeated now, "but I only sleep in it and keep clothes in the wardrobe. There's more room for books and space for my desk in the other room."

"Don't you think it's a bit cramped having all of your books out like this?"

"No." Taamarai couldn't think of anything else to say.

He nodded. Then he looked at a large picture on the wall. It was by the same artist as the painting she had bought Ali for Christmas. High buildings climbed towards a bright turquoise and orange sky. "Babe, do you mind if we take that one down?"

Taamarai frowned. "Why?"

"Well, I mean, it doesn't make any sense. The colors are all wrong. Don't you think it looks a bit silly?"

"I like it." Taamarai couldn't help feeling hurt, and it showed in her voice.

"Really?" He sounded mystified, and she wondered why he thought she had bought it in the first place.

He shrugged. "I guess you could put it in the other room. It's kind of your workspace. Anyway, I brought a great photo from our wedding. Mom had it framed for us. It would look great there and it'll help me feel like this is my home, too."

And there it was. The trump card. Taamarai had talked with him about how good it would be settling in here together, making the apartment into his space as well as hers.

"That sounds great." She headed for the kitchen, trying to stay cheerful. "Are you hungry? I got chicken. I thought I could do a stir fry." He usually didn't mind her stir fry.

Darren brightened up. "I'm starving. I've been craving pizza all day. Is there anywhere good round here?"

"Yeah, JB's, but I thought we could cook for a few days. It's nearly the end of the month and things are a bit tight with the plane ticket."

"JB's? I've never heard of it."

"It's local. I don't think it's even a chain. I've met JB." Taamarai smiled. Darren didn't smile back.

"Tam, you know I don't like taking a chance on independents. You never know if they'll be any good. Isn't there a Domino's or something nearby?"

Taamarai had to turn away to hide her annoyance. She had been so excited to see Darren and felt bad for already being so frustrated.

"There's one a couple of miles away."

"Do they deliver?" He sounded happier.

"Yes. But Darren, it's so expensive!"

"Yeah, but Tam, at least we'll know what we're getting. Come on. I've just arrived. And we saved loads by not getting the direct flight."

She knew what he meant: that had been her decision and it had been awful. This would make it up to him. Taamarai already knew she'd lost.

"Besides, you said the restaurant's been giving you loads of extra hours since Christmas."

"You're right." She took a deep breath. "Can you make the order?" Taamarai had worked the morning shift and then waited up to collect Darren when his flight landed. Tomorrow was another early start. She was tired and didn't want to argue. She just wanted to eat and sleep.

He got up and hugged her, the first time since the airport. His embrace pinned her arms by her sides. "Babe, come on. I've got a headache from the flight, and I'd have to set up a new account. Mom always does it at home."

"I haven't got an account, either."

"Oh. Well, we'll need one so it'll be easier if you set it up now."

Taamarai tried to pull away, but he was holding her tightly and moved in for a kiss. His smell suddenly washed over her. It was probably just a day on a flight. Of course it was. His teeth weren't clean and she flinched away. That had always bothered her, but he got upset if she brought it up. Now she squirmed.

"I'll need my hands then."

He let go of her with a playful pinch at her behind, and Taamarai felt herself stepping back, dragging out her phone and sitting on the couch so that he couldn't invade her space any further. She suddenly wanted to cry. This wasn't how it was supposed to be.

It didn't take too long to set up an account. "What do you want?"

He reached out and took the phone. When he handed it back, it was their usual order – a family feast with soft drinks and ice cream. She didn't even have the energy to argue.

Darren settled on the couch beside her and looked relaxed at last. "It'll be good to have a proper meal after travelling all day."

"Well, I need to take a shower. It's been a long day for me, too." Taamarai kissed him briefly on the cheek as she got up, but as she went into the bathroom, she closed and locked the door. He didn't like her to do that. When it had just been the two of them living together he would come in sometimes when she was in the bath or shower. He liked to surprise her.

Out of the shower, she looked at the clothes she had stacked ready on the toilet. She could have gone back to the bedroom in her towel and got dressed there. He'd have appreciated it. But she pulled on her clothes with guilty relief.

When she came out, he was watching the alert status on her phone. "It's nearly here."

"Great." Taamarai felt so tired. She thought about downstairs. Ali would be cooking a spaghetti sauce that Taamarai had taught her. Ali had offered to cook for all of them, and Taamarai knew she had been disappointed to hear that Darren didn't like to meet new people too quickly. Taamarai didn't want to wish she was downstairs instead of up here, feeling like she was missing out.

As they sat down and opened up the sea of greasy boxes,

Taamarai looked at Darren. "I usually have Carl and Ali up for dinner on Saturdays. It'll be a good chance for you to meet them."

Darren's mouth turned down at the corners. "Tam, I've only just got here. I don't want to have to meet anybody just yet. I just want to be with you."

Taamarai knew she should back down but didn't. "You'll have had a chance to sleep and tomorrow you can unpack while I'm at work. They're looking forward to meeting you."

Ali was. Or at least she was curious. Carl would come to take a look and Taamarai was already apprehensive.

The next evening, Darren stayed mostly out of sight until Taamarai called that the food was ready. Ali had helped to lay the table and when they all sat down, it seemed almost normal for a few seconds.

Taamarai had made a plain pasta sauce. Carl was surprised. He'd expected her to push the boat out with one of her three-course masterpieces. As it was, presenting something so ordinary, she looked more nervous than he had ever seen her about her cooking.

Darren dug in without waiting for anybody at the table, not that they were interested in saying grace. Carl was, as ever, glad of a hot meal he hadn't had to make, but it wasn't her best. However, after a few mouthfuls Darren put his fork down. He smiled and reached across to take Taamarai's hand. "This is great, Tam."

"Thanks." She looked relieved.

"College must be paying off." He sounded slightly skeptical but looked around the table with a smile. "You know, when we first got together I could hardly eat anything she cooked." He squeezed her hand again and Carl saw a strange look in Taamarai's eye, like something sharp had twisted somewhere inside. "I guess it's because she's always trying new things. You remember that cake? The one that went all over the oven?"

She smiled and laughed. It would have sounded almost natural, if Carl hadn't known her better.

"It wasn't that bad. Well, I mean, it was a bit of a disaster, but I made another one the same day and it turned out just fine."

"That's true. She never gives up." Darren grinned at Carl and ignored Ali.

"I think Taamarai's a great cook." Ali sounded determined and a little testy.

Darren smiled properly at Ali now, almost conspiratorially. "Does she keep the chillies out for you? That took a while. I guess it's what you get used to. This is great, though. You can really taste what's in it."

"I like spicy food. Taamarai never makes it too hot." Ali seemed ready to fight it out. Carl could feel his own jaw clenched tight. The woman sitting across from him was exactly like the one he knew and yet so different she seemed like a stranger. She could barely look up and just ate mechanically, as if eating might stop her from having to think.

"Well, you're lucky. Being able to cope with it, I mean. It kills your taste buds, though, you know? Eventually, it'll stop you being able to taste anything properly." Darren smiled, gesturing at Taamarai's empty plate. "Hey, Tam. You must be hungry. I said it was good. You want me to get you some more?"

She looked up but didn't have time to say anything as he filled her plate again. Methodically she ate. When she was done, Darren sat back and looked pleased until his eyes met Carl's.

Carl had already noticed that the other man didn't seem pleased to see either him (which he could understand – hardly anybody did) or Ali (which he found more distasteful). Darren had shown no interest when they were introduced. He shook Carl's hand limply and then retreated into the corner of the lounge. Carl got the impression, though, that it wasn't anything in particular about them. He just didn't want to share Taamarai or make the effort to be sociable.

Again, those were things Carl understood, maybe better than he was willing to look at head-on, but here he was anyway. He knew that Taamarai wanted them to get along. She had seemed excited about her husband getting to town and, in return for all the free meals, Carl had felt like he could try his best, even if he already had reservations about the man sitting opposite.

When they finished eating, Darren seemed happy to let everyone else get on with things. He didn't move as Ali got up with Taamarai to clear their plates away, and Carl found himself standing to help more quickly than usual, just to make the point. It made no difference. As they were coming back from the kitchen, though, Darren called out, "Tam, check the freezer. I got our favorite. I think there's enough for everybody." He added jokingly, "As long as there's enough for me!"

Taamarai returned shortly, looking slightly embarrassed. She was holding four ready-made ice-cream sundaes, the children's-party kind, covered in sprinkles and sweet goo and served in plastic cups with peel-off lids. Carl frowned curiously. They weren't some-thing Taamarai would usually eat.

"I love these. My nan used to get them for me. I found them at the 7/11." For the first time since Carl had met him, Darren looked genuinely cheerful. "I guess we'll have to get some more tomorrow."

"I'm good." Carl nodded his thanks and pushed the offering away gently as Taamarai doled them out. Ali was ready to enjoy the nostalgic novelty of it, though he could tell that she was also unsettled.

"I won't either, tonight." Taamarai said it cautiously, with forced joviality. "I've already eaten too much." She reached out to take back two of the desserts, but Darren put a hand on her arm.

"Come on, Tam. I've just got here. We're celebrating. Besides, you don't look good when you let yourself get too skinny. You deserve this." He nudged it across to her with a smile. For a moment, Taamarai looked like she might stick to her guns, then she smiled back, a bent, broken smile that hung uncomfortably off her face.

"You're right. I'll just put this one back." It took her slightly longer in the kitchen than it should have to put one ice cream away, but Darren didn't seem to notice and Carl couldn't catch her eye when she came back in. He wasn't sure why he wanted to. The whole situation was making him angry, angry enough to be even ruder than usual.

"So, Darren," Carl leaned back in his chair, comfortable in this space that had become almost a home away from home in the last five months. He felt faintly, childishly vengeful and the fact that he could see Taamarai squirming only made him act out more. He stretched out his legs and held eye contact with the younger man, enjoying Darren's awkwardness and sense of displacement from what was supposedly his home. Taamarai continued to scoop the ice cream up as an excuse not to have to talk.

"Must be strange coming down here for the first time. What do you think?" Carl could have gone in harder, but he could see from Taamarai's face that she knew he wasn't even half started.

Darren, however, looked smug. He clearly believed he had measured up the situation and knew how to handle it. "Sure, it's weird having Tam away like this for so long. Of course I'd like to have her at home, but this is something that's important to her, so it's important to me." He reached out and laid a hand over Taamarai's on the table. She smiled crookedly but didn't look up. "And it looks like it's going well, doesn't it, babe?"

"Yeah, really well." She didn't react to being called "babe," though Carl felt a little queasy. It was one thing seeing it written down on a gift tag and another hearing it aloud. At last, she looked at them both, defiant yet pleading. *Don't*, she seemed to beg, without knowing what she wanted not to happen.

"I'm really glad I came to Gabriel Heights. It's been a great choice. You guys have been really supportive and it's easy to get to college and work and there are some great business opportunities around here."

Darren looked at her sharply. "Tam," his voice was low. "Let's talk about this ourselves. I thought we'd decided."

"Well, I.... It's complicated." She said this to Carl and Ali, her smile becoming brittle and pained.

"You not keen on moving out here permanently?" With malicious relish, Carl skewered the question Taamarai so obviously didn't want asked and met her eye with a challenging stare. She looked away. She had never backed down like that before. Carl turned to Darren, who looked back with undisguised hostility.

"Well, Tam's done a great job, but it isn't exactly home."

Carl thought back to Christmas Day. She had looked like it was home then, though he had to admit, she didn't now. Darren gestured out toward the window. "I'm sure this is a nice enough area, if you're used to it. But I don't see how Tam manages without a garden and then all the steps and the noise."

"Darren, you never go in the garden. You don't like the sun or the insects."

"That's not true. I like sitting out in the garden. Just not in summer. We had that great barbecue just before you left. That was in the garden."

"True," she conceded softly. "But we've got the balcony here."

"Tam? It's tiny and covered in pigeon mess! Besides, that's not the point. We're miles from home here."

Taamarai looked up. Her fierce stare didn't last, but Carl felt a glimmer of triumph. "I'm miles from my family wherever we are in the US."

"I know, babe. So you know how hard it is. But you're not as close to your family as I am."

Carl thought of Taamarai's calls with her parents, the regular updates she shared about her brothers' families. If Darren was much closer to his folks than that, Carl wasn't sure what that would look like or that he'd want to see it. Darren wasn't done, though.

"You said yourself, most of your friends have moved away from where you grew up. Besides, you always said you wanted to travel and see the world."

"And you said you'd come with me." Taamarai sounded tearful.

"And I did." Darren's tone declared the discussion over. "I've visited your parents three times and we went to Germany together that time. But that isn't the same as being where I want to live. I've got a home, Tam, and I want to stay there."

Carl watched them curiously. It wasn't a fight. Nobody was fighting. Yet the tension in the air crackled like static. Taamarai seemed to want to sink into the floor. Ali had retreated across the room and was buried in a book, but every so often, she looked up, worried and afraid. Carl knew he should leave. For so many reasons, he should leave. It would be the polite thing to do, not that that mattered much to him. It would give Taamarai some relief, and although he thought that should matter to him, he was more angry at her than sympathetic. He wanted to grab her and shake her, to smack Darren down in front of her just to see how she reacted.

The rage was what eventually decided him. It made him uncomfortable and unsure of himself. He knew plenty of men who treated their wives and girlfriends like shit. He'd watched his mother put up with it. He didn't see that it was his place to judge but watching Taamarai shrivel in front of him caused his fist to clench under the table. Alongside images of shaking some sense into her flashed other visions that he didn't know what to do with: walking out of the place with her, showing her how good it was all those other times Darren wasn't there. How good it might be if.... He shut the thought down.

"Well, we'd best be heading downstairs, Ali," Carl remarked. Ali got up without demur, bringing the book with her. Taamarai wouldn't mind. On her way out, she paused and hugged Taamarai.

"Thanks for dinner."

Taamarai just nodded mutely.

Once they closed the door back in 502, Ali seemed like she might explode.

"Well, say what you gotta say." She didn't deserve his snappiness, but Carl felt tense and tired and wanted to put some distance between himself and the whole evening.

"Dad! What *was* that?" Ali looked on the verge of tears. "Why is Taamarai like that all of a sudden?"

Carl poured himself a whiskey from the bottle on the table. "I guess she's just tired." He couldn't meet Ali's eye but sensed her confusion and frustration. Carl was no kind of father, and he knew it, but he didn't usually palm his daughter off with bullshit he didn't believe, and she was smart enough to recognize the change.

"But stuff's quiet at college right now. And at the restaurant. Taamarai said so!" Ali was pleading with him, desperate for some answer that made sense and Carl didn't have one, at least not one he was prepared to risk putting into words.

He'd decided at the turn of the new year, when memories of Christmas wouldn't leave him alone, that it was just normal, fancying Taamarai a little. She was always there, she was easy to get on with. Not too much drama. Since he'd taken on Ali, there hadn't been any other women he had spent that much time with. And she'd got that smile, and skin so soft he wanted to touch it, then felt cross and stupid for wanting to. And her eyes. He was a man. He noticed. It didn't mean anything.

He certainly didn't want Ali suspecting, and any kind of answer seemed like it would give him away. He wasn't sure he could safely unpick the ways Darren made him angry as one man judging another and the ways he made him angry for Taamarai. Nor did he want to admit how much he recognized Ali's dismay and missed the woman they both knew she could be. He settled for, "Must've been a long day, with Darren moving in," and refused to be drawn further until Ali stumped off to her room, muttering under her breath. It could have been about him or about Darren or neither of them.

Chapter Thirteen

It wasn't possible to avoid Darren completely, though Carl and Ali managed pretty well. Carl found himself back at the bar more often, and Ali stayed late for a couple of school clubs and study halls. Taamarai still came by, though, usually just before her shifts at the restaurant. She never said not to say anything to Darren but, on the rare occasions Carl saw him, he didn't.

Most days, she would come down an hour or so before work and make herself tea. She would sit with Ali, if she was around, or play cards and chat if it was just Carl. When she talked about her work, her college, recipes she was thinking of trying, it seemed like she was saying it all for the first time, and Carl wondered what she and Darren talked about.

Apparently, though, she hadn't given up on the possibility that they might all get along. Every so often, she would try to organize a dinner. Darren would eat with them then go and sit on the couch and play computer games with his headphones in. Ali asked Carl why Taamarai didn't say something, and he grunted. He didn't have a good answer except that sometimes he saw a look in Darren's eye or heard him make a joking comment, and could imagine how it might seem easier and easier as the years went by to avoid those looks and comments.

On this day, Taamarai had turned up in 502 with a strange, determined expression in her eye. She'd invited him and Ali for dinner, and Carl hadn't been able to come up with an excuse fast enough. Besides, he felt bad for her. Taamarai looked almost desperate.

So they headed upstairs. At 602, Taamarai pulled Ali into a warm embrace and looked almost about do the same to Carl before stepping aside and welcoming them in. The apartment smelled mouthwateringly good, and the table was spread with a proper South Indian feast, the sort she had made for them once before, for no particular reason, just after she moved in. Darren looked over from the couch but didn't make any other move.

"Ali, it's so good to see you! Carl, would you mind putting out the cutlery and plates and Ali, can you lend me a hand finishing off the chutney?" Carl was happy to have something to do other than being ignored by Darren and felt himself warm at hearing Ali and Taamarai chattering happily to each other in the kitchen.

After a few minutes, Taamarai called them over and, when everyone was sat down, explained the dishes. In the middle of the table was a huge dish of steaming, fluffy white rice that she served to each of them. Beside each plate except Darren's was a cup of thin red soup with green leaves floating in it. She called it *resam* and Carl remembered sipping it last time, then pouring some over rice.

A thick *saambaar* was familiar - she served the orange-colored lentil and vegetable stew most weeks. This one was jewelled with glistening lumps of eggplant. A vivid yellow potato dish, dotted with green peas and chillies and served with fried breads like golden balloons sat next to a deep dish of creamy coconut chutney. Another favorite.

Other delicacies in reds, greens and browns were introduced as chutneys and vegetable fries and stews. At the end of it all, she said, they should keep back a bit of rice to mix with yoghurt, sitting ready in the middle of the table. When they had eaten like this last

time, Taamarai had shown Ali how to mix and scoop up the sumptuous mixture of hot rice and cold yoghurt with her fingers,
savoring the traces of all the other dishes they had eaten mixing
together. Ali had practiced eating that way until she could do it
with the same ease as Taamarai.

There were a couple of smaller bowls that Taamarai passed
over briefly. They were lightly spiced versions of the main dishes,
without any chilli. She had put them in front of Darren. As they
dug in, Taamarai immediately turned the conversation to Ali, who
was keen to catch Taamarai up on everything going on in her life.
Darren was hardly eating, but Taamarai didn't seem to notice.

In a break in the conversation, he finally spoke up. "Tam, this
tastes funny." He gestured at one of the chutneys.

"It's coconut and red pepper." She had already explained it and
Carl thought he detected a hint of exasperation. But maybe he was
projecting his own onto Taamarai.

"I don't like coconut."

"I know," she said gently, but firmly. "But you don't have to eat it.
I can't make South Indian food without coconut chutney." She
smiled as if they were having a perfectly lovely conversation.

"It's delicious," Ali chimed in, apparently oblivious, though Carl
suspected she wasn't.

"I guess that's why I've never really liked South Indian food that
much."

As Carl waited for the apology, Taamarai just shrugged.
"There's plenty of stuff here you've eaten before and didn't mind. If
you really don't fancy it, there's some of yesterday's pasta in the
fridge that you can warm up." She turned to Carl and passed him
the *saambaar*. He peered curiously at her but she didn't meet his
eye. Darren munched thoughtfully on some plain rice.

"Did your Amma teach you to make chutney?" Ali asked in the
quiet. It seemed to delight Taamarai as much to hear Ali call her
mother "Amma" as Ali calling her Tam had once upset her.

"Yes." Taamarai nodded happily. "We used to make it together
all the time when I was little. You can get proper fresh coconut in

Britain these days. It comes frozen. But before that, we experimented with dried and coconut paste and all sorts until we got it just right."

"That's so cool!" Ali had clearly never considered the possibility of coconut coming in different forms and was about to ask more when Darren jumped in.

"Yeah, remember the last time I came to visit? That weird stuff your mom made. That had coconut in it. It made me feel really sick."

Carl saw something pass over Taamarai's face. He had never seen her really angry before, and almost didn't recognize the emotion.

"It was *pooththu*, Darren. It's not weird and you didn't have to eat it then, either."

Darren looked taken aback.

"You know I didn't mean it like that, Tam. It's just I don't like coconut and it was kind of gross. The rest of that meal was okay, but that spoiled it."

Taamarai's left hand was clenched tight beside her plate. Her right shook slightly, hovering above her plate between mouthfuls. "Yeah, well. I guess we both remember that meal differently."

Darren looked nonplussed for a second, then full of hurt and sympathy. He reached out and put a hand over hers, and Carl thought for a moment Taamarai might pull away, but she didn't.

"Tam, I'm sorry! I'm not saying it wasn't special. You know I'm not saying that. It's just that we were talking about the food, that's all. And that wasn't that great. That's all I was saying. I know it was the last time you saw your brother before his accident."

Taamarai's head shot up and her look as she met Carl's eye was filled with horror.

Carl frowned, catching up to what Darren had said. "Wait," he exclaimed. "You said your brother...shit!" He pushed back a little from the table as a sugary tide spilled across the surface. Taamarai had leaned forward, apparently for more rice, and knocked a glass of soda with her hand. Carl stood up, liquid pouring off his lap and onto the floor.

"Tam, watch out." Darren looked startled and was already dabbing with a napkin at the area around his plate as the spill made a splattering noise from the other end of the table.

"I'm sorry." Taamarai was frantic. "I'm really sorry."

Carl looked down at the puddle around his feet and took a towel that Taamarai was already passing to him. "It don't matter." He wanted Taamarai to stop saying sorry. "Look, it's fine."

He looked over at the bathroom, but now that there was nothing actually dripping off him, it was clear that this would require more than dabbing down at the sink. "I'll be back in a bit." Carl stumped across the apartment and headed for 502. He couldn't tell whether he was more shocked by the half-litre of soda poured so unceremoniously into his lap or what he was sure had provoked it. Still, there was little to do but peel off his sticky, sodden clothes, wipe sugar residue off himself and change.

He heard a soft knock at the door and cursed under his breath as he grabbed a towel to wrap around his waist. He knew who it would be. Taamarai scooted through the door the moment it was open. "I'm sorry. I've left Ali and Darren cleaning up upstairs. But, Carl." She suddenly seemed to notice that he was wearing only a towel. She looked absurdly up towards the corner of the room, turned her head awkwardly then met his eye again.

"I'm sorry about your clothes, Carl. I've got to get back up there." She seemed to want to say several things at once and not be able to get any of them out.

"Carl, please, don't say anything to Darren about Joshua. Don't ask him anything or tell him what I said to you. Please." She took a deep, shaking breath.

Carl eyed her coolly. "He didn't die in Afghanistan, did he?"

She looked down. "I didn't say he did." Her tone was quiet but determined. She didn't apologize and when she looked up again, it was to meet his eye defiantly. "You asked *how* he died. I said Afghanistan. That was true." The defiance fled before something darker and sadder.

"I'm sorry and I don't have time to explain now." She sounded tired. "But I'll tell you anything you want to know, answer any question you want to ask me. Just please, please don't say anything in front of Darren."

He looked at her appraisingly. He waited. He knew what had to come next, the inevitable reminder of his place and of what he owed her. If he had ever been grateful for everything she had done for Ali, if he wanted her to keep cooking for them. But she didn't say any of those things. The silence dragged on and at last he realized that she was begging not bargaining.

Carl just nodded and with a grateful nod in return, Taamarai turned and left. He heard her soft steps on the stairs and wondered why her desperation made *him* feel exposed and unsure. After pulling on a clean t-shirt and jeans, he headed upstairs himself, where the rest of the meal passed in stilted conversation. Darren hardly spoke except to joke about Taamarai's clumsiness and occasionally cast suspicious looks towards both Carl and Taamarai.

When Ali and Carl had gone, Taamarai turned reluctantly to the lounge. She hadn't wanted them to leave. She could see that Darren was upset. Maybe he just wouldn't speak to her properly for a few days. He did that sometimes. All she would get from him was when he was hungry, what was wrong with the food and how unhappy he was. She found herself hoping for that.

"I'm exhausted. I'm going to bed," Taamarai said with forced cheer and headed for the bathroom. She nearly made it but heard him put down his laptop and get up.

"What were you doing, running off downstairs like that?"

"What?"

"Tam, you know what I mean. After your accident at the table."

"Oh." Taamarai hated that she felt guilty. She knew it would show on her face, so she stayed facing the bathroom door. "I just went to check on Carl. To see if he was okay and was going to come back up." With the lie out she made herself turn around. "You know he can be a bit funny."

Darren had complained about Carl's manners and moods quite

a bit, so hopefully this would be enough. Darren's eyes narrowed, though, and Taamarai could see that slithering intelligence coming to life, the one that wormed its way into things and didn't seem to stop. Once she had admired it. Determination had seemed like an attractive quality.

"Weren't we talking about Joshua?"

Fear flared up, but so did anger and she let it win. "No. We were talking about how you don't like coconut."

Darren weighed this up. Even he couldn't miss the tension in the air. His face went from suspicious to petulant. "Oh yeah. You were telling me off for having opinions about food."

Relief and dismay competed and Taamarai hoped neither of them showed. "I wasn't telling you off, Darren. I was just saying that you knew what had coconut in it. You didn't have to eat it."

He shoved his hands into his pocket. "But why should I have to remember which ones are which? Why would you cook something you know I don't like? And then make a fuss like that, in front of everyone?"

Why couldn't he say "Carl and Ali," Taamarai thought. She had noticed before that he almost never used their names.

"I mean, how do you think that makes me look, makes me feel?"

When she said nothing, he barreled on.

"You've changed, Tam. We used to talk about everything and always think about each other. Now it's like you don't even care what I think or how I feel about anything."

"Darren, we're talking about one meal!" Taamarai snapped.

"Except it's not just one meal, Tam." Darren sighed. "You keep having people over. Then you make stuff I don't like, then it's like you purposefully tried to show me up. You know Carl doesn't like me anyway. Now this'll just make it worse."

"What makes you think Carl doesn't like you?"

He rolled his eyes. "Tam, he hardly even speaks to me. I've tried to be okay about it because I know you think he's your friend. But he doesn't even pretend to make an effort with me. And considering you do pretty much all of his cooking, I just think he's really rude."

"In comparison to sitting on your computer with your head-phones in when we've got guests for dinner?" Taamarai's patience was fraying.

He looked at her with wounded surprise, as if she had said the last thing he could possibly have imagined and something so unfair as to make him blink at the injustice of it. "Tam, I didn't invite them over. You know I don't like having people in my space. I never have. I like our evenings together, just the two of us. And it's hard when it's all conversations about stuff I don't really care about."

Taamarai opened her mouth but she had nothing to say that wouldn't make it worse. She turned abruptly and headed for the bathroom. Her skin felt hot and tight from anger and she splashed her face with cold water. She cleaned her teeth carefully and brushed her hair. When she stepped back out of the bathroom, Darren hadn't moved. He had evidently been staring at the bath-room door the whole time she was in there. She headed past him towards the bedroom, and he caught her around the waist, pulling her towards him.

"Hey, Tam. It's okay. I know you get down sometimes, and tonight's dinner reminded you of your brother." Taamarai's heart stopped, but, for now at least, Darren's mind was on other things. "But everybody's gone now." He grinned a grin that she knew looked cheeky, childlike and endearing. She had commented on it before, thought it to herself. She found herself smiling despite the tears in her eyes.

"Yeah. Well, we should probably get to bed. I've got an early start again tomorrow." She tried to step away but Darren kept his arm around her waist and, with his free hand, reached under her clothes and groped at her breasts.

"Ooh, boobies. I've missed these. It's been hard having you away for so long, Tam." He kissed her, but before she could respond or decide not to, he moved to kiss her neck. He pulled her pyjama top quickly over her head and she felt the familiar pressure on her shoulder, the cue to kneel. He had already unfastened his pants.

"You know you look so hot like that, babe. Mmm. I know it's been hard, being apart like we have. We just need to try a bit harder, that's all. You've just gotta think about how you make me feel." He stroked her hair, and took some of it in his fist. "You know nobody makes me feel the way you do, babe. You know we were meant to be together. You know I'll always love you, no matter what."

Taamarai felt herself slipping away from it all into another place, another life. Sometimes she could vanish completely, but tonight, anxiety kept her tethered in the present. She knew Carl would want to know more. And she knew that Darren could never know more, and she knew which of those thoughts concerned her most.

Chapter Fourteen

Taamarai pulled the shutters down outside the restaurant and turned around. It was nearly eleven, and the next bus would be due in a few minutes. These days, she was often the last one out and enjoyed closing everything down. She could almost imagine it was her restaurant.

She caught sight of a figure standing on the corner and stood up sharply. Adrenaline pumped through her. It was likely nothing but the area wasn't great. In a second, the shape resolved. Carl. She breathed a sigh of relief but her heart continued to thump.

"Hi." Taamarai couldn't help sounding pleased, even though she knew why he was there. He just looked over at her and she stared back without thinking. The street lamp's silver light glanced off the angle of his jaw and cast his eyes into shadow. A loose t-shirt accentuated powerful shoulders and left his forearms bare, lined and toned as a statue. She had tried to help it but couldn't. When she closed her eyes sometimes she could almost imagine how those arms might feel around her.

"I was in the area. Thought you might like company. Maybe take a walk home?"

Taamarai looked up at the warm starry sky. This was a conversation she had been dreading but the walk would be welcome.

"Sure. That'd be good." She bent and secured the last of the locks, and they set off.

For a block or two they said nothing, keeping pace easily, sticking to quiet streets. She waited for him to start. If that was why he was here, he would have to ask. He'd waited over two weeks since her disastrous dinner party, but there had always been Darren or Ali around when they had seen each other. Now it was just the two of them.

"You said I could ask you anything I liked. About your brother."

Taamarai glanced sidelong at him. "Well, what do you want to know?"

He shrugged. *Tell me everything; then we'll see if I've got questions.* She nodded and looked ahead, doing better talking to the night air.

"Joshua *was* in Afghanistan." She hadn't lied to him. Not really. "He served two tours and got a bad shrapnel injury. When he got out of hospital, he had tattoos put around it and joked about it at the pub." She smiled sadly at the recollection. "He had other wounds, too, that he didn't talk about in the pub." Her look darkened.

"He drank too much. He was scared of the dark. If he didn't drink, he didn't sleep for days on end. If he drank, then he'd sleepwalk, sometimes break things, hurt himself." She dug her hands into her pockets. It seemed like there was so much and yet so little to say about those times.

"He lost job after job until he stopped looking. His girlfriend left him. We didn't blame her. She didn't feel safe anymore. Nobody should have to live like that."

Taamarai glanced over and Carl met her eye, but they didn't break stride and both looked ahead again. He was listening.

"We tried to get him help but there isn't much of it about and he didn't want to talk, he said. Maybe if they'd let him talk to the same therapist for more than a month at a time, but...."

She pulled herself up sharply. There was no point to "maybe

ifs." They had reached the river and Taamarai stopped, suddenly too tired to carry it all. She turned towards the black, glistening water and leaned one foot and her arms against the railings.

Beside her, Carl leaned against the railings too, looking equally comfortable but more ready somehow. He was close enough that she could detect the faint clean scent she recognized as his. No aftershave or perfumed deodorant. Soap and something like worn cotton. Sometimes it made her shiver and her chest feel heavy. Sometimes, when she sat on the couch in 502 or played cards with him before work, it wrapped around her comfortingly. Tonight, she closed her eyes and let it ground her as she walked with her memories.

"It was a few years later. His accident. He fell in the canal after a night drinking. Drowned." She could hear the moving water below them and was glad not to see it. "Of course it was an accident. Loads of people saw him leaving the club, blind drunk. He didn't have rocks in his pockets or anything like that." She gripped the railing tightly.

"I thought the same thing, until the letter arrived. He'd posted it that morning, but it took a while to get to me over here. Only me."

She felt a tear gather in her eye but knew it wouldn't fall. She had been in that moment, with the letter in her hand, too often. Speaking was a kind of relief.

"He told me he wished he'd never come home from the war. That he hadn't really. Everything after it was just a nightmare, and he couldn't wake up. I think he just needed to tell one person but the last thing in the letter – the last thing he said was not to tell anybody else. Especially not Amma." She looked up at him. "I guess I've just broken that promise."

Carl met her eye but said nothing. She didn't look worried about her choice.

"Because the Army might want their money back?" he asked.

She smiled sadly.

"No. It wasn't life insurance. The money was a compensation package. For his injuries. He never told us the details. We didn't know he'd still got it. We figured he'd spent it all. But he never touched a penny. He left it all to me. To do something amazing. That's what he said in the letter and in his will." Taamarai looked momentarily lost, her view across the river fuzzy with fresh sorrow, then she seemed to remember what exactly she was trying to explain.

"No, it was for Amma's sake. I don't know if she suspects. I think she does. But that's not the same as knowing. She did everything for Joshua – fought to get him help, picked up the pieces over and over, cleaned his flat, got him jobs, held him when he cried at night. Joshua didn't want her to think it wasn't enough, that she should've done more. He knew she could cope with an accident, even if she blamed it on the Army because of the drinking."

They stood on the river bank in silence for what felt like a long time without becoming awkward. At last, Taamarai pushed off from the railings and headed back along the path. Carl caught up in a few steps. He didn't tell her he wouldn't say anything. They both knew he wouldn't.

"Thank you for not asking until tonight. I know Darren noticed something. I never told him many of the details about Joshua, but he's always wanted to know and, well, he...he believes that honesty is always best. I don't know what I'd do if he found out. If he told Amma."

This time the silence felt less comfortable, at least to Taamarai. The words seemed a betrayal of Darren but also a burden eased at last for sharing.

They passed by a row of neons. "Do you want a drink?" Carl asked, slowing down. Taamarai stopped in her tracks. It was late. She shouldn't. She should get back to Darren.

"Yes. I really would."

He led the way to the third door in the row and downstairs to an ordinary, grimy underground bar. As he went to get them beers, Taamarai tapped off a quick text and was glad that Carl didn't ask as he came back to the table. She shoved her phone back into her pocket and they both took slurps from full glasses.

"The book. The one you gave me?" They were about halfway down their glasses. Carl didn't seem to know exactly what the question was.

Taamarai nodded. "He gave it to me for my birthday, the last time I visited before...." she trailed off. "Like I said when I gave it to you, I think he was trying to say goodbye."

Taamarai's heart squeezed tight with too many emotions. She focussed on Carl's hand around his beer glass, the recollection of his hand on the book.

He had large, careful hands with wide knuckles. They were covered with scars and grazed here and there. He kept his nails short and tidy and Taamarai wanted very badly to reach out and touch that hand, to run her fingertips over the rough skin and smooth nails, to feel him touch her in return and not think or feel anything else. It made her dizzy and unsure and she pulled herself away, back into the painful meeting of the past and the present.

Carl waited for a long time as Taamarai seemed to stare at nothing at all, somewhere roughly where his beer glass was. Finally, she looked up with a strange, hopeful expression that vanished a moment later.

"Do you still have his letter?" It wasn't any of the questions on the tip of his tongue. He didn't need to see the letter to believe what she had told him. He asked because his throat was dry and his pulse was quick and it suddenly seemed like a way back to somewhere ugly but safe.

Taamarai smiled again sadly but also with relief. She seemed to agree. Reaching into her pocket, she opened her wallet and pulled out a worn piece of paper. She passed it to him with care, not letting it touch the wet tabletop. Carl unfolded it reverently. He had been going to ask if she was worried about Darren finding it. He went in her wallet for money all the time. When he looked at it, though, the squiggles were alien and opaque. She met his eye and grinned.

"It's in Tamil." As quickly as her smile faded, she looked

anxious at not having the letter in her possession, and he passed it back and waited as she stowed it again.

"You didn't have to tell me." Carl frowned. That wasn't quite what he meant. He'd asked, after all. "Not all of it."

The silence rose up again. He knew the question he wanted to ask took them back in unsafe directions, but he decided it was the beer talking. "What did he think – Joshua – about you and Darren? About you living out here?"

Taamarai took a long drink and placed her bottle back on the table. "You want another one?"

"Sure." He glanced around. He really shouldn't let her go up to the bar. The place looked seedier when he saw it through her eyes, but Taamarai seemed unfazed. He watched as she made her way to the bar and returned with two fresh beers after a short joke with the bartender. She sat back down and spotted one across to him, then looked up seriously.

"What did Joshua think about me and Darren?" She drew the question out into the air between them. "It was really sweet. The day Darren and I got married, he came up to me in the middle of it all. Asked me if I was having a good time. If I was happy." She paused, as if seeing the memory from a different angle. "I think he liked Darren."

Carl didn't think she sounded sure.

"He was glad I'd found somebody. He knew that I loved living in the US. He always enjoyed visiting."

Her face and voice lit up with sincerity as she talked about the US, a change that she maybe hadn't noticed or was too tired to hide.

"He come over much?"

"Three times after he got back from Afghanistan. A couple of times before that, between his tours." She looked sad but as if she was trying to ignore the feeling. "It was difficult. I didn't have the money to travel home and we didn't have much space over here, so he couldn't stay long. But it was always great. It just got a bit hard. Darren found it tough, having my family over so much, in his space." She took another drink.

"The last time I was back was the funeral." She looked up and her eyes begged for confirmation. "It was sweet of Darren's parents to lend me the money for a flight."

Carl knew he shouldn't say it but couldn't not. "Lent you the money? Didn't Darren go?"

To his surprise, Taamarai didn't seem angry at the question. She just looked at him, weighing something up, then drained her beer. "I'll be back in a minute. Are you busy tomorrow?"

He shrugged, not sure where this was going. "Nothing much."

As Taamarai went to the bathroom, he looked around the bar. He got caught up for a few minutes watching a pool game but spotted her the moment she came back out, moving with just a tiny sway. She didn't drink much and it showed.

As she got to the bar, Taamarai gave the bartender a big smile. Carl knew because he could see the man smile back. He let himself watch as she chatted and gathered her bounty. Even if he didn't know her, she would still be the woman he watched.

When she reached the table, she deposited a handful of glasses, gripped expertly between her fingers. Two glasses of water. Definitely a good idea. Two shots. A less good idea. Two more shots. Nothing like Taamarai at all. She pushed two of them over to him.

"Gotta be a bit drunker for this." She knocked back one of the shots. He followed suit without taking his eyes off her. She turned to the water and looked into it at first, without drinking any.

"Is it weird? That he didn't come to the funeral?"

"He didn't, then?" Carl wasn't surprised and didn't hide it.

"No." She shrugged.

He was beginning to recognize the gesture for what it was – a sign that she didn't want to think whatever it was that she did. "It was expensive. My family offered to pay, but he said he didn't like the idea of that. And Darren hates travelling. I know he says he doesn't mind, for my sake. But he does. He gets stressed about it and I couldn't deal with that right then. And we'd have had to stay with my parents. I mean, I wanted to. I wanted to be with them. But he finds it difficult. My family. They're, he says...."

She trailed off again, took a long gulp of water, then swallowed the second shot. "He says they're loud. He.... I don't know. They get on. It's just different. I guess I just wanted to be with my family."

She looked up again. Carl hadn't touched his second shot. His heart felt curiously tight. He could picture her sitting alone in some anonymous bus depot, heading for the airport, and the thought pained him.

"So, is that weird? That he didn't go?"

This time he couldn't dodge the question. He knew what she wanted to hear. That it was normal, wanting to be with her family, that it was okay that Darren didn't like to travel. And he couldn't. "Every family's different."

She looked relieved.

"But from what I've seen, what you've said, if there are good ones, yours might be one. And I don't care if they aren't. Something like that happens, if you can't trust your husband to be by your side?" He let his own unspoken question hang, staring so hard that he seemed to see nothing but her eyes, looking back at him. "I don't think it's weird. I think it's fucking pathetic."

For a moment, Taamarai looked shocked. She drank the rest of her water, then slowly, painstakingly, she put the glass back down as if afraid she might break it. "Yeah, I guess it was." She reached up and swiped at her face, and only then did he notice that she was crying. She looked around, suddenly bewildered by the noise and dark.

"I've got to go." She stood unsteadily.

He reached out and took her hand. It didn't take much to pull her back into her seat.

"I've got to get back. Darren will be worried."

Fuck Darren, he thought, but tears were flowing down her cheeks and he knew he couldn't say it. Not now. "Okay. Let's head home."

He took back their empties, getting her another glass of water.

She drank it obediently, then followed him out. The fresh air by the river helped and after walking with her head down for a few minutes, she stopped and looked up at him.

"I'm sorry. I didn't mean to get upset." She tried to look carefree and lighthearted, but it was thin as a rag over her pain.

"About your brother being dead or your husband letting you down?" It was a cruel question and a fresh tear slid down her cheek. "Don't seem like nothing to be sorry for to me." Though the words were softer, his tone wasn't. Carl hated her apologies. The pretense fell away, and she let her face relax into something natural. Not horror or grief, just something sad and worn and tired and normal.

"I guess not. I mean, he's always there for me, usually. He just doesn't..." Before he could say anything, she interrupted herself. "I'm not even sure why I'm making excuses." Taamarai sounded suddenly angry. She had begun walking again, and he sped up to hear her. "I don't even know why I'm talking about it, like any of it matters in comparison to Joshua being dead! I haven't forgiven him." She said it like a revelation. "Darren, I mean." She paused, then stopped.

"My brother killed himself." She looked straight at him. "I've never said that to anybody else until tonight. My brother killed himself and my husband didn't even ask me how my parents were doing when I got back from the funeral." She looked like something shocking had just happened right in front of her, and she couldn't tell how to process it.

Taamarai turned around and carried on walking again. This time he caught up a bit closer, not sure what he was meant to do about any of it. He could see that her cheeks were wet with slow tears, but she didn't seem to mind.

Her hand brushed against his, just the rhythm of their steps, him walking so close. He felt himself adjust his pace and their fingers twined together, looser than that day at Ali's school, but her hand just as small and warm in his. They walked on through the dark. A few people stared then went on their way. He wondered what they thought was going on.

Carl was surprised when they got back to Gabriel Heights. The walk had seemed to last forever and a moment. He could see from the lights that Ali was already in her room. The apartment above blazed bright from every room. Darren liked it that way and wasn't paying the bills.

They climbed the stairs slowly, both feeling the effects of the shots and the beer and a long day, and she never let go of his hand until they reached the fifth-floor landing. At 502, as he was about to unlock the door, Taamarai stepped away. She looked up at him with a lopsided smile.

"How do I look?" She'd scrubbed roughly at her face and eyes. He knew what she was asking. She didn't want to answer any questions when she got in but the truth was, she looked terrible. Her eyes were red and puffy, her cheeks streaked and pale. He reached up and brushed one to see if the tear stains might rub off, his thumb stroking her skin softly. He couldn't tell if she leaned a fraction into the touch. He took a step closer to see better under the single corridor light, and they came to rest like that, her cheek cupped in his hand. For a few breaths, neither of them moved.

"You'd better come in." He took his hand away with a reluctance he had no use for and no desire to acknowledge. When the door opened, he was relieved to find that Ali was indeed in her room. He waited as Taamarai went to the bathroom. He heard the tap running and when she came back, she looked better. Tired and weary but okay enough to deny that anything was wrong. At the door, they stopped again.

"What will you say? If he asks what's up?" Carl wished he hadn't asked as a flicker crossed her face. He couldn't read the expression but it made him feel complicit in something.

"It's fine. I'll just tell him it's been a long day." She looked about to say something else but turned instead to go, expecting him to step aside so she could reach the door.

"It's not fine." Carl hadn't moved and he caught her cheek

again, as he had on the landing. Her skin now was smooth and silky, freshly washed, and a little cold from the water. "What you told me tonight. That isn't fine."

She just nodded then reached up and touched his hand, holding it against her face, her fingertips tracing the shape of his fingernails and the outline of his knuckles beneath his skin.

"I've got to go."

This time he did get out of the way and watched the door close behind her, listening to her steps on the stair.

At 602, Taamarai opened the door with reluctance. Her mind churned with the evening. The old hurts opened up felt good, like some swollen infection had been lanced. Her cheek was warm where Carl had touched it, though she knew that was just a memory now. As soon as she opened the door, Darren was waiting for her.

"Hey babe, what happened?"

"Hey. I'm sorry. I texted you. You got it, right?"

"Yeah – an electrical problem at the restaurant?"

"Yeah." Taamarai let her weariness show. "I couldn't lock up until it was sorted so I had to wait for the contractor to come out. You know how it is." He nodded even though he didn't know.

"You could have called me. I could have talked to you while you waited. I wouldn't have minded."

"I know. Thanks. But there was plenty to get done – cleaning, odd jobs. I kept busy."

"Have you been drinking?" He had moved in close to her and sniffed suspiciously at the air.

Taamarai kicked herself. She hadn't even thought about the alcohol on her breath. "Um, yeah. There was a party in. Regulars. They bought a round for everyone. All the staff. What have you been up to?" She tried to sound bright and cheerful, not like she was rushing to change the subject.

"Oh, you know. Mostly I just played my new game." Taamarai gently extricated herself from his arms so that she could walk into the apartment. The washing up was still on the side from breakfast, with a plate and a cup from his lunch. A pizza box stood next to the fridge.

"You got takeout? I left you some of the pasta sauce from last night in the fridge. I thought I told you about it. Sorry."

"Oh, yeah. I didn't fancy it. And I'd have had to make up the spaghetti to go with it. And I was missing you, so I thought pizza would make me feel better."

Taamarai nodded but couldn't help the annoyance slipping into her voice. "I know. And it's fine. But things are tight right now. Takeout is expensive." She felt tears in her voice and cut herself short. She hated feeling pathetic but the pizza had probably cost her the last hour of work. He just didn't think in those terms.

"Yeah, I know that babe, but it isn't that much when it's just me. You know I only have the simple stuff, and I didn't tip the delivery guy 'cos it arrived nearly cold by the time he'd climbed these stupid steps, so we saved on that." Knowing how much her tips meant to her, Taamarai felt something like anger and squashed that too. "Besides, I was expecting to have dinner with you tonight. Then I wouldn't have needed pizza."

He came up behind her and curled his arms around her waist. "Look, I know you're worried about money right now, but we've always got your savings if we really need them."

She didn't say anything, and he began to nuzzle her neck. "I was thinking, talking about your brother's money. We haven't been on holiday together for ages. You're working all the time and I'm not doing great here. Maybe we should get away for a week? Go to the beach or something?"

Taamarai didn't want to have the conversation again about how that money wasn't for holidays or pizza, that she owed it to her brother to do something real with it. She didn't want to talk about Joshua at all. Not to Darren. She desperately wanted him to stop talking about "her brother's money" like that was all Joshua was - a bank account that she was being selfish for not letting him use.

Turning in his arms, she kissed him. Darren was already in the mood. Her presence was the only encouragement he needed, and in a few minutes they were in bed, their clothes leaving yet more mess behind that she would clear up in the morning.

She knew all the noises he liked to hear. She made the ones that told him he'd done enough for her as quickly as she could, wanting to turn the light out and close her eyes against the day. He was happy to move on, though he seemed a little off his stride and, a bit sooner than usual, climbed out of bed and waited for her to kneel in front of him. They almost always finished like this these days. She was just so good at it, he said, and he loved the way she looked.

She heard the words and then stopped hearing them, felt his hand in her hair, then stopped feeling it, felt fluid on her face, then felt nothing as he handed her a tissue and she wiped herself down. He pulled on pyjamas and waited for her to do the same. Since she'd moved to Horton, she had taken to sleeping naked but her skin was sticky, he said, and annoyed him in the night if he touched it.

In the bathroom, Taamarai was pleased to shut the door. She washed properly and stayed there longer than she needed to. By the time she got into bed, he'd got the TV on and was already watching one of his favorite cartoons. It would run until they fell asleep. He didn't turn the light out, though, and her heart sank at the prospect of further conversation.

"What's wrong, Tam?"

"What do you mean? That was great." She smiled wanly at him.

"Yeah, you know you're really hot like that." He frowned. "It didn't really seem like you were into it, though. Like, part of it, you were just lying there, and you seemed like you were about to cry."

She curled up on his chest. It was easier than looking at him, though she noticed his smell. He'd stopped washing that much as he didn't have a job to go out to. He said he didn't notice so he couldn't see why she was bothered. He piled on sweet deodorant instead.

"I'm sorry. I was into it. I'm just really tired. That's all."

"Yeah, I know that, babe. I'm sorry you're having to work so much at the moment. Your boss at the restaurant should really work things out better."

She didn't argue.

"But babe, you've gotta see how it makes me feel when you're like this. I know you don't mean to, but when I'm looking at you and it's like you're not enjoying it, it just feels really crappy, like I'm some sort of rapist or something."

Taamarai felt herself twist inside. She had never thought about it like that, about how awful it might be for Darren. On top of the memories of Joshua, she felt acutely that she had failed to give somebody else what they needed.

"I'm sorry, Darren. I am. I'm so sorry." She cried now, and he turned the lights out and held her.

"I know, babe, I know. You just gotta stop working so much. We'll talk about it tomorrow, and maybe we can try out some of those new toys I ordered last week. See if we can get you back in the mood." He groped her affectionately, and she laughed through her tears, feeling relieved when he laughed back. Forgiven. At least a little. "I love you," he murmured.

"I love you too." She curled into a ball, her back to him, and at last closed her eyes.

It's not fine. The words were with her as she fell asleep, and her cheek still felt warm.

Chapter Fifteen

Carl hadn't bothered to put on a top. He'd thought about it when he heard the knock at the door, then opened it anyway. Because it was hot? Because he knew it was Taamarai? They knew each other well enough, right? She was practically family, except that it didn't feel familial.

The moment he opened the door, he wished he'd pulled on a vest but would've felt ridiculous running to grab one, so he stayed put, staring at her as if daring her to say something. She didn't, of course, and that made him feel worse. What had he expected her to say? Had she even noticed? And did he want her to?

"Bad day?" It was an easy question and a mean one. She looked exhausted and fragile and it made her flinch. And that made him feel just a tiny bit worse, and better too. She shrugged, unwilling to meet his eye. That pride, so different from his, but just as strong.

"Just long."

"Isn't Darren off to his new job today?" Touched by something like remorse, he tried to focus on something good. Taamarai had sounded excited, or at least made a good attempt, when she'd told them about the new position.

"Yeah." She didn't look happy. "Now he's got something, it'll make things easier." She didn't sound convinced by her own words or like she was really even listening to them. They had just become something to say.

Abruptly she looked back at him, her eyes hunting. Carl knew what for: anything else to talk about. Her gaze drifted down. "I've wondered what your tattoo was of. Sometimes the top shows over your clothes."

It was a butterfly, its wings flexing inwards, straining to take off in a way that no butterfly ever did outside a cartoon. It wasn't very good. He knew that. But the kid who'd done it had something about him, some economy of lines that made things move. The result was raw, but he had never regretted having it done and never gotten another one.

"The way it's flapping. Like the air's heavy around it." As Taamarai spoke, he saw her hand rise, like it had in the library, as if an imagined touch might tell her something about what she was seeing. "When did you have it done?"

It was a sign of her distraction that she asked, of her desperate desire to be talking about something other than Darren. She had taken on board from Ali that his past was off limits. Carl watched her eyes, fixed on his chest, following the lines of the butterfly with frightening intensity. "In prison." Her face never flickered.

"That makes sense. It's simple. It's beautiful, though."

"I was twenty-three. My first real stretch. Armed robbery." He said it to shock her but she didn't react, or at least, not in any of the ways he might have expected.

"Did you know sailors usually have a tattoo of something with wings? Birds, butterflies.... There's a superstition that if they drown at sea, it will carry their soul up to heaven." Her hand still lingered in the air between them. "Being in prison must feel like drowning sometimes."

Carl stepped forward. She didn't notice in time to move her hand and her fingertips met his body, but she didn't pull away.

"I expect it does. Drowning, that is. The kid who did it told me the same thing. How these wings would carry me straight up and out of there." His voice had dropped very low and stopped completely as her fingers began to move, tracing the lines across his skin.

Taamarai continued to look down, and he couldn't take his eyes off her face. With a shudder, Carl realized that she was beautiful.

He'd never thought about it before, not really. She'd got a smile. A decent figure when she didn't cover it up. There was nothing wrong with how she looked and he'd stopped pretending he didn't notice, even if he still pretended not to dwell on it. This was something else completely; a feeling, not a thought, real the moment he acknowledged it. Not eyes or smile or figure but all of it and none. The woman he knew. He felt his breath catch in his throat and his stomach somersault.

"I don't have any wings," she whispered. The movement of her fingers stopped. Suddenly she looked up at him, straight into his eyes, saying nothing until she pulled her hand back. He didn't stop her as she stepped away. "It's a beautiful tattoo. I'm glad I've seen it properly." She turned towards the kitchen. "Do you mind if I borrow one of your pans? That's what I came down for."

"Sure." To his relief, she didn't look back at him as she found what she was after and headed quickly back out of the apartment. Carl stayed where he was for several minutes, still sure he could feel her fingers brushing over his skin.

At last, he moved, but purposelessly. Ali would be out most of the day. When she first started staying after school for clubs and track meets, it had startled Carl how used he was to having her around. Now, adrift in the empty apartment, he was relieved to be alone. He rubbed a hand over his head and sat for a while, not reading a magazine and trying to ignore the quivering tension in his body.

Finally, he headed for the bathroom, still pretending that he wasn't going to do anything but shower and that, if he did do anything else, he wouldn't be thinking about Taamarai while he did it.

He was about to turn the water on when he heard a soft

rustling. He stopped, listening carefully. The building was in a state, but it didn't sound like a water leak.

The noise changed and, with a strange feeling in his stomach, he recognized the sound of crying. A gasp, a sob, and then back to rustling. He knew immediately where it was coming from and who was crying. He leaned slightly closer to the wall, and the sound grew louder. It was travelling along the pipes.

As he reached for the shower to block out the sound, the noise shifted. The words weren't clear, but he could hear shouting. It was Taamarai. He heard a lower, mumbling sound and guessed that Darren was speaking quietly, as he always did. She cut him off, then there was silence for a couple of seconds. "Darren, get out!" The words were distinct this time and as loud as Carl had ever heard her. A door slammed upstairs and everything went quiet.

Carl turned on the shower and stood under it for a long time. His tattoo seemed to tingle and he couldn't shake a sense of guilt alongside a sharper, more urgent feeling. He leant one hand against the tiles and let the water slide over his chest and legs. He pushed his head into the flowing water too, until he could hear nothing else and had to close his eyes.

It didn't matter. He could only see Taamarai anyway and hear her voice in his head. Just his name. A question. That was all she said. *Carl?* He heaved a ragged breath and squeezed his eyes more tightly shut. He tried to imagine her touch on his body instead of his own, the feel of her kiss, and was overwhelmed and disappointed all at once.

When he was done, he lingered still in the private cocoon of falling water. Inside it he could simply be with all the things he felt. Outside, he would have to weigh them up - what he should and shouldn't have done or said, what could and couldn't be real. What line he had just crossed and how to carry on acting as if he hadn't.

Carl had settled down that night in front of a game when there was a knock at the door. This time he did pull on a vest. He wasn't surprised to see Taamarai, holding the pan she had borrowed.

"I just came to bring this back."

"You didn't have to." He remained standing across the doorway.

"No." She looked embarrassed and perhaps a little hurt. "I guess not. Well, here it is anyway." She held it out and he took it. She was about to turn away when he stepped aside.

"You want a beer?"

She turned back to him with a grateful smile. "A beer would be great." She hesitated nevertheless until he gestured her in, casting back a small, slightly guilty glance up the stairs. Then she passed him and headed straight for the fridge.

He turned down the game but didn't turn it off. She sat down at the other end of the couch and for a while, they sat watching. "Bad pass," she interjected softly. He looked up in surprise and she laughed.

"Darren took me to see nearly a game a week the first year we were together. Then every year since, almost. My first game, I couldn't even see how you were supposed to tell which team was which. Now, I can spot a bad pass when I see one." She was quiet for a moment. "I guess I should be grateful for that."

"How did Darren's first day go?" Back to poking that open wound. Carl wished he could stop himself.

She rolled her eyes at him and downed most of her beer. "This one? Apparently, he didn't like the 'vibe' he got from his line manager." She turned back to the game. "He'd been there for an hour!" She snapped her jaw shut, then shook her head. When she opened her mouth again, words poured out in a bitter rush.

"The one before that, he didn't even make it on the first day. He left it too late, missed his bus connection and rather than apologize for showing up late, he called them to resign because the journey was too long." She breathed in deeply. "*That* was my fault. For living out here."

Carl had known the other jobs hadn't worked out, but she had never said why. They focussed on the game for a while, saying nothing. Suddenly she said, without looking at him, "I'm sorry about earlier."

"What for?" He glanced at her.

"I shouldn't have asked about your tattoo. It's none of my business." From the way she kept her eyes on the game, her fingers tight on her beer bottle, he suspected the apology wasn't really for the question. Again he felt his skin prickle and was disturbed by his own confused guilt.

He kept his face straight, his voice neutral. "I don't mind. If I don't want to tell you something, I won't."

She looked over and nodded slowly, then she said, "Armed robbery?"

"Is that a question?"

She looked away and shrugged. "I guess. Ali's never told me anything about your past."

"There's a lot she doesn't know." He was quiet. He hadn't planned to tell her what he had. He'd just said it to get a rise out of her.

"I guess I figured it'd be easier for her." He turned back to the game. "I was twenty-three. I'd been into stuff for.... I guess I always had been. Breaking into places, shoplifting. I didn't think about it much. You do stuff, you run, sometimes the police catch you. Bunch of guys I was with said there was a safe at this jeweler's store. We went along with our hats pulled down and scarves over our faces."

He laughed gently. "The guy had a silent alarm. Police picked most of us up before we'd made it a block. I didn't even know three of the others were carrying. I don't remember anyone getting guns out, but the cops didn't care. They did us all as if we had. My lawyer got me off with nine years. Out in four and a half."

She thought about this. "Twenty-seven when you got out?" They sat together for a while. "You said it was your first real stretch?"

He gave her another sidelong look. "Two more. Five years the one, the other could've been sixteen, but my lawyer cut me a deal for information. I did two. When I got out after that one, that's when I found out about Ali. That's when she started living with me."

"That's a lot of time."

"You don't want to know what they were for? The other two?"

She looked over at him. "Do you want to tell me?"

"Not sure that I do."

"Wouldn't be much point me asking then, would there?" She smiled.

They turned back to the game. After a few minutes, he got up and returned with two fresh beers. She took one with thanks and Carl looked down at her, still standing. "You don't mind being here?"

Taamarai looked around. "Gabriel Heights?"

He snorted dismissively. "My couch? My place? Watching a game with a man who's spent ten years in prison and won't tell you what for?"

She seemed to consider this. "I hadn't thought about it." She didn't move except to look around the apartment. "I guess I don't." She reached up with her beer bottle and waited for him to clink the neck before adding, "Maybe I'm naive, but I try to take people as I find them."

"And how's that been working out for you?"

Again, she seemed to give it serious thought. "Lately, pretty well." She smiled with increasing warmth then became earnest again. "I've maybe missed some important things over the years though." For a moment, he wondered if he should say something about being able to hear her earlier. Instead, he sat back down.

"We all make mistakes. I figure it's about how we make the comeback."

"Carl?"

He looked over sharply, his heart in his mouth. She couldn't know, but he felt it must all be visible on his face. "Can I spend the night?" He frowned and felt sick and elated and sure that he must have misheard. "On the couch?"

After a moment, he nodded. "Sure." They watched the rest of the match in silence. "I'll get you a blanket," he said as it finished. "You need a toothbrush, too?"

"It's okay. I don't...." She hesitated. "Yeah. That would be great."

He came back a few minutes later. "Thank you." She looked around. "You don't need to go to bed early on my account."

He turned back to the television and flicked channels. "I wasn't gonna." He sat down and saw her smile out of the corner of his eye. She disappeared off to the bathroom and, when she returned, headed for the kitchen.

"You want another beer?" she called.

"Sure."

She brought the two bottles and handed one over. "Sorry for going through your beer. I'll pick you up another six-pack this week." She collapsed onto the sofa, this time closer to the middle, as the blanket was stacked at the other end. She sounded a little drunk.

He looked at her, suddenly annoyed again. "Why you always do that?"

Her head flicked round to look at him. She had felt his tone, and her eyes were deep with guilt and apology. "I'm sorry. What did I do?" She looked like she might cry.

"That." He gestured angrily with his bottle. "You'll buy me more beer, you're sorry before you even know what for." He turned to look at her properly. "Like you're apologizing for taking up space." He breathed in, aware that he was being harsh and cold. He sighed and when he spoke, it was with more emotion than he intended.

"You think after what you've done for Ali, I mind you drinking my beer?"

She looked embarrassed. "I'm sorry." She'd said it without even realizing and laughed nervously. "I guess I hadn't thought about it. You're my friends." She was awkwardly silent for a while.

"You're probably right. I apologize too much. But I guess, I wouldn't want you to think I take it for granted. Getting to spend time with you. And Ali. People like their space." She paused. "It just makes me worry."

Something seemed to burn in the air between them. It made Carl uncomfortable. At last, with a savagery that he hadn't meant to show, he asked, "Darren tell you that?"

"What?"

"That maybe you take people for granted and they wish you weren't around?" He glared at her and she looked away.

"I guess, I don't think so. No. Not those words."

"Let's try this then." He wouldn't let it go. "Did anybody else ever tell you that's how you made them feel?"

She looked down, her brow creased in concentration. When she looked up, it was with genuine confusion. "No. I don't think so."

"Neither did I." He stood up and headed for the kitchen. When he came back with another pair of beers, she was staring down at her hands, her empties on the floor beside her.

"Stand up," he ordered.

Taamarai looked up then did, mute and bemused, clearly ready to be told to go. He handed her a bottle. "Drink this." She did, or at least a good quarter of it. "Now listen to me because I'm only going to say this once." She nodded and didn't break eye contact.

Carl squared off to her. "When you showed up, I thought you were some uppity oddball. I thought you'd fill Ali's head with dreams and then break her heart." Taamarai still didn't look away.

"I never said you were my friend." He didn't like the way the word tasted. "Never had much use for them. But it seems like you decided to be anyway." He frowned. "But whatever you call it, since you moved in, things have changed. For me. For Ali. Seems like life can be better and, like you're always telling me, Ali deserves that."

He took a breath, feeling the rush of words leaving him. He hadn't decided before he started what he wanted to say, but as he saw her, looking at him without nervousness or apology, just those eyes that seemed to take him in for all he was, he felt what he wanted her to hear, rising unstoppably out of him.

"You don't make me feel taken for granted, whatever the fuck that means, but what I do resent is having to sit in my own goddamn living room listening to what that worthless son-of-a-bitch you're married to says you are and ain't, and not a word of it good, even though you keep him, feed him, make excuses for him and let him talk you down. So you choose. Sit down, drink your beer and don't even think about telling me what Darren says you do or how you act or what other people think of you, and believe me that if we've got a problem, I'll tell you myself. Or you can head right on back upstairs and let him tell you some other ways that it's your fault he won't do a damn fucking thing with his life except bring you down."

Carl could feel his hand shaking when he finished, nowhere near shouting but alight with his own anger. He glared down at Taamarai, fully expecting that he had crossed the line, waiting for her to burst into tears, maybe even slap him and storm out.

Her lips were pursed and when she spoke, her words were careful, but that was from the beer. Her eyes stayed steady with the same clear, determined look as when she'd given him a book of poetry and carved herself a hole straight through most of the shit he used to keep people at arm's length. She lifted her beer and took a drink.

"You can call us whatever you like, Carl. I don't need to be your friend. But thank you." She reached out and touched the neck of her bottle to his, but didn't make a sound with it or pull it away, just rested it there as she leaned in closer and kissed him gently on the cheek.

Then she walked past him, placed her beer on the table and headed for the kitchen. When she came back with water for them both, he was already sitting down, apparently absorbed in the game. She took her seat and, within minutes, they were engaged in a running commentary.

Chapter Sixteen

Ali pushed food around on her plate. She'd already had two helpings and seemed to be using this last mouthful as a distraction. Taamarai had started coming down to their place again for dinner every three or four days. Darren never came and she rarely mentioned him. From odd comments, Carl gathered that she usually cooked for him then came down to eat with them.

At first, she had gone almost as soon as the washing up was done, but most times now, she stayed until past midnight. It felt almost like it had before except that Taamarai seemed faded somehow, slower to smile or just a bit too cheerful. It was still better than not seeing her, though, and Ali had begun opening up again, which made her hesitation now surprising.

Carl stared at her across the table, but he was too impatient to wait long.

"Well?"

"Nothing." Ali carried on fidgeting with her food.

Taamarai gave Carl a concerned glance and he suspected that she too was thinking of the boy, and whether he had been causing Ali any trouble. Before either of them could ask more, Ali found her nerve.

"It's parent-teacher conference at school. Tomorrow."

Carl frowned. "Tomorrow?" Ali had told him a few times across the years. He'd never been much of a regular but she'd always given him more notice than this.

"Your parent-teacher conference is tomorrow?" Taamarai echoed. She thought about this, then smiled. "Well, that's great. I can have something ready for when you get back." She looked at Carl and it was evident that she assumed he was going.

Ali still looked like she was desperately embarrassed about something. "The thing is, Mrs Morris said specifically how she was looking forward to seeing you *both* again." Ali looked down at her food and then back up at them. "I mean, I said I wasn't sure if you could make it."

Taamarai felt terrible for her. It wasn't even Ali's lie, but she also knew that, if Carl agreed, she was ready to tell it again.

Carl took very little persuasion, as it happened. He certainly hadn't been thrilled at the prospect of going on his own. As they arrived, the school was brightly lit up. It seemed strange being there at night, surrounded by adults, like a theatre set for the wrong play.

Carl glanced around in discomfort as parents drifted by, looking like they were just coming in after regular jobs. Taamarai walked beside him, apparently looking at everything except him.

In the sports hall, teachers sat in rows with parents milling between them. Ali had given them a list. Taamarai gestured to the far corner of the room. She had evidently already worked out an order, and he just followed along.

"Good evening. We're here on behalf of Ali Grigg." Taamarai smiled.

The teacher stood up and reached out to shake her hand, already and visibly running calculations in her head as she looked from Taamarai to Carl. She shook Carl's hand. "Ali is a lovely girl."

It seemed like something she said about all of her students but then she became more sincere. "She's really come on this year. She's taking her studies seriously, and there is a very bright spark there when she lets it shine." Beside him, Taamarai smiled more broadly. Carl didn't know what to do with his face.

"So what does that mean?" he asked instead. "I mean, she's coming on. She's bright. That's like, what? That's a pass, right?"

The teacher looked surprised then critical. If he'd bothered to come to these meetings before, she seemed to imply, he would already know that. But maybe he was imagining it.

"Oh, that was never in doubt, Mr Grigg. I mean that Ali is working towards a straight A in my course."

They talked for a bit longer, and he heard Taamarai asking all the questions he wouldn't have thought to, about how to help her with her homework, or think about extra credit. In a few minutes, they were shaking hands again and moving around the tables, Taamarai still taking the lead.

The next teacher in line was younger and less good at hiding what she was thinking. She shook Carl's hand first and looked confused as she greeted Taamarai. Throughout their meeting, she kept glancing at him as if trying to work out what he'd got that might explain the situation in front of her. It certainly wasn't youth, money, class or charm, her expression seemed to say.

The story was the same, though. Ali had finally figured out what trying looked like and was taking them all by storm.

After half an hour of talking to teachers, Carl felt an unfamiliar nervousness as the principal hove into view. This time she made no mistake. Her skepticism was entirely intentional and perfectly pitched. He still wasn't up to scratch.

"Mr Grigg, Ms Calder. It's good to see you both."

As if she sensed his uncertainty, Carl felt Taamarai's hand in his, the straightening of her back palpable as a tiny change in the shape of her grip.

"Alison has been doing wonderfully," Mrs Morris continued. "There is even talk of college scholarships among the faculty. I can only think that she is receiving the proper support and guidance at home and we are all delighted for her."

Feeling Taamarai about to step in, Carl got there before her. Just once, he would show the woman in front of them that he could be the conscientious and respectable figure she so clearly felt him not to be. Or at least he could pretend.

"Thank you, Mrs Morris." He surprised himself at remembering her name. "Ali's always been smart. She and my wife," he stole a glance at Taamarai but looked away before he had to see her reaction, "it's just great seeing how well they get on. Ali's getting the help she deserves."

"It makes all the difference, Mr Grigg," Principal Morris agreed primly.

He felt Taamarai squeeze his hand and open her mouth to speak, but before she could, Mrs Morris was off, pinning down another set of parents.

They looked around and made for the exit and out into the evening streets. This time, Carl knew he could let go of her hand any time. He didn't, though, and neither did she. Near the bus stop, they came to a halt, looking out over the river.

"It sounds like Ali's doing amazingly." Taamarai turned her head to look at him at him. "The principal means well, but she was wrong to say what she did."

The river lapped below them, and traffic and pedestrians alike went past unnoticed and indifferent. Carl wasn't angry as he said, "No, she was right." He looked out at the water. "What you've done, with Ali. The way she carries herself now. Thinking about the future. All of that. My girl. College." He looked back at Taamarai and felt her squeeze his hand even tighter. She looked horrified.

"No, it's not. It's not! Carl!" She was staring intensely at him. He felt something inside him quake and might have taken his hand back out of shame, but he couldn't be sure, and she was still holding on anyway. "Ali was wonderful the day I met her. She always has been. And that's because of you."

"After you telling me all the time how she needs to be a kid?"

He felt that she must see his every failure and couldn't understand why she didn't just say it. Or walk away.

Taamarai shook her head with a dismissive smile though and did finally let go of his hand. "I don't have to agree with you about everything to know that Ali got very lucky when you decided to step up for her."

He wasn't sure what he might have said next because her phone began to ring.

"I'm sorry." She scooped it hurriedly out of her pocket. "It's Darren."

She turned away and he heard her voice change. She didn't even realize she did it. "Hey. How are you?" Just a touch higher, sharper. Less able to cope. "Sorry I missed your calls. I was at that thing I told you about. At Ali's school."

So she hadn't told Darren that she was going to Ali's parent-teacher conference, then, just "that thing." Darren had been upset when Ali accidentally mentioned their last visit to her school. It was dishonest, he'd said. And that was never okay. But it had helped, Taamarai had replied. Surely that was more important?

Carl had caught Darren looking at him and sensed that dishonesty wasn't what bothered him most. At the time, whatever his own occasional flashes of attraction, he'd thought it was a bit pathetic that Darren might see him as any kind of threat. Now Carl had to admit that Darren might not be completely stupid.

He watched people walking by and tried to tune out the one-sided conversation happening beside him. At last, she hung up.

"I'm..."

"Yeah, I know. You're sorry." Carl couldn't help sounding bitter and knew he had no right to. The bus pulled up, stopping him from saying anything else and by the time they sat down, he managed a wry smile.

"Guess you didn't tell him you were out pretending to be another man's wife, then?"

The last time they'd joked about this, Taamarai had shut him down. He'd figured then that her and Darren's relationship was too sacred to be laughed about. That wasn't how he remembered the conversation any longer. It felt in his memory now like she had been pushing hard against a door to something she didn't want to see, shoving it closed and scared even to know the door was there. It had taken him longer to realize what was on the other side.

Behind that door, Darren wasn't perfect, their relationship wasn't strong and fair and equal. She was not happy. In the months since, that door had refused to close, and Carl was increasingly sure that Taamarai lived most of her life on the side of it she didn't want to see. He felt for the tiredness it gave to her eyes but resented the way she kept trying to live in two worlds, two lives, without knowing what he wanted if she ever slammed that door shut on her broken illusions. Did he want it for the right reasons, as her friend?

Sometimes he knew exactly what he wanted, but that didn't make it possible. Right now, Carl was hoping she might shut him down again, show him that the lines were still in place and that some jokes were off-limits. He made himself hope for that. Taamarai flexed her hand, looking momentarily at her ring and then back at him.

"It didn't come up." She smiled a little smile that looked almost wicked, and then it turned into something more serious. "I didn't tell him. I couldn't be bothered to explain. But if you want me to, I will. It isn't a secret."

He shrugged magnanimously. "Hell, what you tell your husband's up to you. I guess that ain't me anymore, till the next parent-teacher conference." He couldn't help pushing harder, trying to find the point when she shoved back, knowing he would resent it when she did.

She grinned instead. "Mrs Morris's face! I don't know what she thinks is so strange." She looked like she genuinely didn't. Sometimes Carl couldn't tell if Taamarai was naive or just oblivious to the rest of the world. She glanced at her hand again and the ring which hung loosely on it. "We should get you one of these for next time – look the part."

His heart skipped a beat that wasn't just because the bus had hit a pothole. "And how would you explain that to Darren?"

"Who says I would?" She grinned again then her face closed off. There it was. She had crossed the line only she could see. It had taken him a long time to work that out, too. He couldn't guess why the ring was it this time, but something in the joke had come too close, felt too real. For a second, it had exposed how much of her life was lived in fear of upsetting Darren, even by thinking things he wouldn't like. She retreated.

"I mean, of course I'd tell him. Darren would think it was a laugh. We tell each other everything." That was it. The lie that tripped her up. They didn't tell each other everything, and she didn't want to deal with that or the deeper, secret pain that only Carl in the whole world knew she carried.

Taamarai looked over her shoulder, checking on reflex that Darren wasn't there, that nobody had overheard, even though Darren knew nobody in Horton. They were uncomfortably quiet for the rest of the journey until Carl hauled himself out of his seat near their stop. They didn't talk up the stairs either.

Ali was waiting for them when they opened the door. She had cooked *saambaar* and rice, and it wasn't half bad. Maybe as good as Taamarai's. Taamarai beamed. As they told her everything, Ali listened and interrupted in equal measure. Then she looked slyly at them both and asked, "What about the two of you? They all still think you're my stepmom?"

Carl turned to Taamarai, willing to let her decide. He promised himself that whatever she said, he'd play along. Taamarai grinned almost defiantly. "Nobody questioned it. How could they, anyway? It's hardly any of their business."

Ali laughed back. "You guys hold hands talking to the principal, or what?"

Carl actually felt himself flush a little and was absolutely prepared to brush that one off with a curt "none of your business." But again, to his surprise, Taamarai answered, without hesitation. "Actually, yes. It seems to help Principal Morris remember to be polite." Ali laughed right out loud, Taamarai laughing with her. Carl got up to get them sodas and was glad that when he returned, the subject had changed.

They sat around the table chatting until Taamarai's phone rang again. She didn't answer but looked like she had been caught stealing from the cookie jar. "I'm sorry. I'll have to head up."

Ali got up and hugged her goodbye. "Thanks for going tonight."

"I wouldn't have missed it for anything!" Taamarai held Ali's arms and stared at her affectionately. "You're quite a favorite by the sound of things, and you deserve it. We were both so proud of you." She looked over to Carl, suddenly a little embarrassed at including him like that, as if she really did have some right to speak for them both. He just lifted his soda bottle in a silent salute.

He knew he should get up and...and what? Hug her? He'd never hugged Taamarai before. Why would he start now? He didn't really hug anybody, even if Ali seemed to hug him more and more these days. Shake her hand? That seemed even weirder after an evening spent holding it like a ten-year-old at a milkshake bar. But then she was gone and the moment was over and he felt resentful and a little deflated instead of relieved.

"Dad?" Ali asked as soon as the door was shut. She sounded serious and curious all at once.

"Yeah?"

"How do you know when somebody's the right person for you?"

He frowned in surprise then lifted a sardonic eyebrow and gestured around – the apartment, his life as Ali had always known him. "How in the hell would I know?" His frown deepened. "You not thinking of throwing away all this great progress on some kid telling you you're the love of his life, are you?"

"No!" Ali looked confused and a bit embarrassed. She glanced back towards the door as if Taamarai's presence, lingering in the room with the warmth of her laughter, might be able to overhear. "I was thinking about Taamarai and, you know, Darren. She talks about him like he's definitely the one. Like she couldn't imagine being with anyone else."

Carl thought about it. It was true, or at least, he'd certainly heard her talk like that. Not so much lately, but that wasn't an observation he felt like sharing with Ali if she hadn't already noticed herself. He didn't want Ali accidentally bringing it up with Taamarai, for a start, and he definitely didn't want his brilliant and perceptive daughter thinking that he was paying too much attention. He wasn't, after all. It didn't mean anything to him.

Instead, he said, "Well, isn't that how you're supposed to think when you're married to somebody?"

"That's what I mean," Ali replied thoughtfully. "I guess so, but when he used to call her, and now he's here and they're living together again, it always seems to be a downer. For her, I mean. I guess, with the right person, shouldn't they make things better?"

Carl stared at his drink. His tattoo itched under his clothes. The room smelled of cooked food. He looked around. Ali was leaning over the table asking for his advice, chatting to him about life, doing brilliantly in school.

It could be a scene out of a life somebody else might want to live. Somebody like him might want to live. He retreated from the thought but remembered what he'd said to Taamarai. It seemed like things could be better, ever since the day she moved in upstairs.

"I guess they should." He paused. "But we're all looking for different things. Better for one person don't always mean better for someone else. They'll work it out."

It was a lame answer and Ali looked like she knew it, but she didn't push. Instead, she came over to the table and dealt a quick hand of cards, a companionable half hour before she headed to bed. Carl picked up his hand and wondered what *working it out* would mean.

He hadn't meant what he said about different kinds of better, at least not about this. Taamarai was miserable and it made him sick to see it, and angry that he felt anything at all. It wasn't give-and-take or learning to compromise. She'd compromised almost everything about herself for what Darren wanted. But the accusation had come on swift wings as Ali asked her questions that he might be no different.

Taamarai made things better, but wasn't she just doing what she did with Darren, now with him and Ali as well? Giving whatever she could to make things better for other people until she disappeared completely?

The thought was a kind of comfort. It let him breathe after the intensity of the day, but it didn't feel right. Could he do more? Sure. But even in his darkest moods these days, Carl knew that it was possible to be less of a man and more of a failure than he often felt, even when it looked like you'd got everything made. In other moments, it was possible to believe that he might actually be of some use to Taamarai. That was a thought to keep him awake at night.

Chapter Seventeen

Taamarai had eaten with Darren that evening, so Carl looked surprised to see her when he opened the door, but not too surprised.

"Can I come in?"

He stood aside and gestured her in. She went straight to the fridge and grabbed two beers. He took one without a word and waited.

"Is Ali in her room?"

"Yeah. Some project for school. About rainforests."

She nodded. It made things easier. Ali would have her headphones on, and Taamarai felt she could speak more or less freely. She drank most of her beer before she could say anything at all. She was so angry.

"I told Darren about Ali's idea. The food stand."

Ali had come home from school a week earlier raving about a new pop-up market downtown. The kids all went there for their lunch. The local chamber of commerce was offering some sort of regeneration package. Ali was vague but excited. None of the stands did anything as good as Taamarai's South Indian stuff. Why didn't

Taamarai try opening one? It wasn't a restaurant, but it might be the beginning of one.

To Taamarai, it had seemed serendipitous. The head chef at the restaurant had left. She didn't get on as well with his replacement. The erratic shifts they kept calling her in to cover were getting harder and harder to live with. Her college course would be over in a few months, too, so it was time for a new challenge.

Still, Taamarai had brushed it off. She'd had a plan: her college course, getting a job as a head chef, then opening her own place. She wasn't ready to start skipping levels. She wasn't up to it. She didn't have the skills.

Except that, as she and Carl and Ali talked, she began to think she might. Back when she was doing the publishing stuff, she *had* run her own business, though she'd never thought about it in those terms. At least she knew her way around a commercial tax return. She'd done her own marketing, budgeted for projects. And she could cook. She bounced out and headed straight for her laptop to find out more. Her excitement had only grown.

"I told Darren right when Ali mentioned it but I don't think he was listening. I've done my homework since then. And it could work. It really could!" She looked at Carl suddenly, begging him not to contradict her.

"I don't think I could do it on my own, though. Most of the stories on the website are couples. There's a pair of brothers. It's just logistics. You need somebody to do the cooking. Maybe they can serve too, but it's easier with two. And you've got to keep the place tidied during the day, take breaks, then there's all the inventory, buying and stuff." Taamarai still felt dizzy imagining it but not enough to back down.

"So I talked to Darren about it properly tonight. I showed him the scheme. He's still got no work. It could be great. We could open it up together. I'd be doing most of it. I'm the only one who could cook and buy ingredients, and I've always done our tax returns, so I'd keep doing that. And I know he doesn't like the idea of retail, but even if he just helped out with taking orders, cleaning up a bit."

Taamarai ran out of steam and went quiet. When she spoke again, she was tired and sad.

"We could have done it." Her voice cracked with tears that weren't falling yet. "He just refused."

Taamarai looked at Carl as she said it. He wasn't even trying to hide his lack of surprise. What she had once read as scorn or cruelty felt different now: a refusal to let her hide. She felt the tiniest flicker of the crazy fire that had blazed in recent weeks whenever she remembered the feel of his skin beneath her fingertips. She was too angry for that right now, but it remained in the background – the unsettling intensity of a connection unspoken, and deeply confusing.

"How come he won't do it?" Carl asked.

Taamarai laughed and was shocked at her own bitterness. "He doesn't like the idea of us working together. It might make things less special between us. And he'd feel like he wasn't contributing equally with me doing such a big share of the work."

Carl felt this was a very Darren-shaped argument for the way it conveniently ignored that right now he wasn't contributing anything at all. Taamarai wasn't done, though.

"And he doesn't think he'd be any good at sales even though I told him I'd do all the advertising, but he said he was worried he'd be rude to customers and spoil it for me." Her eyebrows rose angrily. "I told him to just not do that then. How hard is it just not to be rude to people?"

Carl didn't feel especially qualified to comment, but she evidently didn't expect him to.

"I tried to talk to him, show him how it would be okay and he just kept pushing things back at me until eventually I asked him what he really thought was so terrible about the plan." Unshed tears choked in Taamarai's throat.

"He says he thinks I'm being stupid thinking of opening a restaurant at all. That it's all been stupid. College, moving out here. I mean, I knew he thought that already." Her shoulders slumped and her voice fell. "But I thought he at least understood why I had to. He told me he doesn't think my cooking's that great. 'Faddy,' he said."

The words seemed to crush her anew as Taamarai said them. She stared up at him, a terrifying want in her eyes. For reassurance and comfort. His reassurance and comfort. Carl felt its pull and gritted his teeth against temptation.

"So fucking what?" Her eyes opened wide and he waited until he could tell she was listening to what he was saying and not the defeat inside of her. "Taamarai, when has Darren ever said a thing worth hearing about food? Your cooking's great. Course you've got what it takes to run a business. And the reason Darren doesn't think any of it is a good idea is because he knows that, too." He let out his contemptuous huff now.

"He's worried about you working too much, him not contributing enough? Bullshit! He's worried you might stop paying him to sit on his ass all day doing nothing while you're out there working till you fall over. He's worried you'll finally do something on your own and do it well and decide you'd be just fine without him."

Immediately, he sensed that was a sentence too far, but he didn't regret it.

She looked awkward and unsure and sounded tentative again. "He's always been really supportive. I mean, when I first moved here, he didn't like it, but he didn't try to stop me. And he's always said he doesn't like working with people. I shouldn't be asking him to do something he's always hated."

Carl could almost hear Darren's voice hijacking the sounds coming from Taamarai's mouth. When she stopped, he looked at her, letting his own disdain show.

"He let you come out here? You shouldn't expect him to do something new 'cus he's always told you he don't like to? You want to dig a hole and rest that bar in it? 'Cus from where I'm standing, the floor ain't low enough."

He turned away, disgusted, though he couldn't tell whether at her or himself for being such an ass about it. He drained his beer and then looked at her again.

"You remember what you told me when you first got here? After we'd emptied that damn U-Haul?"

She looked puzzled.

"'I'd have managed,' you said. Stairs and all, and you know what? I thought back then you were just talking but once I knew you, I knew you would've." He looked her over, much as he had that day.

"Way I see it, what you've gotta decide is whether you want this bad enough. If you do, you'll manage."

There were so many other things it would be easy to say. How Darren would always find a reason why her dreams weren't important, and about her own self-respect and watching it erode day by day, but none of that would help right now. Instead, he saw the angry torrent in her head shut down.

Carl knew the blind rage of feeling like every way he turned, there were more reasons why something wouldn't work out. He loved watching Ali figure out that might not be true, and he knew she would never have learned it from him. Now he saw the light returning to Taamarai's eyes as she also saw that she had choices. She nodded and drank some beer.

At last, she looked at him with a frankness that had no visible anger in it anymore, just years of exhaustion. "I knew he wouldn't. Even before I brought it up." She headed for the door and, just as she was leaving, remembered to murmur, "Goodnight, Carl. Thanks."

"No problem," he replied to the closing door and her departed ghost. The whole thing might have seemed like a dream if he wasn't listening to her steps on the stair, even and slow.

Taamarai opened the door to 602 and headed for the kitchen. She had been putting away the washing up earlier, and talking to Darren about the food stall, when one asinine comment too many had blinded her with rage and stopped her mouth, and she had turned and left.

Everything was exactly as she had left it. Darren was on his computer. He seemed to spend more and more of his time in chatrooms. At first, she'd hoped it might help ease the loneliness he constantly complained about. She asked after his friends and family, but he hadn't been in touch with any of them. When she asked who he was talking to then, he shrugged. "Nobody. Just people."

Once she might have asked. Tonight, she just left him where he was and carried on cleaning the kitchen. She had almost got it done, was hoping that maybe he would stay there until she had gone to bed, when she heard him move and caught his smell as he crowded into the kitchen behind her.

"It's not safe walking around here at night."

"You don't seem to mind me doing it when I'm walking back from the bus after work."

"That's different. I know you've got to work."

"You could walk out to meet me at the bus stop." Her voice was robotic. She couldn't feel anything.

"Tam, don't start that again. We've talked about it. It's like saying I've got to give up half an hour of my evening every time just because you want to work some low paid job miles away. And anyway, nothing's ever happened."

"Nothing happened tonight."

"Tam! Stop putting things away and look at me!"

"Somebody's got to put things away." She carried on with what she was doing. "Anyway, I didn't go for a walk. I went downstairs."

His silence was heavy with disapproval. When she'd finished putting away the dishes, Taamarai turned around. Darren loomed in the doorway, though he was shorter than Carl. She looked him up and down and felt suddenly claustrophobic.

Clenching her jaw, she took a deep breath. "I'm going to open a stand through the chamber of commerce scheme."

She tried to get past him. This wasn't a conversation. He didn't move, though, and she leant back on the sideboard rather than actually push. She didn't say anything, though, relishing the idea of making *him* have to ask for once. He didn't.

"Tam, we've talked about it. It's not a good idea."

"No, Darren," she said, surprised at her own calm. "We've talked about it and *you* don't think it's a good idea. I think it's a great opportunity."

"And that's it, then? That's all that matters? What happened to always making decisions together? Thinking about what's good for both of us?" He started angry but by the time he was done he sounded tearful and looked broken. Taamarai felt her resolve weaken.

They had always agreed to share decisions. If it wasn't right for both of them, then it wasn't the right decision. She had always thought that mattered, that it was how a relationship should be.

Taamarai reached for the certainty she had felt minutes before. It came to her in a familiar voice. *It's not fine.*

When Darren hadn't come with her to her brother's funeral, they'd had a similar conversation. She had to go, obviously, but it wasn't the right decision for them both. Something that eluded her then seemed clear as day now.

"Darren, not doing things is a decision, too."

He looked non-plussed.

"You say that opening the stand isn't the right decision for you. Well, fine, I've listened to you. I'm not asking you to come and work with me. I can manage it on my own. But not doing it isn't the right decision for me. And that means it can't be the right decision for us either. I'm offering a compromise. We can talk about the details. It's not like you don't have any choices here."

"I don't, though, do I?" He stared at her resentfully. "You're talking about compromise but you've already said you're going to do this even though I think it's a stupid idea, so you don't really care what I think or how I feel."

Taamarai could feel herself getting angry again. He never seemed to listen except to the bits that suited him. "How is that different from you saying that I just can't do it, no matter what it means to me?"

"That's completely different!" He looked at her like she was an imbecile. "You're talking about a big risk. It might not work. I'm just saying let's not change something that's working. That's completely different."

Without warning, Taamarai felt tears and rage break like a storm inside her. She held them in but could only manage through grinding teeth, "You think this is working?"

The kitchen closed around her. Darren's smell choked her and she hurried past him into the lounge.

"Tam." He turned to follow her. "Tam, I'm worried."

He sounded suddenly terrified, childlike and pathetic, and she stopped.

"Tam, please look at me." Slowly, she did. Tears were streaming down his cheeks. "Tam, I've never been worried about us before. Never. I've always known we'll be together forever." His lip shook. She knew this was the part when she was meant to rush over and tell him she would love him forever, but although her heart ached with guilt, she couldn't move or speak.

"Tam." Her silence encouraged him. "You said, when you first signed up for this course and moved away, you said if I ever asked you right out to quit and come back home, you would."

It had been one of many late-night conversations that began with him telling her how proud and supportive he was of her, and ended with her pouring out reassurance that she would always put their relationship first.

"So Tam, if I asked right now, would you? Would you quit and come home?"

Taamarai blinked tears back and swallowed but she knew the answer and not saying it wouldn't change anything. "No."

Darren looked crushed. His shoulders slumped and he began to cry again. With shock, Taamarai realized that she was almost hoping. Poised and tense, she was waiting for the words: *well, maybe that's it then, maybe we just can't make things work.* As soon as the thought crystallized, terror consumed her.

She had never been with another man. She had made every promise she knew to this one. A self-protecting part of her pushed back against the hope. On one hand, she might just have to stay silent a few moments longer for the choice to be made. On the other, if she did, she would have to confront every humiliating, degrading moment they had shared. She would have to figure out who she was and how she could have been so stupid.

Darren seemed to see her waver. He looked pleadingly at her, broken and desperate.

"It's okay, Tam. I understand. I shouldn't have dropped it on you like that. I know I'm not the man you deserve. I'm just scared because I don't know what I'd ever do if I lost you. But it's okay. If this is important to you, we'll work it out."

He walked over and took her hands in his.

"You're right – I wouldn't ever have to go there or be involved in it, and it's your money so we're not really losing that much if it fails." He smiled sadly. "I'll miss you when you're out at work, but I guess I do now. It'll be okay, Tam."

She stumbled forward into a hug, relief lapping over her like an oil slick. He kissed her hair and then her ear. "I love you, Tam."

"I love you too." The response was learned and Taamarai felt sick, but she kissed him back and he whispered in her ear, "I love you so much. You know nobody could ever love you as much as I do."

His hands crept under her clothes. "You're so beautiful. You turn me on so much, babe. I don't know what I'd do without you." He was unfastening her bra. "To me, you're the most beautiful woman in the world." He was groping to pull her pants down, his hands digging into the flesh of her hips, which Taamarai had always been self-conscious about and which now revolted her beneath his touch.

"No one could ever love you like I do or find you as hot as I do right now." The words vibrated against the skin of her neck, and she felt them with confused horror. Gratitude and disgust curdled in her stomach.

Darren pulled her top off, letting it fall to the floor with her bra. Taamarai caught sight of her reflection in the window, lumpen and misshapen, and could only close her eyes as he ran his hands hungrily across her body. He was unfastening his pants and, this time, pulled her over to the couch.

He was rough and it hurt, but Taamarai knew the feeling would pass. "You're so gorgeous, babe." She could feel her stomach wobble and his fingers gripping hard and Taamarai closed her eyes and tried to be somebody else with somebody else. It only took a few seconds. She had been doing it for so long.

When he was finished, Darren did up his pants again and walked to the kitchen. He usually didn't like to touch too much right after they made love, when their skin was sweaty. Once it had made Taamarai sad. Now, she hurried to the bathroom and showered for a long time, glad to be left alone. For the first time, he had been afraid. Taamarai remembered the hope but heard in her ears, "Nobody will ever love you like I do."

He wasn't wrong. She'd had crushes over the years. Friends, colleagues, one boss. Taamarai had felt guilty about them, tried to hide the feelings even from herself, but not one of them had ever shown any sign of noticing her, of desiring her. Men didn't ask for her number at bars or chat her up on the bus.

As she climbed out of the shower, Taamarai wondered if it mattered. If she spent the rest of her life alone, would it matter if she never had to feel his touch again? The thought flared brief and bright against the habit of love and disappeared from sight.

When she got out of the bathroom, he was waiting for her. She was wrapped in a towel because she had forgotten to take clothes with her. He was facing away from her, naked, and as he heard the door open, he turned to present her with the glory of his own arousal.

In two steps, he was beside her, peeling at the towel, smiling and pinching playfully. The trauma of less than an hour ago seemed forgotten. Sex meant forgiveness, or more correctly, admission. She was wrong to cause him fear and doubt and with that admission, his confidence returned. Taamarai was not forgiven, but the sin had become venial. She could make amends.

Taamarai disappeared to that other place where they were other people, and when they were done, she pulled on her pyjamas gratefully and turned away, saying she wanted the light of the cartoon out of her eyes so she could sleep. He curled against her back, cupping her breast in his hand through her clothes.

"Booby!" He giggled softly. "You know I love you, Tam. I think you're making a mistake, but I'll always be here for you, no matter what. Just promise me something?"

"What?" She asked it warily.

"When this is done with, we can go home."

Taamarai felt her stomach knot. When what was done with? Her dream, her life? And what home? Christmas Day flashed into her mind, and the thought that this apartment might be as much of a home as she had known for years. She let out a sigh that could be an *mmm* or an *mmhmm*, and he seemed to hear it as an answer.

"I love you," he whispered.

For a second, the reply wouldn't come and Taamarai felt him tense. She knew the conversation that must follow if she hesitated even a microsecond longer, another night of lost sleep before another long day. "I love you too," she murmured.

Darren nestled against her contentedly, and Taamarai tried to reach for the memory of Christmas again, but what she found instead was Carl. Shame and disgust overwhelmed her. That night with Darren became Carl, seeing her body as she did and as Darren treated it. Tears trickled silently down her cheeks and she pulled the pillow over her mouth to hide the sound.

Chapter Eighteen

Ali, Carl and Taamarai got to the fifth floor, and Taamarai felt the ache in her legs. Often she didn't notice it anymore. It had been a twenty-hour day, though, and she was about ready to collapse. Not completely ready, though. She was riding an intense buzz and could feel it bleeding away as she got closer and closer to her door so, despite her exhaustion, she paused at 502.

"You want a beer? One for the road?" Carl didn't look tired at all. He really was nocturnal, and looked more cheerful than she could ever remember seeing him. It suited him and she couldn't stop grinning as he smiled back at her, all rough stubble and sparkling eyes.

The three of them piled through the door and Ali hung off Taamarai but was clearly almost unconscious.

"Ali, thank you so much." Taamarai could feel tears welling up in her throat and laughed a little to keep them at bay. Ali laughed back and squeezed her.

"You were amazing, Taamarai! They loved the food. I always knew you were the best cook ever." She was grinning like a Cheshire Cat but her grip was getting looser by the second.

Taamarai laughed again. "You get used to the late nights, but it's hard when you start. You've been incredible tonight. Thank you! Now," she held Ali away from her, hands on her shoulders. Again, she felt tears in her eyes. Ali looked back at her, smiling and full of joy. Part of her wanted to clutch the girl to her and freeze time, but instead she turned Ali physically around and pushed her gently towards her room, "Go to bed!"

"Yeah, okay, *Mom*." Ali turned her head back and rolled her eyes sarcastically but her smile was bigger than ever. Then she stumbled into her room and closed the door behind her.

Taamarai was still staring after Ali with stupefied delight when Carl re-emerged from the kitchen with two open beers and his own smile, more subdued but still looking like it wouldn't scrub off his face without some real effort.

"Ali gone to bed?" He nodded his head over to the closed door.

"Yeah, she was practically falling over she was so tired." Taamarai took the bottle he held out, and they toasted. "Cheers."

Carl was staring at her. "You put on quite the show."

"I couldn't have done it without you." Suddenly, Taamarai felt very foolish, as if he might be able to see straight through to her most secret thoughts, which these days seemed mostly to be about him. She took a deep breath.

"Thank you." The buzz of the night inside her and the beer mixing with it made her feel reckless and lightheaded. "I mean it. I didn't think I was going to pull it together."

He took a drink at last. "You'd'a done just fine. Like you told me and I told you – you'd've managed." Taamarai laughed but he didn't. "And anyone tells you different...."

She was glad that he didn't say any more. Neither of them wanted Darren any closer to this moment than he had to be.

Taamarai nodded carefully. "Yeah. I would have done." She let the words sink in. She would have done. It might have seemed impossible, but she would have done it. "Still, I really appreciate it. You and Ali, both."

They both knew what she meant, though Taamarai would swear she didn't. Ali was thrilled to have helped and would have done anything Taamarai asked, but when Carl had turned up at lunchtime for the grand opening of *Amma's Kitchen*, wearing jeans and a clean white t-shirt and asking what he could do to help, Taamarai had been openly incredulous before remembering to set her face straight.

For the first hour, she worried it might be a joke or a well-meant disaster. Then the rush picked them up and the orders flowed in and the food went back out, and Taamarai didn't have time to worry and didn't need to, anyway.

Carl knew what he could do and what he couldn't. He left Ali to the front of house and washed cookware, stacked ingredients, piled up and sorted rubbish, passed Taamarai water and occasionally reminded her to eat. At the end of the night, he and Ali helped her clean up and close down, then push the cart over to a nearby lockup.

Embarrassed by the silence, Taamarai took another sip of her beer. She took a step forward, heading for the couch, expecting Carl to turn with her. When he didn't, she nearly walked into him and felt the clumsiness of exhaustion and the rush in her fingertips. "Sorry." She was about to step back, but he caught her gently at the waist.

"Careful there." Carl looked down at her with slightly narrowed eyes, and Taamarai could hardly breathe. "Somebody else nearly falling-over tired."

His eyes were fixed on hers again but she couldn't read what lurked in them. Something uncertain.

"Carl?"

Taamarai wasn't completely sure what she was about to say but before she could, he let go of her and stepped away.

"You should get some sleep. Gotta do it all again tomorrow." His smile was gone.

Wired and tired and suddenly confused, Taamarai was through the front door before she knew what was happening.

She stood in the hall, staring at the scuffed wood, unable to make a single decision, her face still fixed in a grin and tears in her eyes.

Inside, Carl kept his hand on the door. He knew if he opened it again she would be there. There had been no steps on the stair. His heart was racing and he closed his eyes against a thousand thoughts.

He hadn't meant to catch her the way he did. He hadn't expected her to come in, though he remembered offering her a beer. He'd helped out at the stall because he wanted to see her win. Then she'd looked up at him with the question from his dreams. Her eyes were wide and full of fire.

She had pulled off something amazing today. Carl knew he couldn't have done it. In the weeks gone by, her idea had taken shape at the table here in 502, one recipe and color swatch and font choice at a time. Tonight was hers, he told himself, and she didn't deserve regrets. And maybe that was most of it – not getting in the way of her victory. Not wanting to be a regret – that wasn't something he'd ever worried about before, but it was there too, in a swirl of feelings that he didn't want to look at any closer.

At last, steps moved away and he retreated to the couch, putting on a late-night movie about something he likely wouldn't remember in the morning.

As Taamarai faced the last flight of stairs, each step loomed like a mountain. She dragged herself up them, one by one. The energy of the night was gone. She felt hollow and lost.

At 602, she opened the door quietly, hoping Darren would have gone to bed. He appeared in the hall before she had even taken off her shoes. He glanced down at the half empty beer bottle in her hand and she saw his lips purse disapprovingly.

He smiled, though, and came forward to crowd her into a hug. She could still almost feel Carl's arm around her waist, and recoiled towards the wall.

"How did it go?" Darren's smile was unsure. Taamarai felt her heart rate speeding up, racing towards a blind panic and she breathed as slowly and shallowly as she could. Sickness rolled up and over her and her vision blurred.

"Tam?" Darren stepped forward again. "Tam, are you okay?"

She managed to wave him off just in time. "I'm fine, Darren. I'm just tired." No need to pretend about that. "It was good. It went well."

He looked sincerely glad and relieved and she wondered where those emotions came from, that he wore on his face as if they were his. "That's great, babe. I knew you could do it."

He'd said the opposite, so many times and in so many ways that in the end she'd told him, as her mother had told her when she was a child, that if he had nothing good to say he might as well say nothing at all.

"So it was okay, doing it by yourself?" He was solicitous, as if the fact of her being on her own had nothing to do with him.

"It was fine." It was tempting to leave it at that, but there were other temptations. "And I wasn't by myself. Ali and Carl came by." She met his eye and saw his lips press together again.

"That's nice," he said after a moment. Taamarai just nodded. "I guess you don't know if it's going to work out after all then. Until you've managed a day or two properly." She nodded again, staring at Darren as if from a huge distance.

It was harder and harder to see him for how he was, not how he wasn't. Who he wasn't. Taamarai tried to remember the day in the canteen, when they had both been so young and her heart had fluttered because he noticed her.

When she still didn't say anything, Darren reached out to take her into a smothering hug. Taamarai was stiff as a board. He stepped back a little, holding the tops of her arms, as she had Ali's. Suddenly, he reached for her ribs and the places he knew she was ticklish.

It was something he did when she was depressed or they had disagreed. "Ooh, who's my ticklish girl? Who's my cute little baby girl?" His fingers dug into places that would normally make her laugh painfully and writhe to get away. This time, Taamarai was still and silent. She couldn't feel anything and wondered for a moment if she had ever felt anything all her life.

"Come on, Tam!" He let go of her and looked dejected. "This isn't my fault." He reached for her beer bottle and she let him take it. "Maybe if you hadn't gone out drinking when it was done...." He frowned. He set the beer bottle down on the table. More mess. Taamarai felt a tear trickle from her eye and turned away to hide it. She was too late.

"Tam, babe." He was back again, his arms around her. The wrong arms, the wrong smell. "Babe, don't cry. It'll be okay. I know you thought you could do this. And you said it went well. At least you'll know you tried." He rubbed her back. His hands began to wander. "Come on. It's been a late night."

Taamarai turned towards the bedroom door, already drifting mentally away from where she knew they were going. He would take out his frustration – first at her insistence and now at her silence – in the punitive, performative sex she couldn't tell him she didn't like because she had said she liked it a bit rough before. How was this different to that, he would ask if she even tried, and she wouldn't be able to explain, because how do you explain a feeling?

Tomorrow they could wake up and she could make it up to him with how she dressed and what she cooked, by coming home early and talking quietly about nothing very much and offering him more of whatever he wanted. She had done it all before.

The numbness shattered like some vast dome beneath a raging storm. Her hands came up to ward him off and she took a step away.

"I'm going to go and sleep downstairs." For a second she didn't think she'd said it aloud. But Darren was blinking in shock.

Like a robot, Taamarai collected pyjamas, wash things and clothes for the next day. For a long time, he didn't even follow her around. He only stopped her as she got to the door.

"Tam?" He looked lost. "Tam, what's going on?"

Taamarai couldn't speak. She could hardly breathe and just shook her head.

"Look, I...I can sleep on the couch," he offered desperately.

Taamarai shook her head again and moved to get past him. He grabbed her arm.

"Tam, look at me." She did. "If you go down there tonight, I don't know how I'll feel about you coming back up here tomorrow."

It wasn't a very effective threat.

"Goodnight, Darren." She squeezed past him and said over her shoulder, "It's my name on the lease so if I need to come in to get anything, I will, but if you need some space too, that's fine. I can stay downstairs for a few days."

Before he could reply, she shut the door and headed quickly down to 502. Taamarai wasn't completely sure what reception she would get. She didn't understand what had happened earlier, when Carl had closed the door in her face. But she had nowhere else to go and an instinct to go where he was that was stronger than a single, confusing moment in a crazy day.

Rather than knock and risk disturbing Ali, she texted Carl.

> Can I come in?

The door opened seconds later. Carl had clearly been awake and close to his phone, but he also looked ready for bed, wearing just his baggy sweat pants and looking freshly washed. Taamarai was almost too tired to notice, but only almost.

He gave her an unreadable look then stepped aside. As the door closed behind her, Taamarai felt some tension break. Even if Darren came looking, Carl wouldn't let him in without checking with her. She was safe from so many things she had never thought to fear. *Not fine.*

"Sorry." She gave him a searching look but he didn't react. "Can I sleep on the couch?"

He looked at her again as if wondering whether to ask a question, then turned away. "I'll get you a blanket."

Fifteen minutes later, Taamarai was curled up under a thin blanket, the rough fabric of a cushion against her cheek. The tears came then, though she wasn't sure what she was crying for. About an hour later, she got a text.

> Babe, I luv u mor than nething. Ur my soulmate. U no we r ment 2 b 2getha. Pls cum bac 2 me.

Taamarai turned her phone off and finally slept.

Chapter Nineteen

A week after *Amma's Kitchen* opened, business was booming. Taamarai feared it couldn't last, but it was great to get things off to a good start. Ali came to help when she wasn't at school. More surprisingly, Carl had carried on showing up. And Taamarai was still sleeping on the couch in 502.

Darren had begged her the second night until she had told him firmly and a little crossly that, if he wanted to be able to discuss any of this, he needed to respect that this was what she needed now. He looked like a man plunged into icy water.

It seemed never to have occurred to him that she might be thinking about the future of their relationship. That had been a consideration in his purview alone. Since then, Darren had been quieter but had still asked her upstairs every night to talk. Taamarai felt she owed him that.

The conversations wound on and on. They covered all the same ground and he never seemed the following day to have understood any of the things he said he had the night before. Instead, he would try to explain to her why she didn't really feel the things she said she did or why she shouldn't.

Every night, he tried to keep her there, and every night she left.

Taamarai kept expecting Carl to say something, but he didn't. Ali kept her counsel too, but gave Taamarai significant hugs and sometimes came and sat with her on the couch in the mornings, chatting about school and the stall.

That night their talk went round again. By the end of it, Darren looked stubbornly at his hands as he sat cross-legged on the couch, refusing to admit that Taamarai had a right to feel angry.

"You say I should be doing more to support you. I know you've always done more work than me, but Tam, you like work. You always have. And I always told you I was lazy. I enjoy not having any pressure. I thought you were okay with that. You always were before."

Taamarai felt the tears in her eyes again that came with pure frustration.

"I know you always said that, but I never thought you meant it! Not in the way you do. I thought we'd work together to build a life for ourselves. Not something stressy or hectic. I know you don't like that. But *something*. A life that was ours."

He looked pityingly at her. "We had one of those, Tam. You just weren't happy with it, so you tore it all up to come out here." He looked suddenly thoughtful.

"You know, Tam, you've never really been happy for as long as I've known you. Have you ever thought that maybe you just want to be unhappy? That you maybe need therapy or something?"

Taamarai wobbled inside. She couldn't deny it. She couldn't remember when she had felt happy. No, that wasn't right. She had been happy lots of times, but she had always been anxious and focused on what could be better.

As a teenager, she'd been insecure. When she met Darren, some of those insecurities seemed to go away, at least for a while, but she had worried about her college grades. She got all the grades in the end, but finding work and keeping the rent paid had still been a struggle. Then there was the worry about Joshua and after that, the horrible truth of never having to worry about him again and the secret she carried because of it.

Through it all, the work hadn't stopped – the short contracts, the poor pay, stitching together jobs to keep them afloat, while Darren never seemed able to think about what he spent or to hold onto a position. The housework and the cooking all fell to her. But what if those were excuses? The thought terrified her. What if she just was a naturally unhappy person, doomed to feel like this forever?

Darren leant forward and took her hand. "Babe, it's okay. We've all got issues. And I love you no matter what. I bet we could get you some sessions to talk to somebody if we head back home. We'd be saving on rent living with Mom and Dad and I bet you could get some of your old publishing stuff going again or maybe take up teaching. You were great at those cover jobs. Whatever it takes. If that's what you need, we'll do it." He squeezed her hand gently, finding his confidence again.

"It could be really good. Maybe it could even help you with your weight issues. I know that doesn't help with you feeling down, but it's like you always seem to let it go when you're nearly winning. Like with the publishing, too. You're a great editor, Tam, but you've never achieved what you're capable of. I just wish you could see yourself the way I see you."

Taamarai's thoughts whirled. It seemed suddenly too true, the story of her life cast in new colors – Darren putting up for so many years with his depressed, overweight, underachieving wife who worked all the time and never felt happy. She felt tears on her cheeks. Then she remembered Ali sitting on the couch with her that morning, Carl shuffling a deck of cards at the table when it was just the two of them. Joshua's letter. *Do something amazing.* Because he knew she could. Taamarai couldn't make the thoughts make sense, couldn't shout them back as a story to contend with his. If she opened her mouth, nothing would come out but a wild scream. She disentangled her hands from his.

"Maybe you're right, Darren." Her voice was hesitant but grew stronger. "But at least I've always tried to make things better. And

I'm happy *here*. This is my home and I like it. I have friends and I enjoy what I'm doing."

Again he looked very sorry for her. "Tam, you cry almost every night. That doesn't seem like someone who's happy."

Taamarai bowed her head. When she looked up, her eyes were dull but determined. "But I only do that when I talk to you. Maybe you're right, Darren, and I'm just a miserable person. But maybe I'm not."

She knew he wouldn't like what she said next.

"I think maybe you should go back to your parents for a while. We both need some space."

He looked shocked. "You're throwing me out? Tam, I've only just started feeling settled here."

Taamarai looked around the apartment that she had cared for so lovingly. Now that she mostly stayed downstairs, it was dusty. There were socks and bits of rubbish and laundry across the floor, washing up piled around the kitchen, and most of her wall hangings were stacked in a corner.

"Come on, Tam." Darren was pleading. "It'll be so embarrassing. What do I tell Mom and Dad? Tam, don't throw this away. You're the only woman I've ever loved. You're the person I want to spend my whole life with."

She felt her resolve breaking. "I'm not throwing anything away. I just think we need time apart to think about things. It'll be good for both of us." Her voice got harder. "I've told you what I've got to say, Darren. Maybe you should think about making some changes as well."

That had been another set of painful conversations. They began with her asking whether he wanted anything out of his life beyond living off her earnings in his parents' back bedroom. They turned into her asking for them to make just a tiny bit of space in their lives for her interests and preferences. They devolved with wearing predictability into increasingly minute nit-picking as Darren challenged her tell him one time when he had ever been unreasonable or inconsiderate or immature. That was hard to do, because it was more about the things he didn't do than the things he did, and that was a logic he refused to recognize.

So she told him how much she hated that he still dressed like a grungy teenager, how he didn't wash enough or keep his teeth clean, how he always wanted to eat bland, unhealthy foods that made her feel fat and bloated, how she sometimes wanted for them to watch a film or read a book together that she picked instead of him.

And he replied that she was being shallow and controlling to care about his wardrobe, that he went to the doctor and dentist so why couldn't she just accept there was nothing wrong with him, and anyway, he was healthier than her because he wasn't over-weight, and if she didn't want to eat what he did that was fine. She could always cook something else for herself.

It wasn't his fault she had no self-control. It wasn't his fault that all the things she suggested to do or read or watch were just preten-tious and boring.

Now he looked desperate and hopeful. "I'll do anything. But what do you want me to do, Tam? I don't understand."

Finally, it was enough. "I can't face having the same conversa-tion again, Darren. I've said what I need to. This is why we both need time to think."

He didn't seem to know what to do with his face, then sighed. "Okay, babe, if this is what you really want."

"I can stay downstairs while you sort out travel," Taamarai said with barely concealed relief.

"No, it's okay. Mom will give me the money. I'll get a flight tomorrow." He moved back towards her.

"But babe, can you stay tonight? Don't go back downstairs." He looked like he might cry again. Taamarai felt herself being pulled into an embrace and then a kiss. She could already feel herself shutting down, numb to what would follow even before he started taking off her clothes.

Chapter Twenty

Taamarai cleaned 602 herself, even though Ali offered to help. She was embarrassed at the state Darren had left it in. When it was done, she rehung her pictures and reorganized her kitchen. Working her old restaurant job, even on reduced shifts, was becoming impossible. Within a few weeks, she'd quit to focus on the food stall full-time. Her college course was nearly over. Evenings and any free days went to her final project, but mostly she was at the market square or prepping food and trying recipes. And if she was at the market stall, so was Carl.

In the evenings, Taamarai cooked for them again, mostly at her place, or Ali did, nudging hot food at them when they came in late.

A month in, Taamarai had tentatively raised the question of paying them for their help. Carl had brushed her off. Paying Ali for the occasional Saturdays and Sundays she helped out was fine. He liked the idea of Ali knowing her time was worth something. But he didn't want a dime. He'd managed to pull a couple of jobs with his usual contacts as they were getting the stall up and running. It was enough to keep him and Ali going for now and that was all he'd ever worried about.

A week later, Taamarai had brought it up again, and this time she insisted. If she couldn't pay him, she couldn't accept his help.

Carl had tried to get angry. "Friends" still sounded wrong in his head, but that was the essence of it. Friends helped each other out. They didn't get paid.

Taamarai had looked pained but let it drop for another few days. Then she cornered him again, and he knew from the look in her eye that this was the final showdown. Friends helped each other out, she agreed. That covered the grand opening, maybe the first couple of weeks when everything was riding on hopes and dreams. She was grateful and always would be. But friends didn't exploit each other by accepting six days a week of unpaid labor. And anyway, how was he going to keep the rent paid and Ali fed if he was at the stall all the time instead of doing whatever else it was he did?

On the verge of telling her to mind her own business, Carl suddenly realized that he really didn't have money for the rent. More troublingly, the prospect of heading down to his regular clubs or calling up Jackie was downright unappealing. He didn't even consider Taamarai's suggestion that he could leave her on her own at the stall. But that meant he'd be picking up anything extra in his free time, of which there was now precious little.

As he stood there, saying nothing, running an unfamiliar collection of thoughts and numbers in his head, Taamarai made her offer: half of any profit they turned, week-on-week, backdated to the week after they started. Because of upfront costs, they hadn't actually made any money that first week anyway, despite a fantastic turnover. Besides, she wouldn't want to insult his friendship. What she was offering was still a decent sum of back pay, plus whatever they managed to keep coming in from now on.

A gentle laugh had hovered in Taamarai's eye, and with hardly a word said on his part, Carl had lost. The feeling was strange. He didn't work with people or for people, or at least that was what he always told anyone who'd listen.

At first, he'd stubbornly taken on a couple of extra jobs anyway.

It didn't do to alienate some of the people he worked with and besides, some part of him whispered, all of this could vanish any day. But those jobs felt like work, whereas the stall didn't, really. Two months in, he noticed that he was thinking differently. He never technically quit his other work. It was never that kind of business. It just didn't factor in his life much anymore.

That didn't mean he could ignore a direct call from Jackie.

It was a quiet Thursday and Taamarai just nodded as he said he had to go. An hour later, after washing and changing, he ducked into a small kebab shop.

"You took your time." Jackie eyed him from behind two heavies who looked slow and comfortable but were neither.

Carl shrugged. Anybody who worked with Carl knew he came and went on his own schedule. Disconcertingly, he felt more like apologizing because of working a food stall in the market with his painfully proper neighbor than if he'd been out on somebody else's illegitimate business. He didn't, though, and Jackie just shrugged back.

"Whatever. You got your business." He adjusted himself against the counter. "And I've got mine. Shipment coming in tomorrow."

Carl raised an eyebrow. Jackie was a drug dealer. A shipment coming in was hardly a big event in his world and he didn't usually call Carl.

"Rumor is the kids over on 17th think they can cut in. They've been after some of my dealers. Join them or get cut." Jackie frowned and Carl watched the other man's face, seeing the tension there that had always kept him off anybody's permanent payroll and, therefore, out of anybody's day-to-day affairs.

"Point is, I'm beefing up security, making a point. I want someone there with some experience. I want you there." When Carl said nothing, Jackie added, "Your usual plus fifty percent when I've got the goods safe. Danger money." He laughed but didn't look like he thought it was funny.

Carl weighed up his options. With the back pay Taamarai had insisted on plus what the stall was making now, he didn't actually need the money, which was weird. What he also didn't need, he suddenly sensed, was the intense feeling that this could all turn to shit quicker than he could say, "I didn't plan for it to be like this."

Something had changed while he wasn't looking. Some sense that he *could* plan. Even if Taamarai vanished back to wherever she came from or the stall went under, he *could* find something legit and hourly paid and make things work without Jackie's perpetual tension seeping into his life, too. He nodded decisively.

"You can keep your fifty percent. I do this, and you don't call me again." He looked Jackie in the eye. "Nothing personal. Just wanting to switch my business up. I do it and no matter what, you don't call and you don't pass my name to anyone. If it goes bad, you don't even have to pay me. But either way...."

Jackie thought about this, then nodded slowly. "Yeah, I get it. You're out. Shame. Hard to find steady guys, but...."

Carl also had a reputation as a man not worth arguing with. Jackie reached out his hand, a shake on many years rather than one job. For a while, they chatted about the details. As Carl got up to leave, Jackie looked at him. "Chick?"

Carl paused. "Something like that."

Jackie nodded. "Well, good luck to you." He looked Carl up and down and laughed. "And good luck to her."

As Carl headed out, he wondered what he'd even meant by "something like that." He had decided as he said it that he was talking about Ali. Also, it was what Jackie expected and was therefore the best thing to tell him. But it was Taamarai's face that he'd seen in his mind. As he stepped into the street, he felt somebody walk over his grave.

Chapter Twenty-One

When Taamarai looked down she could hardly believe what she was seeing. Carl's body was a mass of blood and bruising.

"Ali, what happened?"

"They've just fixed the elevator. He came out like this. I got him to the couch, but he's...."

On each breath, he seemed to gurgle.

"Okay. Okay." Taamarai knew she had to calm down, if only to stop Ali's spiralling panic. She reached out to take Ali's hand. "You did well, Ali. You did really well."

"He said never to call 911."

"That's okay." Taamarai couldn't think about that now. "Can you get me some scissors, Ali, quickly?" Ali returned in a few moments and handed them over. Taamarai was surprised that her hands weren't shaking as she cut through his clothes. Everything she saw only made it worse. There were lacerations and swollen red weals and seemed to be blood everywhere. In his stomach, a hole bubbled and dribbled.

"Ali, quickly. Here. Bring a towel." Again, Ali did what she was asked. "Press here. Whatever you do, press down here." Ali squeezed on her father's stomach. Carl groaned but he was getting weaker. Taamarai pulled his eyelid up and one bloodshot eye stared back at her but there was nothing there. Her hands sticky, Taamarai registered that she was dialing only as the call went through.

"911, what's your emergency?" It sounded like a movie.

"We're at 502 Da Vinci Towers, Gabriel Heights. We need an ambulance."

"What?" Ali practically screamed it, but couldn't move her hands off Carl's stomach.

Astonished at herself, Taamarai was entirely calm. "He'll die if we don't, Ali. Don't worry about what happens after that. We'll deal with it." The operator prompted her for more information. "I don't know. It's my neighbor. He's been beaten. Maybe stabbed. Yes, we're keeping pressure on the wound. Thank you."

The distended minutes seemed like hours until they heard pounding on the stairs. They were pushed gently aside. Medics began to carry Carl out the door, and they both went to follow.

"Family only."

Ali looked terrified.

"I'm the stepmother." One of the medics nodded. They hadn't been on the 911 call to hear any different. Ali clutched at Taamarai as they headed down the stairs. In the ambulance, Ali held her father's hand. Extraneous sounds drifted away as Taamarai focused on watching Carl breathe. Each gasp and rattled exhalation was another proof of life and she prayed, willing him to live.

At the hospital, the medical team and gurney disappeared down a long corridor and then nothing seemed to happen for a very long time. Eventually, Taamarai tugged Ali gently to her feet and over to a restroom. She cleaned Ali's hands and her own, both caked in drying blood.

"Here. Take off your top."

Ali looked numb but did as she was told, peeling off her bloody t-shirt. Even her bra was stained red but there was nothing Taamarai could do about that. At least she could put the girl in her own sweater, warm her up a bit and hide the worst of the awful ichor.

She brushed out Ali's hair with her fingers. "Now, wash your face. You'll feel better." Taamarai knew from too many long-haul flights that the mechanical act of washing, the feel of cool water on the face, could make things better even if the world was collapsing.

"Good." She stroked Ali's arm, washed her own face, then pulled her into a big hug. "Let's get ourselves some coffee and something to eat and see if there's any news."

"I'm not hungry."

"I know. I'm not either. But," Taamarai checked her watch, "it's nearly midnight. We might be here all night. We've got to stay strong for your dad."

Ali just nodded. Out in the corridor, they grabbed weak coffee and snacks from a vending machine. The food disappeared even though neither of them wanted it. There was no news, so they waited some more.

Ali was asleep on Taamarai's shoulder when a doctor came over. "Mrs Grigg?"

Taamarai looked up blearily. It had to be nearly three in the morning. "Erm, no. Ms Calder."

"But you are...?"

"I'm Ali Grigg. How's my dad?" Ali was awake like a shot, her eyes wide.

The doctor was sympathetic and kind, but left no room for misunderstanding. "Your father has been stabbed and beaten badly. He lost a lot of blood. Fortunately, there were no severe injuries to the internal organs, and we've managed to stop the internal bleeding."

"Can we see him?" Ali was breathing shallowly, managing to keep her panic at bay but only just.

"In a moment. I'll take you to him." The doctor's calm seemed to settle her. "He's unconscious but stable."

"Can we stay with him?"

The doctor frowned, taking in Ali's frantic, exhausted look. She glanced at Taamarai, who gave her a firm stare. Whatever was best.

"No. You can't stay overnight. He needs to rest." As Ali was about to jump in, the doctor continued. "But you can go and see him now, and you can come back tomorrow in the afternoon."

She looked sternly at Ali. "You can have a few minutes now, then the best thing you can do for him is go home, get yourself washed up and get some sleep. If anything changes, we'll let you know." She smiled wearily past Ali at Taamarai. "You both did well. If he'd gotten here a few minutes later or you hadn't put pressure on the stomach wound, he'd be dead. Now, come with me. Don't be shocked when you see him. He's getting the best treatment possible."

Ali had taken Taamarai's hand again and squeezed, childlike and suddenly afraid. Inside a private room, the doctor stood aside and Ali rushed forward, then stopped. Hooked up to innumerable wires and tubes, with one down his throat, Carl looked like himself but not. The bruising was still shocking, his face almost unrecognizable. The blood had been washed off, though, leaving other parts – his hands and shoulders – strangely familiar. His knuckles were cut. Taamarai had never thought before about how often she had seen them that way.

The doctor took Ali's shoulder and guided her over. "It's okay. You can hold his hand. Don't touch any of the equipment but you can talk to him quietly. When you come tomorrow, do the same. Touch and sound can often reach people in your father's condition."

Ali took his hand and Taamarai moved on autopilot to take the other. It felt weak but still warm and familiar.

The doctor turned away. "A nurse will come by for night checks in about fifteen minutes. You'll have to leave then. May I have a word?"

The doctor gave Taamarai a final tired smile and Taamarai followed her out.

In the corridor, the doctor spoke carefully. "I don't know what your husband was doing, Ms Calder." She looked up and gave her the smallest of nods. "Maybe you don't either. He's stable. We've done everything we can. The injuries to his torso were serious but the bigger problem now is the swelling around his brain. We're monitoring him, but there's really no way to know. If he wakes up, that will be a start, but even then, we could be looking at temporary or permanent brain damage."

Taamarai tried to take it in while simultaneously feeling horribly fraudulent. She touched her wedding ring, a complicated symbol of multiple betrayals, but which the doctor read differently.

"I know it's frightening. We hope that Mr Grigg will make a good recovery. He's in very good shape, generally. But I need to be honest with you, and you may want to prepare your daughter. He may not be quite who he was if he wakes up."

Taamarai just nodded, then at last remembered to say, "Thank you, doctor," before hurrying back inside.

Ali was staring fixedly at her father's face. She looked up at Taamarai. "He'll be okay, won't he?"

Taamarai tried to radiate calm. "Remember, the doctor said he's in the best place, getting the best care. He's going to be fine. And he can probably hear us, unless he's asleep, getting some rest like the doctor said he needed."

Ali thought about this, then nodded slowly. "Dad. You're going to be okay, Dad. You always told me to fight." She lifted his hand and kissed it. Then they stood in silence until the nurse came by. Ali took Taamarai's hand and let herself be led out of the hospital and to a cab. In the foyer of Da Vinci Heights, however, they both stopped dead. The blood trail Carl had left behind still ran to the elevator, smeared by the boots of the ambulance crew. Taamarai took Ali towards the stairs instead.

They made it up to 502 like zombies. Ali was dragging her feet and simply handed Taamarai her keys. Taamarai let them in and they took in the state of the apartment with the same shock. Abruptly, Ali burst into tears. Taamarai just held her until Ali began to sag, then steered her up to her own apartment and straight to the bathroom.

"Ali, Ali, look at me." Ali's eyes swivelled like glassy red marbles.

"Ali, I need you to take off your clothes. They're all dirty." Taamarai didn't say *bloody*. Ali looked around as if she didn't know where she was, but complied. Taamarai turned on the shower. "That's good. I'll bring you some clean night clothes. I want you to get in the shower. Take your time. It'll help you relax."

"Taamarai?" Ali's voice was shaky.

"Yes?"

"Can I stay here tonight?"

As if she needed to ask. "Of course." She squeezed Ali's hand. "I'm going to get you some clean clothes and put them just outside the door. I want you to have a nice long shower and I'll make us some cocoa."

In the kitchen, Taamarai worked on autopilot. She heard Ali finish her shower. They sat together without saying anything, then Taamarai got Ali into bed and took her own turn at washing, watching the water turn pink as she stood under the faucet.

By the time Taamarai crawled into bed, she hoped Ali would be asleep, but wasn't surprised when the teenager rolled over and nestled up to her. Taamarai was exhausted but her skin felt like it was on fire. All she could remember was Carl's head lolling. The feel of his limp hand in hers was so real he might have been lying next to her. He had to live.

Hours later, her eyes heavy and thick, Taamarai came round to a sense of acute stress that she couldn't place. The memories rushed at her in a wakeful moment. She could feel Ali beside her, and she slowly rolled onto her back and reached for her phone. It was nearly noon. As quietly as she could, Taamarai got up and, just as she was putting on coffee, Ali emerged from the bedroom, bleary-eyed and confused.

"What time is it?"

"Coming up to one," Taamarai replied quietly. "I've just put coffee on. I'll make us eggs for breakfast." She was already chopping onions, tomatoes and tortillas.

"We need to go to the hospital." Ali sounded like she could only just remember why but knew it was urgent.

"I know. And we will. Visiting starts at two. We'll be there by two. But we might be there until late. I brought you some clean clothes. Try to have a wash and get dressed, then we'll eat and go right out." She turned and smiled gently at Ali. "I can go and get you something else if you want different clothes."

Ali shook her head. "Whatever you got, it's fine."

As promised, just over an hour later, they arrived at the hospital and made their way straight to the same room as the night before. It looked as if nothing had changed and Taamarai felt a sudden wave of nauseating déjà vu sweep over her. All she could do was follow Ali to the bed, taking up their positions from the night before. After maybe an hour, Taamarai pulled a chair over for Ali, and after another half an hour, she found one in the hallway for herself.

The hours passed. They talked about nothing, just chatting. Taamarai went out for food, leaving Ali to say anything privately to her father that she needed to. She came back and they talked about the food. They ate. Taamarai cleared away the rubbish. They talked some more. They were silent. Evening turned into night. The nurse came in and checked the equipment but this time didn't ask them to leave.

Eventually, Taamarai looked over at Ali. "Do you want to stay or go home for the night?"

"I want to stay."

"Okay. I'll see if I can get us some blankets." Taamarai enjoyed stretching her legs but was glad that Ali had wanted to stay. She would have done whatever Ali needed but knew she couldn't have slept if they had gone home.

Even as her legs relaxed from walking, she felt the desire to be where he was again. It seemed like the worst time in the world to think about whatever she felt about Carl, and the only thing in the

world that mattered, except for how Ali was doing. For the first
time, she noticed the buzzing in her pocket.

She had texted Darren the night before in the cab on the way
home, then again as they made their way to the hospital and that
evening while she'd been out of Carl's room. He knew that she had
to be with Ali.

Darren was calling and Taamarai fished her phone out and
watched it ring off. She felt a twitch of anxiety pass down her spine
as she saw the screed of messages.

> Tam, call me.

> Is everything OK?

> Babe, Im worried bout u. R u stil out.

> Tam, I luv u. Cal me.

> Hey babe, do u no wen ul b bac?

> Babe, I hope ur neighbor is OK.

> Tam, I need 2 talk 2 u.

She felt her anger well up. He knew Carl's name. He knew
where she was. He knew why she couldn't call. Guilt followed. All
he'd had were a few text messages for nearly a day and a half. His
parents would be out at work, so he was by himself. He was already
stressed by the situation between them.

Knowing she should step out and give him a call, Taamarai
checked the time. Either way, he'd give her a hard time – for waking
him up so late or for keeping him awake so long. But Ali needed
sleep and so did she. Taamarai fired off another text.

> Still at the hospital. Carl seems stable.
> Going to get some sleep now.

She paused before adding 'love you' but knew it would cause a fuss if she didn't. Then she headed back. Ali was already half asleep, leaning her head forward onto the bed. Taamarai draped a blanket over her before adopting the same position on the other side, her hand gripping Carl's tightly.

Chapter Twenty-Two

There was a persistent beeping that Carl couldn't quite place. Then came the pain. It was muted, distant, but locatable – in his stomach, chest, head and arms. That didn't leave many places that didn't hurt. His throat felt thick and sore and his mouth was dry. He was neither warm nor cold. Carefully, Carl tried to open his eyes. The light at first was blinding. As his eyes began to adjust, he found himself looking across a short expanse of crisp white cotton and into a sleeping face.

For what felt like a long time he lay back, listening to his own breathing and looking at that face. It was pale with exhaustion but peaceful and unexpected. He had never seen Taamarai asleep and didn't know why she should be here now. As slowly as he could, he rolled his head on the pillow. The face asleep on his other side was more deeply familiar, though just as unexpected. Maybe none of this was ever expected.

"Ali?" The word came out as a croak and he was about to try again when Ali's eyes shot open. He felt her grip tighten on his hand.

"Dad?" Ali looked frantic. "Taamarai! Taamarai!"

"Carl?"

Both of them sat up so that he could see them at the same time.

"Thank God." Taamarai closed her eyes and whispered something. "I'll go and get a nurse." She stood up stiffly and seemed to find it hard to let go or step away.

"Dad?" Ali repeated it with traumatized relief.

"Where? How long?" The words were rough and hard to form. "Water?"

Ali passed him a cup with a straw and he drank a sip before she took it away. "You can't have too much. The doctor said. Not at first." She looked apologetic. "You're at St Mercy hospital."

"Hospital?"

She nodded and looked afraid. "Dad, you were dying."

"How long?"

Ali took a deep breath. "You've been unconscious for three days."

"Three days?" His brain was foggy and dull, like the pain. "St Mercy?"

It was hard to put everything together. Ali gave him another small drink of water.

"Taamarai?" he asked.

Ali took his hand in both of hers. "I didn't know what to do. When you got home, I knew. I knew it was really bad, and you always said no hospitals, no police. Don't worry, I didn't call the police." She added it quickly. "I went to Taamarai. She called 911." He was processing this as the door opened.

"Mr Grigg." The doctor smiled and walked over, letting Taamarai go and stand beside Ali. She checked the monitors and his chart, then turned to him and asked a series of simple clinical questions. He was relieved to be able to answer them.

"You've been on quite a bit of morphine to control the pain. We'll start reducing the dose. That'll help you to think more clearly. We'll also need to check your movement and coordination. We'll want to keep you in for a little while longer."

"Want to go home."

Ali squeezed his hand but didn't say anything.

"It's fine, Doctor. However long he needs to be here." Taamarai's voice was assured.

"Your wife is right, Mr Grigg. You should listen to her." The doctor turned to go, missing his bewildered frown.

He waited for the door to close before looking between them. Taamarai appeared mortified, but unrepentant. "It was only family in the ambulance. Ali was on her own."

"I needed her, Dad."

He wanted to go to sleep. But mostly he wanted to get out. "You know we got no insurance?" The words still came out half-formed but perfectly intelligible.

A strange look passed briefly across Taamarai's face before she said, "I know, but don't worry about that."

"What?" He reached out again and Ali passed him the water. He could feel anger rising up inside him, forming a seal around the fear that lay at the heart of him. Before it exploded, though, Taamarai reached out and touched his hand. Her voice was calm and he felt it cut through him.

"You don't need to worry about it. There's a scheme for people with no insurance. The paperwork is all done. No charge for treatment, no police. You just need to focus on getting well."

He closed his eyes. None of it made sense, but he was so tired. The next time he woke up, it was dark and he was alone except for the beeping.

Chapter Twenty-Three

They had insisted on a taxi and Carl didn't argue. He'd been injured before, but he needed no doctor to tell him that this was different. When he moved, something tenuous seemed to strain inside him. Every movement hurt, but there were particular motions that caught him sharply, a visceral warning of mortal danger.

At Da Vinci Tower, with Ali on one side of him and Taamarai on the other, they got him into the elevator. He was disturbed not to remember anything of the last time he'd been in there.

Ali had slowly told him everything she remembered and he was shocked at the pain and fear in her eyes as she clung to his hand. For his own part, Carl could remember leaving the apartment to do this one last job for Jackie. He'd checked out the dockyard, knew who was on his team, but he still had a bad feeling. He couldn't remember anything else.

After he'd been in hospital for a week, two police officers came by. They asked him the usual questions and he told them the usual lies but about the attack itself he could honestly declare that he didn't remember a thing, and with nothing more to go on, they told him it was unlikely anybody would ever be charged. That was just fine by him. Carl was relieved to see them go and to hear that they had left Ali and Taamarai alone after only a few searching questions.

Taamarai unlocked the door to 502. Apparently, she had keys now. He didn't question it. Inside, everywhere looked spotless. Not just clean of blood but tidy, fresh. There were flowers on the table and new curtains at the window.

They helped him to the sofa. It was covered in a throw. Taamarai had picked it out with Ali and apologized to him for the bleach stains it was covering. He didn't have the energy to respond. Ali hugged him carefully before heading for the kitchen. He could smell baking in the air.

"Carl." Taamarai was kneeling beside the sofa, still holding his hand from helping him sit. "It's good to have you back." She smiled and he managed a hint of a smile back before Ali appeared, carrying an elaborate cake on a plate. She switched suddenly, from jubilant to shy.

"I made you this." She placed it on the coffee table and then backed away, not sure whether it was a big deal or not. *Welcome Home, Dad.* The icing letters were painstaking and careful, perfectly inexpert.

Taamarai drew back, leaving room for Ali to sit beside Carl and grinned with pride. "Ali didn't need my help with any of it."

Not with the cake maybe, but as Carl looked around, Taamarai's help was everywhere. Shame surged around him like a tide. The quiet became choking and as he always did, he turned to anger to make the discomfort go away. Why couldn't they just leave him be? Why couldn't they have just *left* him be? Ali would have managed. Taamarai would have looked out for her. He took it for granted she would, as certainly as that he'd been about to die. Ready to snap at them both to leave him alone, he saw Taamarai gesture briefly to Ali.

Before he knew what was happening, Ali sat herself down next to him. She reached out, about to take his hand, then leaned over instead and wrapped her arms around him sideways, squeezing his shoulders where she knew she couldn't aggravate his wounds.

"I'm glad you're home, Dad." She whispered it into his side. Carl couldn't move for several seconds, then reached up to hold Ali's arm with his hand, bending his head into her hair.

"I'm real glad to be back, too." He closed his eyes and breathed in the smell of Ali's hair. They simply sat together before he said, "That looks like a great cake." Ali looked up, only just letting go of him, and grinned, apparently not caring if he saw her tears.

"I'll go get us some plates." Ali began to get up, then leaned in suddenly and kissed him on the cheek. Taamarai was about to get up too, to get them tea or drinks or something else unobtrusive and useful, but Carl reached out instead and caught her hand. She looked over at him, her eyes deep and warm and full of feeling.

"You've took real good care of her." He spoke low and nodded towards the kitchen, where Ali was rummaging in the cupboards.

Taamarai smiled and shook her head. "We've been looking after each other."

He had only taken her hand to stop her getting up. He should let go now, but as he did, she gripped his fingers instead.

"We were worried for a while. It's very good to have you back." Then she let go of his hand and he wished she hadn't.

Ali reappeared with plates and Taamarai went off to make them tea. When she returned, Ali sat beside him again and cut the cake for all three of them. They ate and joked. He tried not to laugh and Ali rested her head on his shoulder. After a while, Ali got up, collected their plates and headed for the kitchen again.

"Carl?"

Taamarai stared down at her own hands then at him, still smiling but looking like maybe she shouldn't be. He turned to look sidelong at her, careful not to twist too much. "Whatever happened...." She looked up resolutely. "Ali doesn't blame you. You know that?" He flinched away. How did she know? He sometimes felt that his eyes were glass when he looked at her.

"What about you?"

It was mainly to turn the question away, except that he realized he cared about the answer. She looked at him thoughtfully and glanced at the kitchen. Ali seemed busy enough.

"I thought about it in the hospital. About if you...." She squeezed her eyes closed for a moment then stared at him. "I don't blame you. But I was angry at you." Her eyes bored into him and Carl couldn't look away. "For nearly being gone. Forever. I could see how much Ali needed you."

To his surprise, she reached out and touched his arm. That was all. A touch to confirm that he was still real, still there.

"I didn't...." Carl couldn't say the things in his head about the things he never meant to happen. He tried again but the words just wouldn't form. He stopped trying. She didn't move or ask any questions.

"You can't blame us either," she said at last, "for wanting you with us, for doing whatever it took."

He looked up quickly and caught a small smile, tentative but unapologetic. Then she seemed to take herself in hand. "Anyway, you should get some rest. Doctor's orders." She stood and he tried to get up but had to wait for her to hold out a hand. He shuffled towards his bedroom, feeling every step in his stitches. He stopped in the doorway to the kitchen.

"Ali, I've gotta get to bed. Thank you."

She smiled at him.

"For the cake."

Ali put down the cloth in her hand and carefully, but without embarrassment, walked forward and kissed him again. "Sleep well, Dad."

As he closed his bedroom door, there was a smile Carl couldn't hide twitching at the corners of his mouth but something beneath it too – confusion about how everything had got this way and what way that was. When he lay down, the feeling changed again. He felt ashamed, knowing that sleep would find him soon enough, that he felt safe and glad to be home and that he didn't deserve any of it.

Chapter Twenty-Four

Carl stretched to pull down the shutter on the storage bay. His stomach twinged. It had been nine weeks since he was discharged from hospital, since Taamarai had manned the stall by herself with Ali helping on weekends. Other stall holders around the market had chipped in, too. It turned out they didn't need to know the details to feel that something terrible had happened and that one of their own needed help.

Now, at the end of his first week back, Taamarai was beginning not to treat him like he was made of glass. Nevertheless, as he locked the security shutter in place, she appeared beside him.

"You didn't need to do that." Almost without thinking, she placed her hands on his sides, as if to check he hadn't come apart in the middle.

"I'm fine," he muttered gruffly. Something about his time in the hospital and the weeks afterwards when he had struggled to do even the simplest things, when Taamarai had seemed practically to live downstairs with them, had changed the ways they moved around one another. He told himself he could do without her fussing, but knew he couldn't have until pretty recently.

He didn't tell himself anything at all about the way she placed a hand on his back to check if he was okay or how he still reached for her arm. It had been to steady himself when he first started moving around the apartment on his own. Now it was just a gesture as he passed her, a touch of acknowledgement. Satisfied that he was, in fact, fine, Taamarai handed him an envelope – his share of the week's earnings.

"Still doing well?"

"Yep!" She looked triumphant. "Beating all the odds!"

They took the bus back. He had insisted that morning that he could walk but now he was exhausted. It was a cellular exhaustion that Carl had never experienced before – a body bringing itself, piece by piece, back from the brink. As the bus pulled off, Taamarai stared out the window.

"What are you going to do with your day off?" she asked as the city rolled by. The market was closed that Saturday for maintenance work. Some of the stallholders were annoyed but, with a rent rebate and a day off, Carl could see the bright side.

He contemplated the question for a while. It seemed strange – thinking about what to do with time. Mostly it just passed and he reacted when he needed to. He shrugged thoughtfully. "You're the one's always got plans."

Taamarai laughed easily. He wasn't wrong. Darren said it made him tired being around so many plans, stretching out into a crowded future, but Taamarai no longer felt bad about it. Watching some of them come to life had given her confidence. While she had plans for the stall and for opening her restaurant and maybe for the recipe book she would like to publish, though, plans for free time had gone by the wayside. Between helping Carl and Ali these last few weeks, keeping on top of final college deadlines and increasingly long online chats with Darren, Taamarai didn't have a clue what to do with herself on a day off.

"No. Not this time." Taamarai said the words as much to herself as to Carl, feeling their strangeness. "My college work's done till the end of the month. And Darren's got a game, so he'll be out all day."

She felt bad as soon as she said it. Like he was just another chore and a less important one than her college work.

"And with Ali being away...." Ali was going to be on a track-and-field residential Saturday morning to Monday evening. It had surprised Carl that she wanted to go and that he was happy to let her, and that he was able to pay for it.

Carl gave Taamarai a sidelong glance. He had caught something as she said Darren's name, but wasn't sure what and didn't want to ask. Instead, he said, "So?"

"So what?"

"So, what are you gonna do?"

Taamarai looked around as if a plan might fall from the sky. "I dunno." The answer didn't seem to please her. She looked around again. A plan had to be somewhere nearby, her look seemed to say. "Could be good to get out of town, maybe?" She mused on this then turned to him more seriously. "Is that possible?"

"Anything's possible," he contributed noncommittally.

She took this on board and then asked, "So if you needed to get out of town for a day, how would you do it?"

Carl frowned. "*Needed* to, needed to? Like, no paper trail and no cameras *needed* to?"

Taamarai laughed out loud then put on a mock-serious expression. "Yeah, okay. *Needed* to."

He nodded and considered the possibilities. "I'd catch the bus from 9th. It's the first stop after the bus station. No CCTV except the one on the bus, and you can always wear a hat. But it's a long journey, so you want to get a seat. Pay in cash. Stay on until Smithson. Change there. Buses every hour out to the national park. Leave by seven, and you could be in the middle of nowhere before lunchtime."

Of course, if he really *needed* to get out of town, he'd borrow a car from the sort of person who didn't ask any questions and whom Taamarai never needed to meet. Or he'd just steal one. Those answers didn't seem in the spirit of the question, though, and his scar twinged at the memory of people Taamarai never needed to meet and choices with painful consequences.

At least, since he'd left the hospital, Jackie had been as good as his word. An envelope of cash had arrived with a note – "Good luck to you" – and nothing since. Carl didn't even know whether the job had gone well or badly but whenever he wondered about finding out, he wound up distracted by other things. Finally, about a month after coming out of the hospital, he admitted to himself that anything he did to discover what had gone down would pull him back into conversations and relationships that he felt surprisingly relieved to be out of.

Taamarai seemed to appraise his answer, looking over at him as the bus bounced along, a smile sneaking onto her face. "Sounds good." She grinned properly. "You wanna get out of town? I can be up before seven."

Carl thought about it. It seemed like something he would normally say no to, but he couldn't think of a single reason why. "Sure."

Her face glowed with excitement. "I can come down and make us breakfast, say around 6:30?" He could practically hear her mind whirring. "I could make us lunch, too."

"Ain't you sick of cooking, just for a day?"

She paused to think about this.

"How about I at least get us dinner?" Carl offered. "There's a place off of 9th, just where the bus comes in." He suddenly felt embarrassed. Before he could backpedal or make excuses, though, she nodded.

"That sounds nice." Taamarai turned to stare out of the window again, but Carl could see her reflection in the glass. She looked happy. He felt happy. It was weird.

The next morning, she knocked on the door to 502 just before six. He could smell pancakes even before the door opened and Ali, who had listened with delighted incredulity to their plans the night before, set the table in moments. She had bought a jug from a thrift store a few weeks ago and seemed endlessly delighted at pouring orange juice from the carton into the jug then setting it on the table with fresh glasses for everyone. Like something out of a movie about a happy family, he thought, with the cutting guilt of revelation.

Taamarai couldn't seem to stop grinning, either. Looking at their stupidly happy faces, Carl put on a sneer that even he knew was unconvincing. "What's up with you two?"

They looked at each other and then just burst out laughing. "It's a good day," Taamarai responded when they stopped. "Now, eat up. We've got a bus to catch!"

They saw Ali off in the direction of her school on their way. The coach was leaving at 7:30 and she promised to text Taamarai when they arrived. It seemed obvious it would be Taamarai. When Ali had disappeared around a corner, the two of them continued in silence. Carl had offered to carry the rucksack that Taamarai had brought and she had refused.

As they walked through the dawn light to 9th Street, Taamarai looked around as if she had never seen the town before. Carl found himself doing the same, seeing moments of light and shadow, graffiti and the tops of glorious buildings that he had never noticed before. At the bus stop, they had a while to wait. Taamarai leaned back against the window of a closed shop. "I haven't been out on a trip like this for years. It's exciting!" There seemed no artifice, no embarrassment about the words.

"You and Darren didn't take trips? Back in Massachusetts?" He knew it was a dig and so did she. He waited for the excuses, for the reasons why Darren not liking something was completely reasonable.

"No, not very much." She stopped. "But he isn't here." It came out as something like an oath. Then she turned and stared down the road as if willing the bus to arrive.

Carl was sorry he'd said anything and relived when her smile bounced back, broad and irrepressible. The bus was predictably a few minutes late but where once she would have been tense with anxiety, Taamarai still looked excited and full of joy. When it came into view, Carl made sure he was there to flag it down ahead of her, unsure why it should matter.

On board, they paid cash, as he had said they should, and he almost laughed aloud as Taamarai headed straight for the back seats and sat in the window with a grin splitting her face in two. If this had been an escape, it would have been a dismal failure. People on the bus and people passing by on the street turned to stare, most of them smiling back as Taamarai met their eyes. He knew they would all remember her.

Carl followed her as the bus lurched forward, holding onto the backs of seats and taking care not to pull at his injury. He flopped down next to her and then thought maybe he shouldn't have. The bus was nearly empty, so there was space for him to sit a couple of seats over. He stayed where he was, though.

For her part, Taamarai didn't worry about the grin on her face. Darren would tell her that smiling too much risked hurting other people's feelings, but happiness seemed to carry her along with it. Watching Carl head down the bus towards her, she felt a flutter in her stomach.

She really had tried to ignore that Carl was a very good-looking man. It had gotten harder and harder as the months eroded his grumpiness, and easier to feel the subtle charisma he exuded without apparently noticing. Now he was smiling, a smile almost embarrassed by its own existence. Taamarai didn't worry about trying to ignore the smoothness of his movements, the lean strength coming back to him day by day after his injury, or the peculiar delight of knowing that he didn't do this sort of thing with anybody else. The smiling or the adventure.

Taamarai had confronted the fact several years ago, without liking it, that she was capable of being attracted to men who weren't her husband. They weren't always strong attractions and she would never do anything about them. But even the emotions made her feel disloyal to Darren, who she told herself was a better man than any of them.

She never told Darren about these crushes anymore. Darren

believed that if you really loved somebody, you could have eyes only for them. Like he did for her. When she had mentioned other attractions, they had ended up in long, desperate conversations about how she would leave him one day because he loved her more than she loved him.

Taamarai would protest that she had meant their vows as much as he had and had never done a single thing to merit his suspicions. Darren would be soothed only by escalating declarations of undying love and fidelity. At last, snuffling into her shoulder that she would never understand how much he loved her, how nobody could ever love her like he did, he would forgive her. They would make love. After the third time, Taamarai said nothing. It didn't matter, anyway.

Well, that wasn't completely true. A couple of times it had seemed to matter. A colleague at an editing job, for example. He wasn't her type, but he made her laugh. They could be witty with one another and talk about life and careers – things Darren either wasn't interested in or said she was being neurotic for worrying about. That connection had felt different from the random crushes. It had been a physical pain sometimes, imagining that they might go on like that forever and yet never be together.

There had been a course mate too, on some training she'd done. With him it had been scary. She had never felt a physical attraction like it. Not even to Darren, she stubbornly refused to admit to herself. It would never have worked. They were different in every way, but she had felt alive around him. Those attractions had fizzled out over time, though, and she was friends with both of them still.

And now, Taamarai knew, there was Carl. She stared out of the window, watching the sky lighten. With those others, she had tried to imagine what a life with them might be like, but it had always been unreal. In those fantasies, Darren had left her – a thing she knew would never happen – or died tragically – something she could never wish for, so she would shy away from the thought as soon as it formed. That left the third option, her favorite daydream. To be somebody else completely, who could think and feel like her but wasn't her, and even better, didn't need to look like her.

As she felt Carl's eyes looking past her through the same window, Taamarai found her own gaze wandering over the bus and the sidewalks, trying to guess who might catch his eye. She knew with a familiar sadness that it wasn't her. And anyway, what did it matter? It was harder and harder to feel lucky to have Darren, easier and easier to imagine being alone, with the simple freedom to make her own choices, but she knew Darren was right that nobody else would ever feel the desire he did for her.

As the dawn broke, Taamarai felt her mood shatter with it. Excitement and adventure was swallowed by bitter self-recrimination and the recurring question of what she had got wrong, and when, to end up here. Carl sat beside her in silence and she didn't realize he could see her fading smile reflected in the glass.

Twenty minutes later, they climbed down from the bus. Carl headed out first and waited a little awkwardly for her at the bottom of the steps, not offering a hand, which she didn't need, but looking for all the world like he might have been thinking about it.

In Smithson, they had a quarter hour's wait for another bus. As the silence stretched out, cut loose from the busyness that carried them along on the stall, Taamarai felt an odd comfort. She and Darren could spend hours together and only talk about whatever he was playing on his computer, but their silence always felt like a failure. This was different.

She looked around the small-town square. The road had a crossing with high traffic lights but little else. A gas station advertised light beer in faded blue. The morning still looked fresh and clear and it was difficult to stay defeated and sad. A few cars slid by, followed by a startling procession of heavy flatbed trucks.

"Logging," was Carl's brief but sufficient explanation. After a while, he asked, "You ever seen a bear? Up in Massachusetts?"

Taamarai laughed. "In the zoo." She frowned. "Do bears even live in Massachusetts? In the wild?"

It was a rhetorical question. Carl's shrug indicated that he had no idea either.

"Are there bears out here? Where we're going, I mean?" She hadn't even considered it and now wondered if she should have.

Carl didn't answer right away. "I dunno." He stopped. "Think I heard somewhere there are. Mountain lions, too. But I can't remember if it was these mountains." He stopped again but it was from habit. With Taamarai he always seemed to say more than he needed to.

"Saw it on TV in prison. Before that, me and some other boys, we'd come out here to the edge of the park and hang around by the river." He felt a mild and unexpected nostalgia. "Wonder if I could find the spot again?" He shook himself. "Anyway, if you're looking for some sort of park guide, it ain't me. We never got any further in than that."

He'd seen Taamarai's smile slide from her face on the bus, without knowing why. Now it seemed to well up again from deep inside and Carl's stomach dropped a few inches.

"Then it's a perfect adventure!"

The bus pulled up just in time for him not to have to react, and they rode the last leg talking about how they thought Ali would be getting on. The kids had a long coach journey ahead of them, so they weren't expecting news for hours. Not so long ago, Carl thought, he might not have noticed his daughter being out of contact for most of a day. He didn't say this, even in jest, and felt the flexing of that other emotion that seemed more developed in his life these days: shame. Today, at least, he didn't think he was letting anybody down.

The bus pulled up next to a sign for the national park and nothing else. A trail led away to the left and Taamarai breathed in the thick forest air and enjoyed the softness of leaf litter under her feet. The weather was damp and a bit chilly, and they seemed to have the world to themselves.

In the bushes things scurried and she watched birds dart, moving too fast to follow. The path forked a few times, but Carl chose their direction without hesitation. At a turning she hadn't even realized was there, he ducked past a hanging branch and they began to push through thicker undergrowth.

Then, suddenly, they were in a small clearing beside a river that ran smooth and silent but fast. Right in front of them, the bank had eroded to form a kind of pool. In an instant, Taamarai could see in her mind's eye a gaggle of young boys, nearly men, lounging on the grass, splashing in the river under a warmer sun than today. She couldn't imagine Carl's face as that boy, but she could make out his build and movements.

"I knew I could find it again," he said softly. Taamarai stepped up next to him and they both stayed quiet, listening to the noises of the woods.

"God, we were young," he muttered at last, with unexpected feeling.

Taamarai wasn't sure what she was supposed to say and wasn't sure she trusted herself to. Her heart was pounding in her chest, making her feel sick and excited and foolish. He seemed to be waiting for something, though, or at least, he said nothing else.

Eventually she asked, "What would you tell yourself then? If you could go back now?"

"Don't get caught!" A single bark of laughter was glib and bitter in equal measure. When Taamarai only smiled, he stopped and thought again.

"Being some lone wolf, don't-need-nothing-from-nobody. It's bullshit. You gotta choose people, same as anything else, and if you pick people who treat other people like shit, some time they'll do the same to you."

Taamarai felt like she was holding her breath as Carl talked to the moving river, just as she had told the river about Joshua while Carl stood beside her.

"Best thing I ever did, takin' in Ali. Maybe not the best thing for her, but I don't know if I'd be standing here if I hadn't."

He wasn't talking about the national park, and seemed to shiver a little at the thought. "What about you?" he asked, abruptly, retreating from his own thoughts. "If you were sixteen again?"

Somehow Taamarai hadn't expected the question. She hadn't had time to think about her answer then filter it for what was admissible to think or feel. She made herself open her mouth, talking without checking first.

"Don't be so afraid. That nobody'll ever love you, that you'll never be beautiful, that you'll fail. Some of it doesn't matter and the rest of it, it's not something that's already decided." The words disappeared into the wet air and left her feeling lighter, filled with guilt but exalted by their honesty, like throwing open the windows of a sick room.

Carl looked sideways at her. "Good advice."

Taamarai smiled. "Yours too." She knew her cheeks were flushed and even though he likely couldn't tell, she looked away. "I guess we all have to figure it out in our own time, though."

"I guess."

He looked back to the river, then turned away, and they tramped back to the main trail. After that, they just wandered. It was easy enough to keep track of where the road was and the paths were marked. At lunchtime, they found a rock, and Taamarai unpacked a sumptuous selection of delicacies – samosas with chutney from the stall, fruit, and dry, lightly spiced snacks that she had found in a store near Ali's school.

When they talked, it was mostly about the stall or Ali, but sometimes it wasn't. They saw birds and clouds moving in the sky and pointed to them with increasingly unabashed enthusiasm. In the afternoon, Carl lapsed into an old ghost story that Taamarai only figured out was a tall tale some way in.

Later on, she got him back by pretending she could hear something that might be a bear. It made him look a bit unsettled until she gave herself away grinning.

By midafternoon, they were back on the bus, relaxed and mostly silent, and Taamarai began to feel cold. Their clothes were soaked from the wet undergrowth. She hadn't noticed herself getting quieter or starting to shiver until she felt Carl rest his arm over her shoulder, pulling her gently to rest against him. The next thing she knew, he was shaking her awake. They were nearly back. As the bus pulled up on 9th Street, she felt a twinge of regret that the day was coming to an end.

They trudged back to the fifth floor and Taamarai was about to say goodnight, perhaps suggest she could cook something, when Carl said, "You wanna come back down and knock the door when you're changed?"

"Changed?" Taamarai felt foggy and tired.

"Figured with you being so cold you'd want to come back here first, get some dry clothes, instead of going straight to the restaurant." Taamarai's face lit up with surprise. She remembered him offering to take her to dinner but hadn't honestly believed it. If plans needed making, she was used to having to make them herself, and she just hadn't had time. She nodded and considered this novel turn of events. "Yeah, sure. I'll come down. Ten minutes?"

He checked his phone. "Table's at half past. Take your time."

Upstairs, Taamarai was grateful there was time to shower. The hot water struck her clammy skin and revived her. She hadn't thought about what to wear because she hadn't thought they were going anywhere. Knowing Carl, she guessed that lowkey would be fine, but she was still enjoying an adventure outside the everyday.

By the time she climbed out of the shower, Taamarai had made her mind up and ignored the guilt and shame as she pulled it on, whispering that she never wore it for Darren.

A stern and competing voice in her brain said that she *had* worn it for Darren. He had said nothing until the end of their evening, when he'd told her, reluctantly, as if he didn't want to but had to for her sake, that he thought she'd made people uncomfortable by dressing the way she had. Taamarai had been horrified at the thought of hurting their friends' feelings.

Darren had hugged her. It was alright. It wasn't a big issue, but it was too bright and too...ethnic. Maybe it was fine to dress like that for a party with her family but around their friends, it was like she was trying to make a point about being different. And anyway, it was a bit clingy. He didn't like other men looking at her that way. That was just for him, he'd said with a lascivious grin. Maybe that grin had made her feel better back then.

Now, with a twirl in the mirror, Taamarai smiled at her own reflection and put the old conversation out of her head. She looked good and she felt good. Leaving her phone behind, she pulled the door to.

Waiting on the landing below, Carl felt unreasonably impatient. They weren't late and he'd said to take her time, but Taamarai wasn't the type to fuss over her looks. He just hadn't expected her to take this long to put on some dry clothes.

At the sound of steps from above, he headed over to the stairwell. Taamarai was making her way down in a black coat, which hung open to show a fitted tunic with a flared skirt almost down to her ankles, in bright cerise with embroidered patterns and glinting sequins swirling over its surface. Beneath it swished wide trousers in deep purple and a pair of delicate beaded pumps. Her hair sprang out around her rounded face like a mane.

On the bottom step, she smiled shyly. "Amma got it for me a few years ago. Darren doesn't think it suits me and it didn't really fit for a while but—" the words came tumbling out full of apology. Carl couldn't take his eyes off her. "Is it okay? I mean, for the restaurant? I can change." She was evidently on the verge of turning round and doing just that.

Carl took a breath. All he could manage was, "Looks fine." She caught his eye and seemed to radiate a little more brightly still.

"Thanks."

The restaurant was a couple of blocks away and Taamarai gamely kept the conversation flowing. Carl couldn't think of much to say and noticed people looking at Taamarai as they walked by. He wished he could do the same.

At the restaurant, she gave her coat to the waiter and he watched from behind as the gown was revealed in its full glory, hugging her figure in some places, skimming over it in others, moving like water as she did. On her wrists, bangles jangled, and when they sat down, he noticed the star still resting between her collarbones. And he realized that he had never seen her without it since he'd given it to her.

They both ordered beers and clinked glasses without quite looking each other in the eye.

"Thank you," Taamarai said softly.

"This was your idea." Not the restaurant maybe, but the day out.

She shrugged. "Maybe, but I wouldn't have done it on my own."

Neither of them seemed to have anything to say and this time they felt awkward, until the waiter came to take their order. A comment about the cutlery was enough to get them into new grooves, comparing notes on the décor and menu. It seemed to occur to both of them at the same time that they were talking about plans for a restaurant that they would open together and they fell silent again.

At last Taamarai asked, "How did it feel today, going back to that spot by the river?"

Carl had been asking himself the same question. He inspected the beer in his hand. "I guess I never expected my life to be much different than it has been. 'Cept the last year. That's been different." He looked up and couldn't help staring at Taamarai, at her rounded cheeks that he knew made her self-conscious, at the wild hair she so often wished was straight or curly and those serious eyes, so much older than her face, which watched him with a sympathy he couldn't have tolerated in any other person.

"I ever tell you about my ma?"

She shook her head, a miniscule gesture. They both knew he hadn't. He leant back a little, uncomfortable, but not so much that he wasn't going to finish what he'd started.

"I guess she was trying. She could be fun." He paused. These were doors he usually kept shut. "Never knew my father, but folks about where we lived, they were all into stuff."

Taamarai nodded tentatively. She knew what he meant and they both knew that she didn't know at all.

"It was normal. I guess I never thought how it was." He fell very quiet and she didn't interrupt.

"Always living like any minute the cops could come by, or maybe somebody'd get angry with you for some reason or be mad at somebody they thought you knew. Maybe one week there'd be a crackdown and no food on the table. Maybe one night, Ma won't come home." He sank into the past, shocked at how deeply it made him feel. He didn't remember that he had felt anything much at the time.

"When that's normal, I guess you don't think about how it could be different." He paused again, considering.

"I wanted things different for Ali." He felt his own shame again. "Least I made her go to school."

Taamarai still said nothing but he saw movement and glanced down to find her hand resting on the table, reaching for his. He took it without thinking and felt her squeeze gently and then let go again. Finally, he looked at her steadily. "I've never had plans before. Not until this year." The quiet dragged on, their fingertips almost touching on the tabletop.

She smiled. He did too. He wondered if he should have said so much and wanted suddenly to be in less sensitive territory. Obligingly, she asked with mock theatricality, "Oh, so what are you planning?"

He laughed gratefully. "I planned this, didn't I?"

As their meal finished, he managed to find a moment when Taamarai went to the bathroom to pay the check, not sure why that made him feel satisfied or why he knew that she would have insisted on paying her way if he hadn't, or indeed, why he felt so sure she shouldn't. It wasn't like they were on a date or like that was a thing he did.

In the cold night air, Taamarai pulled her coat closed around her, and they began the well-worn walk home, their steps matching easily. After a few minutes, they both began speaking at the same time. Carl stopped, glad to have been interrupted. "You go ahead."

"I was just going to say this has been a wonderful day. We should do it again next time we've got time off from the stall."

"We should." He meant it.

"What were you going to say?"

"Nothing."

She raised a skeptical eyebrow. "Carl, you never open your mouth to say nothing."

He shrugged. "Wasn't important."

"Fine." She smiled and they continued in the quiet, their destination in sight. Only when they got to 502, having already reluctantly agreed that a nightcap would be a bad idea, did he turn back, just as Taamarai was headed for the stairs.

"I was gonna say you're beautiful."

She turned on the first step, apparently caught off-guard by his tone, casual as if he'd been telling her tomorrow would be a rainy day. A smile crept over her face but before she could say anything, Carl muttered, "Goodnight," stepped inside, and closed the door.

He felt stupid. Not for what he'd said. It was true. But for how and why he'd said it. The how was juvenile. Like some nervous kid he'd never been, scared to tell a girl he liked that she looked pretty. He'd gone for swaggering self-confidence back then, even when he didn't feel it, and the assured projection that he didn't much care what girls thought about him had gotten him more than his fair share of attention. Since Ali had come into his life, he'd kept things casual, and pretty infrequent at that, but it was still strange finding himself recast as some blushing loser.

The why was confusing. She was beautiful, and he knew she was nervous about the outfit. Shouldn't a friend let her know that Darren wasn't the only person with views? But if that was all, why not tell her tomorrow when they'd be working together all day anyway? And why be so unsure as to nearly not say it, practically run away into the apartment, then feel disappointed that the night was done with?

Frustrated and sore and angry that a good day had left him feeling that way, Carl headed for bed and lay awake thinking about the shapes of his life, subjecting it in his imagination to the warm stare of a beautiful woman he didn't know how to feel about. He was at least surer than ever, after his revelations of delinquency today, that she would never see him the way he saw her.

Outside, Taamarai felt heat in her cheeks and paused for a few seconds on the stairs, as if hoping that the door to 502 might open again. Some fantasy she couldn't deny saw Carl step back out, sweep her into his arms and kiss her, a kiss she couldn't quite make real in her imagination. She couldn't picture what might happen next, either, but when the door stayed closed and she finally headed up to 602, a grin flickered like low flames at the corners of her mouth.

A message from Darren was waiting on her phone. She read it and replied as briefly as she could, trying not to let it touch her mood. It didn't work. By the time she'd sent it, she felt ugly and idiotic and more sure than ever that whatever Carl might feel for her as a friend, he would be disgusted to know what she had done with that in her head.

She peeled off the outfit and put it carefully into her closet, squeezing it to the back where she wouldn't have to see it when she opened the door again tomorrow. She felt mortified now for wearing it, as if she had proclaimed some secret to the world. As she lay in bed, though, she also felt the simple excitement of the day, a pleasure that wouldn't just disappear.

Chapter Twenty-Five

Taamarai and Carl, apparently by mutual consent, didn't talk about their day out, beyond answering Ali's questions about whether they had, indeed, seen any bears, whether they had got rained on, whether they had come back with bug bites and if their feet hurt. She seemed bewildered by the notion of wandering around in a wood for most of a day in early March, and Taamarai resolved that they would take her out there in the summer. Ali was also more than happy to fill any gaps in conversation with excitement about her trip, which had been a huge success.

As a week turned into two, Taamarai didn't stop feeling physically fluttery when Carl leaned close to her at the stall but told herself that the fever of her emotions had passed. They could coast now, back to being friends. Planning her final project for college and running *Amma's Kitchen* gave her blessedly little time to dwell.

Fridays were always crazy and, as Taamarai and Carl got into the elevator at the end of the day, their feet ached. Ali was already deep into a school assignment at the table, so Taamarai offered to serve dinner at hers. It was leftovers from the stall, anyway.

Ali practically inhaled the hot food, thanked Taamarai for it, then vanished again, muttering about an upcoming deadline.

As they cleared up, Taamarai sensed that Carl had something to say. She waited for it, feeling like she knew where it was going. Somehow or other, shortly after they got back from the national park, she had let slip that, despite the stall doing so well, she was tight on money.

"Oh yeah? I thought we were doing better than expected," Carl had said.

Taamarai had known she looked evasive and should just have shut down the conversation but she was also getting used to checking her sanity when it came to Darren. "We are. It's just, well, with paying the rent here and making sure that Darren's got what he needs. We agreed he should get a share each week."

"For what?" Carl hadn't been able to hide his scorn.

"We're married." Taamarai had tried to sound sure of all the things that had once been obvious. "We have what we have jointly." She had paused. "If one of us is earning more one time and the other is another time, it doesn't matter."

"Huh." Carl had looked her up and down. "And how often's that meant he's been paying for you?"

Taamarai had found nothing to say.

"Yeah, that's what I thought."

Since then, Carl had come back to it now and again, making snide comments about household expenses and kept men and today Taamarai didn't want to end another day being reminded of a situation that was harder and harder to justify to herself. She was, therefore, surprised and pleased when Carl appeared to go somewhere else entirely.

"Saw you looking at that vacant place again." It was right off the market square and had been a diner until it closed. Taamarai had indeed gone to look on her lunch break, but she didn't think Carl had seen her.

"Oh! I was just getting a feel for what's available." She shrugged dismissively.

"It could be a good spot," Carl encouraged. "Decent front and plenty of seats, and our locals'd know where to find us." It would also get them out of a glorified horse wagon, which was fine with summer coming on, but would be punishing come winter. Mainly, it would represent what Taamarai had come here to do.

"I guess it could," she agreed, not bringing up the details that she had imagined as she looked through the window of the empty restaurant. The color of the chairs, the specific glasses she pictured on the tables. Instead she said, "Still a long way off that, though."

"Longer if you're still sending half what you make up to Boston."

There it was. Taamarai sighed inwardly but she didn't tell him to leave it alone. Part of her welcomed his needling skepticism and he didn't let her down.

"It's still half, right?" Carl found the whole situation ludicrous and it made him weirdly angry that he himself had never felt so financially stable in his life. There she was, day by day, putting in the same work and more and having nothing to show for it. Her response made him want to laugh and yell all at once.

"Not exactly." At least she looked embarrassed. "Darren said if I'd been managing on what we were making at the beginning, we should keep doing that."

"We're putting the rest into savings. Darren's been talking about maybe looking for somewhere down here."

Carl was temporarily thrown off his stride. Most of the time, he didn't even think any more about how one day she would inevitably leave with Darren. The blunt reminder was a shock.

"That what you want?" he asked coldly.

Taamarai looked down. "I like it here."

"So?"

She began to twist her fingers round one another. "Darren hates it here. He says he'll only come to stay again if it's to look for somewhere else."

"You want him living here with you?"

She shrugged again, still not looking up. "He's my husband. We've been together for nearly ten years." Neither of these seemed like an answer to Carl, but the feeling rose up again that stopped him pushing, the feeling that he wasn't being completely honest. Instead, he said, "Isn't something like this what your brother left you his compensation for?"

He held his hands up quickly, not wanting to be anything like Darren. "I'm not telling you how to spend it and I can understand not wanting to take risks, but if you see a good place, least you can do is look, right?"

Taamarai nodded but still seemed oddly evasive.

A cold sliver of doubt disturbed him. "I mean, that was always the plan, right? Paying your college fees and getting you set up somewhere?" He peered hard at her.

"I guess." She physically cringed. "And the place by the market looks good, but it's not that simple." Taamarai paused. "I don't get a good feeling about it. It isn't the right time yet."

"Maybe, maybe not. Carl wanted to let it go but couldn't. "But you've talked about wanting a location like that. You've gone over there a couple of times. What's wrong with looking a bit deeper, maybe talking to the bank, weighing up your options?"

Taamarai squirmed and still didn't meet his eye.

"So, what is it?" Carl got a sick feeling in the pit of his stomach. He was suddenly impatient, desperate to hear something that would make it go away. "Look at me!" He was sharper than he intended. "Taamarai!"

She did, and her eyes were clouded with tortured tears but she wasn't crying.

"I didn't know what else to do. You would have...."

Carl frowned. He had no idea what she was talking about. "I would have what?"

She didn't look like she was trying to change the subject, but what she was saying didn't make sense either, and he was becoming too anxious not to ask outright. He remembered her words only minutes earlier, about her and Darren owning what they had jointly.

"You didn't give it to him, did you? Your brother's money? Tell me you didn't give it to Darren." Carl waited, nauseous with expectation. It had never occurred to him, whatever else he might think or feel, that he might simply not be able to respect Taamarai.

"What? Of course not!" Her affronted grimace was some kind of relief. "I would never do that to Joshua." She walked abruptly to the balcony doors, dragged them open a few inches and sucked in the fresh air. When she turned back, she was calmer. "I didn't. I couldn't. But...." She stopped, then rallied.

"I should have told you. I didn't know what else to do – everything was happening so fast."

Carl still didn't understand. He felt better that she had given him a straight answer but was still anxious and confused without knowing what was wrong. When she continued, his world shifted on its axis again and this time he couldn't tell what was up or down and what feeling it was that he wanted to stop.

"We couldn't not take you to hospital and I thought, if you were worried about insurance, it would make things harder for you to get better. For Ali to keep on track in school."

For a long minute, Carl was silent. "The hospital?" His voice was weak.

She nodded.

He nodded back, just checking he'd understood. "You used it on the hospital?"

She nodded again and he tried to order his thoughts.

"How much?"

She looked away and shrugged as if it didn't matter.

"How much?" Carl could hear that he sounded angry without being sure that he was.

"What does it matter? It paid everything off." She looked at him pleadingly. "You're alive."

"How much is left?"

"What?"

"Of Joshua's money. Of your money. How much of it is left? How much do you still have for the restaurant?" His words came faster, full of desperation. "I mean, you can't afford this one, sure, but...."

"I'll find something," she interrupted with a small smile,

looking hopeful that the conversation might be over, but Carl was having none of it.

"Sure. With how much?" He moved closer but remained at arms' length.

"It doesn't matter. When the time's right, I'll figure something out."

Carl thought he might throw up or faint. "All of it?"

She had never said how much money Joshua had left her, but it was obvious from conversations about her college fees and plans for the future that it must have been a lot. His hospital visit was cast in a new and horrifying light, and he could begin to calculate something like how much: an ambulance, emergency surgery, blood transfusions, three days in intensive care....

Numbers spiralled in his head. Tens of thousands. At least. Hundreds, maybe. A life-changing amount. A chance to change *her* life. And it was gone. Carl was aware of the scars on his torso, burning suddenly, and he looked up at her with hollow, disbelieving eyes then down at himself. "For this?"

Taamarai seemed equally bewildered. "For you. And for Ali. I couldn't just let you die, or come out of that with so much debt you'd never be free of it!"

"All of it?" The anger was gone and he just felt empty, unable to think about anything clearly. She reached a hand out but he pulled away. He couldn't bear to be near her but didn't know why.

"Carl, I...I didn't know what else to do."

He rubbed a hand over his jaw, turned away, then back, so full of things for which there weren't any words. "All of it." The sounds were just dumb repetition.

When she spoke again, Taamarai's tone was harder and cut through his stupor.

"I'm not sorry and I never have been."

He looked up and could see no doubt in her eyes. He said nothing.

"I can tell you the exact amount if you like, but I'd rather not. It doesn't matter. And it wasn't all of it." Her tone softened. "I'd already paid my tuition for college and got the stall set up. Joshua's given me my second chance."

She was the one who looked hurt and confused, though Carl was sure he was the one who'd just been blindsided.

"Whatever happens, I'll find a way." Taamarai tried to smile. "I know I can now. And you've been part of that. You and Ali. You think I could just have let you die or be buried in debt and carry on with my plans like nothing had happened?" Her anger surfaced now, too. "Is that who you think I am?"

Carl felt dizzy and couldn't stop staring at her. Part of him wanted to reach out, steady himself on her shoulders and feel her arms wrap around him like he somehow knew they would, like they did sometimes in his dreams as he drifted off to sleep. Most of him wanted to be anywhere else, not to have to look at her or hear her voice or think those thoughts. She took a step towards him and he shied away again. She stopped as if she'd been burned.

"Does Ali know?" he asked quietly.

"No. I told her about the insurance scheme, like I told you. She didn't ask for details. She just wanted you to be okay."

"And you won't? Tell her?"

"No, of course not. Carl, please. I'm sorry I didn't tell you. I should have when you'd recovered enough. But what else could I have done?"

His reaction was unfair, ugly and defensive, but he let it out anyway. "You could have kept your goddamn money! Walked the other way! It wasn't none of your business!"

"You'd have died!" She sounded equally angry.

Carl felt like he was being pulled under and didn't know where. "So what?! What difference does it make to you?" He didn't like how his voice sounded – ragged and angry – but desperate too. It was a real question, with an answer he wanted to hear. His eyes were wide and hungry, searching hers.

So, before she could say a word, he turned and stalked out, slamming the door behind him as he left. He headed towards 502 and then remembered that Ali would be at the table, working on her assignment. He couldn't hide that something was up and couldn't trust that she wouldn't ask. She did so more and more these days.

He continued down the stairs, his hands shaking and mosquito clouds of emotion whirling through his head. He'd started the conversation completely in control. In fact, he'd had her on the ropes. He shouldn't like to do it, but somehow it was where they ended up so often, him pushing Taamarai to say the things that lurked behind her eyes. Then, without warning, everything had changed.

The abyss had looked bottomless for a second. If she'd given the money to Darren, he would have lost something for her he could never get back. The thought had been painful but with a strange appeal – the possibility to walk away, to write her off as just like everybody else, to step away from the cliff-edge of which he had become more and more conscious over the passing months. Then the strange had become incomprehensible.

He owed her his life. He'd already known it in the most literal sense. When he first came out of hospital, he had tried to be angry about Taamarai calling the ambulance, but he was genuinely glad to be alive and had come to terms with the fact that she had probably acted reasonably in the circumstances. Or he thought she had. Numbers jostled in his head like bingo balls, but she was right. The exact amount didn't matter. It was more money than he'd ever seen. He was sure of that. And more than Taamarai had ever expected to have until her brother left it to her.

Carl thought of the book she had given him the first time they met, inscribed by Joshua on the front page. It was stuck behind his bed, where he could reach it to read sometimes when he woke early or couldn't sleep or just found himself opening it for no reason at all. She had talked about how much Joshua had meant to her. What the money meant. Her future. Gone. For him. She wasn't sorry. He believed her. But where did that leave him?

Chapter Twenty-Six

At the door to the bar, Carl registered where he was. He hadn't been near the place since he left hospital. As he ducked inside, the dark drew him down. A few people looked over. One or two nodded, but they gave him space. He ordered a whiskey, then another.

Two or three drinks in he found he was talking to a couple of people he vaguely knew. Five or six drinks down, maybe more, some of the faces had changed. The barmaid had finished her shift and stuck around. She was leaning on his arm and smiling. They were both drunk and he thought her name was Reggie, but he couldn't quite remember.

She was looking at him like lots of women had looked at him over the years. Carl was easy enough on the eye and he knew plenty of women liked the hint of trouble that hung around him too. Right now, he needed that look and the promise in it. They would spend the night together and part in the morning. She'd seen him around enough to know she didn't want any more than a few hours of fun. She knew he wasn't worth any more than that. Certainly not a dream, a future. He knocked back another drink.

"You wanna get outta here?" He was slurring badly, but so was she, and she grinned as she helped him stand.

"My place or yours?"

"Yours? Got my daughter at home."

"Aw, you got kids?" She sounded surprised. He nodded and grabbed her playfully around the waist. They stumbled onto the sidewalk kissing.

When Carl woke up the next morning in a room he didn't recognize, the night was a blur. It was the afternoon. Reggie was nearly dressed and passed him a coffee with a straightforward smile. "That was one hell of a night, cowboy."

He wondered what he'd said or done to make her call him that, or if she just called everybody "cowboy." He could remember flashes. They had been clumsy but energetic. Other parts of the night were a blank. She gestured towards the door. "I gotta go, honey. I'm opening up the bar in half an hour. You look like you could use a night off."

Carl dragged on his clothes. "That I could."

He walked out with her and at the bottom of the stairs, she kissed him on the cheek and walked off with a cheerful wave. "See you around, cowboy!"

He rubbed a hand over his stubble in the weak afternoon sun and felt nothing. Maybe it was still the numbness of alcohol from the night before. He felt in his pocket for his phone and saw a screen full of messages and missed calls.

> Dad where are you?

> Are you OK?

> Dad let me know you're OK.

He relived Ali's rising panic as the night before wound on and he never came downstairs from dinner.

> I'm fine.

He sent it hoping it would make him feel better, but he actually felt worse. Carl felt physically sick, decided it was his hangover, and staggered unsteadily home. After a long shower, a large glass of water and a cautious handful of pills, he felt a little better physically but worse mentally.

Wherever his brain turned, there seemed to be something he couldn't face. Ali's helpless terror hurt. She had replied to his short message with relief and concern and he wanted to shout at her that she'd never dared ask him where he was when he'd stopped out before. Before his injury? No, it had happened more slowly than that – the questions, the unconcealed caring. Before Taamarai. Ali wasn't there, though, and he didn't want her coming back and seeing him like this.

He didn't want to think about Taamarai, either. She would have been expecting him on the stall that morning, though she'd have managed on her own. He knew that. These days, she seemed to know it as well. But it would have been hard. She hadn't texted and that also bothered him. It shouldn't. He didn't need somebody else checking up on him, but her silence felt angry.

It was tempting to pour himself another whiskey or grab a beer, but instead, he drank a couple more glasses of water and crawled back to bed. By the time he woke up again, it was dark and he only felt sick. It was a significant improvement but he was still constricted by guilt and anger. There was a knock on his door, gentle but insistent. "Dad, Dad? Are you in there?"

"I'm here!"

Without waiting, Ali pushed the door open. She rushed over and as he struggled to sit up, his head pounding, she hugged him tightly and then began to check him over.

"Dad!" After she had confirmed that he was physically unharmed, Ali looked at him with distraught eyes. "What happened? Where were you?" A tear welled up and slid down her cheek.

"Quit whining! I don't gotta tell you where I go."

Ali stepped back, curling her arms reflexively around her body. Then she turned and walked out. Her silence thumped in his head and followed him as he got up and made himself a coffee. He sat and drank it with Ali sitting at the table doing her school work and he noticed for the first time how much they would usually talk. He felt angrier with every second and wanted to march into his own room and slam the door. Knowing it would make him look ridiculous kept him where he was and further stoked his resentment.

There was a knock at the front door. Before he could move, Ali had got it and he heard low voices. It was Taamarai, getting back from the stall. He caught fragments of conversation. "Yeah, he's here." That was Ali.

"Thank God!" Further words that were almost certainly *is he okay?*

"Fine." Ali sounded dull and resentful. "Just wasted." More words he couldn't hear, then Ali muttered, "Yeah, I'll tell him." The door closed again and Ali came back on her own. Carl felt his mood worsen.

Ali said nothing as she went and got herself water, then, without looking at him, "Taamarai says she's got some food from the stall if we want to go up. Or she can send something down. I'm going up." She didn't wait for his answer.

Carl opened his mouth to shout after but didn't have anything to say. He could just text Ali or Taamarai to send him something down but that felt somehow like admitting to something: that he had been drinking? Well, so what? That he was ashamed to see either of them? What did he have to be ashamed of? Lit by a righteous determination, he stalked out and up the stairs. At 602, he knocked and Ali opened the door then walked away again, helping Taamarai to lay the table.

"Yeah, he's here," he heard Ali say listlessly. Carl headed for the kitchen, but Ali and Taamarai were already bringing the food out. Taamarai looked at him with a questioning, worried expression. He turned away from his shame and sat down in stony silence.

Carl felt he should say something but focused on eating instead, like Taamarai had with Darren there. He disliked the comparison and wondered why his brain had made it. In the end, Taamarai broke the silence first. "How was school?"

Ali didn't look at Carl as she mumbled, "Yeah, it was okay. I couldn't really focus, though. In class." Taamarai nodded sympathetically, keeping her eyes focused on Ali. "Got a good grade on my English project," Ali continued, looking like it was something she had wanted to smile about that had been taken from her.

"That's great!" Taamarai managed a smile for her but it looked like something practiced. They stumbled on for a little longer. The day at the stall had been okay, too. Taamarai wasn't really able to concentrate either, but sales were good and some of the same stall-holders who had helped before – she didn't say aloud what she meant by before – had stopped by to lend a hand.

Eventually, Ali hauled herself to her feet and took her plate to the kitchen. "I've got homework and an early practice tomorrow."

Taamarai nodded and looked like she might try to stop Ali, then got up and hugged her instead.

"Tomorrow will be easier. You'll see. Sleep well, Ali."

"Yeah, you too."

Carl couldn't see Ali's face but could hear that she was close to crying, refusing to let herself. Then she was gone.

The silence fell again, but before it could land, Taamarai headed for the kitchen, where the sounds of rinsing and clattering seemed to last longer than usual. Seething, sore and knowing beneath it all that it was his fault and that, like so many times before, wanting to go back in time didn't make it possible, Carl rose and followed her. She didn't turn around.

"Taamarai."

She carried on washing up.

"Taamarai!" He reached out to touch her arm and, slowly, sluggishly, she turned around.

He was startled to see the look in her eyes, deep and painful, then she smiled thinly. "I'm sorry about last night." She was stealing his lines.

"No, I'm sorry." Carl hadn't expected that to be his opening gambit. He felt adrift. "Can we sit down?"

Taamarai nodded and headed into the lounge. He had imagined the couch, but she sat at the table, gesturing to the seat opposite. He took it with a feeling of being summoned to the principal's office. Still, he knew what he needed to say.

"I'm sorry. About what I said last night." Sitting down was suddenly unbearable. He jumped up, heading for the window and the comfort of fresh air. He heard Taamarai get up too, but he didn't turn to look at her.

"What you did. I still, I don't understand." Carl was still drunker than he'd thought from the night before. He couldn't think straight. "Your brother. That money was for you."

He leaned forward on the windowsill and his reflection in the glass sucked him back into the look in Reggie's eyes at the bar. She'd known men like him all her life and knew just what he was good for.

"You know me for what? A few months?" His voice was getting harder. "That money was your whole life. I mean, if you didn't want it, you could've given it to some charity!" He breathed in deeply, then out again. He couldn't hear her – didn't know where she was. He wanted her to say something, preferably to shout something.

The silence grew heavier until he couldn't hold his anger up beneath it any longer. "Shit. This isn't...I just wanted to say, I don't get it. But I'm glad. I am. You saved my life and I don't know what to do about that, but I know I'm glad to be here and how you looked after Ali...." He felt real, undisguised guilt for Ali now, phoning and texting him all night and all day, not knowing if he was alive or dead. "That was real good. That was real."

When Carl turned around, he was only slightly surprised to find Taamarai standing close enough to touch him. She didn't, though. She hugged herself and stared at the floor.

"You don't have to do anything." Then she looked up, those fierce eyes uncertain. "You don't owe me anything." She searched for an answer in the corners of the room. "I didn't want to get rid of the money. You're not a charity." She paused, holding herself tight. "You say I don't know you. I never said I did." She hesitated. "But I do."

Carl looked up but something in her eyes stopped him from interrupting.

"Not everything. Maybe not even much. But I do know you, Carl. I know when I got here you helped me stand on my own two feet. I see how you've looked after Ali. I've trusted you with something I wouldn't tell another soul. You're my...friend. Don't you see?" She sounded frustrated, as if she finally wanted to shout at him, but the possibility no longer filled him with relief at the chance to shout back. Then she was calm again, and sad.

"That money – that was what they paid Joshua for taking away his hope. Do you think I'd have spent a penny of it if I could have had another day, another minute with my brother? That money wasn't worth his life! And it wasn't my life. This is my life!" She flung her arms out, reaching for the apartment, the stall, the whole world perhaps, then hugging them back to herself.

"This is what he wanted for me. Getting up every day feeling like I've got a chance. Like every day is worth it. He gave me that but you, and Ali, you've been there for me when I felt like giving up. God, it's all so confusing," she muttered at last, almost to herself.

"But it isn't," she answered herself. Taamarai held his glare again. "It's really simple. You're alive. That's all that matters."

Carl stared at her, the sun lancing in through the window behind him and casting golden flashes on a face that took his breath away. His knees felt weak and his chest tight. Then she turned away and walked back over to the table.

"I'm sorry I didn't tell you." She sounded tired. "You had every right to be angry. But what you did yesterday and today. Disappearing." She looked back at him with burning eyes. "Do you know what Ali's been through? Where were you? What was so important you couldn't even text her?" Her voice was rising with a rage Carl had never seen before. It brooked no response and seared the air between them.

"She had to watch you bleeding while the paramedics carried you away, sit by your bed for days not knowing if you'd ever wake up, see you stand and talk again and then you just vanish!" The rage became a disbelieving whisper and Carl was consumed by his shame.

"Don't you tell me about how I take care of my daughter!" He yelled it and saw Taamarai recoil. It made him feel better, or at least, it made the worsening feelings less acute. "She knows how to look after herself. You drop something like that on me! Any wonder I needed time to think?" Her eyes narrowed accusingly: he didn't look like a man who'd spent the night thinking.

"Ain't none of Ali's business where I go or who I spend the night with." Carl wasn't talking just about Ali and he saw the words land. The pain and shock on Taamarai's face made his heart skip a beat. His first reaction was vindictive. He had hurt her and that offered an illusion of solace for his own hurts. His second was something else that he didn't want to name – the realization that he'd said what he did to see if it *would* hurt her.

"And the stall?" Taamarai's voice was soft, shaking but determined. Her shoulders sagged and before he could answer, she did. "We've never agreed you work except when you want to. I pay you for the days you work." She looked at him, then away. "I'm sorry – it isn't your problem. And you're right. It isn't my business how you spend your time." She just managed to whisper, "It is Ali's, though. You owe her an apology." Then she nodded towards the door. "I've got to be up early tomorrow."

Carl opened his mouth to tell her to go to hell, then closed it again. He turned around and headed for the door. He stopped and turned back. Taamarai looked wretched. She was still hugging herself and all he could think was that he didn't mean for it to be like this. He had thought he was apologizing, trying to make it right. But there was nothing else his anger would let him say so he could only leave. By the time he got back to 502, he wanted to lock the whole world out.

Upstairs, Taamarai folded into a dining chair. She had been

anxious about the way things had gone when Carl found out about her paying for his treatment. That had turned to fear, rising to terror when Ali began to text and call to say she hadn't seen him since dinnertime. Taamarai had spent the night downstairs on the couch, waiting with her. Then they had both had to go to school and work and he didn't show up at the stall either.

She had gotten through the day seeing flashbacks of him lying on the couch and in the hospital. She prayed, as she had then, just for him to be alive. He had been, yet she still hurt all over, an ache that reached from her heart to the tips of her fingers.

The tears came slowly at first, but when she gave in, they fell freely until Taamarai sat rocking back and forth on the chair, trying to suck in breaths between her sobs, hurting for something she had never had and told herself she never could. That didn't matter. It still hurt worse than anything since her mother's call to tell her that Joshua was gone.

Chapter Twenty-Seven

Carl had hardly slept after his argument with Taamarai, but when his alarm went off the next day, he pulled on jeans and a clean t-shirt anyway. Ali had already left for school and laid out breakfast for him on the table. He could picture her doing it and felt his own selfishness. He almost couldn't stomach the food, left for him because she loved him more than she was angry with him. Because she was angry with him, because she loved him.

Taamarai wasn't waiting for him on the stairs and the walk to the market was long enough that he couldn't spend it all replaying his own self-justifications in his head. Eventually, his mind drifted away and he found himself back in 602 and the look on Taamarai's face when she realized how he had spent his night. It caused him a different kind of pain.

At the stall, Taamarai had started setting up for the day. When she saw him, she turned away for a moment then spun resolutely back and began to talk matter-of-factly about stock levels. He replied in kind and they slipped into a work routine that, however strained, Carl was surprised to find was still better than any fantasy he could conjure of running away. He had no desire to show her or

himself that he could still get by doing jobs for his old acquain-
tances and even less to lose himself in another bender.

In the evening, Ali cooked for them all and Taamarai ate with
them. He knew it was because it would have hurt Ali's feelings if
she hadn't. As soon as they were done, Taamarai headed upstairs,
pleading exhaustion and saying she needed to make a phone call.
They knew to whom, but she didn't say Darren's name often these
days.

As the week wore on, things got easier. At first, Ali withdrew
into a quietness that had once been normal, but she couldn't keep it
up for long and slowly began to mention things from her day or
show him videos and jokes she had found online.

Carl couldn't have said what he and Taamarai normally talked
about at the stall, but he noticed its absence. Their conversation
now was functional, but they did begin to move around one
another again without the caution that manifested as constantly
getting in each other's way. Their coordination was a soothing
intimacy.

By Friday evening, Carl began to wonder if tonight he might
find a way to frame an apology that his pride rejected but his
conscience ever more insistently demanded. He thought about
suggesting the three of them go out for dinner. Perhaps they would
accept generosity as a proxy for culpability. As they were packing
up, though, Taamarai got a series of text messages. Her face
changed; she walked away around a corner, already placing a call,
and came back fifteen minutes later, shaken and unsure.

"What's up?" Carl knew he had no right to ask. Not now. She
just looked glassy-eyed, though.

"Darren's coming back here to stay. Tomorrow. He called me
from the airport."

Carl felt nearly as shocked as she looked. "How come?"

"He says we've been drifting apart."

That seemed obvious, and Carl realized he had been
assuming that one day Darren simply wouldn't be part of her life
anymore. The text messages and calls would grow fewer and

shorter. The remittances might stop eating into her finances, keeping her poor however hard she worked. She would take off her ring and he.... Well, whatever he might have done didn't matter now.

"He says he wants to try and make it work," Taamarai murmured. "That he's had time to think and he'll make all the changes I asked for." She sounded wooden – a bad actress repeating empty lines.

"Sure." Carl's voice was hollow and disbelieving. "How do you feel about that?"

She seemed bewildered by the question. "He's my husband." She looked at him questioningly. "I've got to give him a chance."

Carl didn't agree. He also didn't like how Darren's choices were turning him back into a trusted confidant, who had to say things that made him feel worse not better because right now she needed a friend. "You think he's changed?"

Taamarai shook her head but what she said was, "I don't know."

He looked at her seriously and asked the question he knew he had to. "You still love him?"

She looked back then away and his heart sank, but she didn't say what he expected and feared.

"I.... He says that doesn't matter. He says we promised to stay together. No matter what. We just need to figure out how to do that." She turned her back on him to fiddle with one of the locks on the shutters. Carl felt something inside him flex in pain. It wasn't his scar. It wasn't even his unresolved guilt about her lost fortune or his battered self-respect.

He took two steps to stand close behind her and was about to remind her angrily that she was talking about a man who hadn't even gone to her brother's funeral when a vision flashed through his head. In it, he pulled her into his arms, buried his head in her hair, kissed her neck. Carl stepped away sharply, conflicted and uncertain, and just waited for her. After a few minutes, Taamarai turned back and pulled a desolate smile onto her face, looking as if some desperate hope had been snuffed out. They said very little as they walked home and, over a subdued dinner, Taamarai gave the news to Ali, who only managed, "Oh."

The following day, Taamarai was quiet at work and Carl kept his distance. They got in each other's way. Text messages came in steadily, no doubt charting every step of Darren's journey. While they were closing up, Taamarai seemed to linger and though Carl would have been just as happy to take the bus he didn't have the heart to suggest it.

As they walked this time, they chatted more easily than they had during the day and without ever mentioning Darren, but Carl felt his steps getting heavier. Back home, they climbed the stairs in ominous silence and at 502 parted without a word. Only as Taamarai reached the steps did Carl turn back and say, "If, you know. Whatever. You know you can come down here."

She frowned and then seemed to understand what he'd said and nodded.

At 602, Taamarai knocked rather than use her key. It didn't feel like her home. She wasn't surprised that Darren was waiting right behind the door. He looked hurt. "I thought you'd be waiting for me when I got here," he said as she came in.

"I told you I had to work."

"I didn't think you meant it."

Taamarai didn't really know what to say except, "It's what pays the rent."

He seemed confused then shrugged. "Anyway," he moved towards her and tried to take her into a close embrace which she returned only briefly, "it's really good to see you, babe."

"Darren, I've asked you not to call me that." It was one of many conversations they'd had about what might have to change if their relationship was going to work. Taamarai felt disappointed that so little seemed to have got through.

"Oh yeah. Sorry. You know I'm trying."

She didn't, but let it pass.

"How was your day?" He asked it dutifully – one of the other things they had discussed. It would be great for him to show an interest.

"It was okay, thanks. We had a bunch of new customers come over from the office block on 14th."

"That's great." He listened for a minute or so while she talked then jumped it at a pause that wasn't really there. "My journey was better this time. There weren't any delays and I got pizza while I was waiting for my transfer. Then there was a taxi right outside the airport as I arrived."

Taamarai felt herself grinding her teeth. They had talked about saving money. All he had to do was bring sandwiches. Yesterday, in the rush to get everything ready, she had texted him the bus route from the airport.

Darren just smiled at her, apparently not seeing the clench in her jaw or the look of disappointment in her eyes. He came over to her again as she was trying to maneuver herself to the bathroom to change out of her work clothes. He reached out and pinched at her playfully. "I've missed your boobies."

Taamarai felt her stomach turn and knew she would scream if she didn't speak. "Darren!" She took a step back. "You decided to come here with no notice. I'm pleased to see you." It felt like a lie. "But we can't just carry on like nothing's happened, like the last few months have just been us taking some kind of long vacation or something. You can't come back here and expect me to just pick things up and be up for..." her stomach heaved, "anything."

Darren looked crushed. "Tam, I came here because this is important to me. I thought it was to you. We haven't been talking as much lately. It's too difficult when it's all over video and phone and text messages. I thought we should be living together again, working things out together."

"And I said I was only willing to try that if you showed me that you had listened to any of the things I said weren't working for me." Taamarai had wanted to sound angry but to her own ears, her voice was full of weariness.

"I have been listening!"

"So?"

"So what?"

"So what's changed, Darren?" Anger was back against her lips now. "You turn up with no notice because you've decided it's the right thing to do, without checking how I feel. You call me babe and immediately complain that I didn't drop work for you even though it's my work that paid for your plane ticket and your pizza and your taxi from the airport and now you've started again with that way you...you...treat my body as if it's some toy you can just play with when it suits you! So what's changed, Darren?"

He looked tearful, then upset. "So that's it? You say you want to try but then I come all the way here because it doesn't seem like you're really bothering anymore and all I get is you talking like I'm the worst husband in the world? It's like you don't even care how hard any of this is for me, Tam. I mean, how am I supposed to keep motivated to try to change when it feels like you've already made your mind up?"

Taamarai felt simultaneously the injustice of the question – there had been so many months and years in which she would have been thrilled to see him try – and its fairness about the situation in front of her. It made any reply difficult.

"Look, Darren, I know this is hard. It is for both of us. But I need to see some sign that things won't just go back to how they were."

"That's just it, Tam." He scuffed his foot at the floor. "I liked how things were before. I thought we were happy."

"Darren, I cried nearly every day!" As the months had gone on, living on her own, not crying every day, Taamarai had found it harder and harder to understand how that had never seemed to trouble him. "And I've told you I wasn't happy. I was miserable. I'm not asking for much. Some time on my interests and hobbies instead of yours. For you to think about what you want to do for a job and just be a bit more grown-up. Shouldn't you want me to feel happy and supported? Isn't that what loving somebody means?" By the time she finished, her voice was high and strident.

Darren glowered at her but didn't raise his voice. He'd

explained to her long ago that he thought somebody who shouted had already lost an argument. "I thought loving somebody meant accepting them for who they are, not asking them to change everything about themselves to suit you. You're asking me to change my whole life because suddenly you're not happy with how things have always been."

Taamarai glared at him. "This isn't sudden, Darren! I've been changing for years into somebody you want, who does things the way you like them. I'm just asking for some balance." Before he could say anything else, she lowered her voice but spoke decisively. "We can work on things while you're here but I'm going to sleep downstairs tonight."

He walked forward and put a hand on her arm. His voice trembled. "Tam, please don't do that. I've only just got here. I didn't come to argue."

"But apparently you didn't come here to change either." Taamarai couldn't let her anger go so easily. She pulled her hand back.

"Tam, come on." He stared at her pleadingly. "Spend the night with me, at least?"

She looked at him in astonishment. "What? You said to me this morning, Darren, that you were fine taking things slow."

"I thought then that we were definitely going to work things out," he muttered sullenly. "We'd be together forever, like we promised. Now I'm not so sure."

Taamarai couldn't fault his analysis, however late it came. He looked up at her. "So tonight might be the last night I ever get to spend with my soulmate."

Taamarai turned pale with horror. She wanted to scream at him that that was the problem, right there. That, to him, it would be a night to remember regardless of whether she even wanted to be there. Instead, she simply turned away. "Goodnight, Darren." This time he didn't say anything or follow her.

Chapter Twenty-Eight

The door upstairs opened and closed. Carl hadn't been listening out. Not really. But his attention had been caught by anything that might be a sound from the apartment above. Footsteps followed and the distinctive sound of somebody on the stairs, apparently going up.

He swigged his beer and sat back, pushing himself into the sofa in a weird parody of relaxation. He tried to focus on the game. He could follow every play, see every move coming, but he couldn't make himself care and kept forgetting who the teams were. After less than a quarter, he set down his nearly-full beer and headed up the stairs himself.

At 602, he passed the door with a venomous glance. He could think of at least one solution to his anger and Taamarai's situation, but he kept going. The roof terrace was a dingy covered storey with open sides. It served no particular purpose, but he sometimes came there to work out on an old boxing bag. Other residents stacked furniture and rubbish up there that they couldn't be bothered to get rid of any other way. It was a strange place for Taamarai to go, but the only place she could have done. He hadn't heard the elevator and nobody had come down the stairs. Of course, it might have been somebody else, but he knew it wasn't.

The door opened quietly and he moved out into the space, lit up by the horizontal rays of the setting sun. He couldn't see anything from the top of the stairwell and took a few paces forward then Carl stopped dead as he saw Taamarai, silhouetted on the waist-high ledge that ran around the whole floor.

For a moment he couldn't breathe, then he scuffed his feet on the rough floor, trying to make sure that she knew he was there. He didn't want to startle her by calling out. The sensation of panic was unfamiliar, dimly remembered from when Ali was small. He'd never felt it for anybody else.

"Hey there." It was impossible to see in the slanting light whether she was looking backwards at him or out towards the city. Or down. "Taamarai. It's me. It's Carl." He moved, getting the light out of his face. Suddenly she was in full view. Her knuckles were pale where she sat on the edge of the concrete and she was gazing out into the orange glow of the sun. She wasn't looking at him but he could tell she knew he was there. "Hey." He took a few steps closer, keeping his voice low.

"It's okay. I'm not going to jump." She tried to sound light-hearted, as if it was funny he might even think it, but her voice was detached and faraway. At last she turned to him, her eyes slightly red. "I couldn't do that. Not to Amma and Dad. Not after Joshua." She sounded completely calm. It bothered him.

"That's good." He took a couple more steps forward and didn't breathe until he had a grip on Taamarai's arm tight enough for him to be pretty sure he could stop her falling. She didn't react. "Why don't you come back over this side anyway? The view's just as good." She looked down curiously at his hand.

"I told you, I'm not going to jump."

"Sure. Easy to slip, out on the edge like that, though."

Taamarai nodded as if only just noticing where she was. She pulled one foot up onto the ledge, looking like she was going to stand up and clamber back inside. Instead, Carl caught hold of her other arm and summarily hauled her back inside the parapet. She half fell, half staggered and turned to face him as he planted her, feet first, on the ground.

Carl finally let go, leaning forward to rest his hands on the concrete to either side of her. Terror drained out of him, leaving other emotions to sweep into the vacuum.

"What the fuck do you think you're doing?" He was practically shouting in her face. His hands were shaking and his heart was racing. Taamarai didn't react. "Well?" He pushed himself backwards off the ledge and turned away, enraged and desperate for her to say something.

"I'm sorry. I didn't think anybody knew I was up here."

"What the hell is that supposed to mean?" He turned back to her in angry confusion. She was still speaking barely above a whisper. "That it would've been okay if nobody had been here? What if you'd slipped?"

She shrugged and seemed to writhe under his stare. "I just thought, if you weren't here, if nobody was here. Nobody would need to worry. I'd have sat somewhere else if I knew you were here." She turned her head and looked out over the city then back towards him, her face becoming unreadable in the shadows again.

"I just needed to be up here to...to try and figure things out." She looked at the floor and whispered to herself, "How did I manage to fuck everything up so badly?"

Carl could almost hear the question in Darren's voice. He felt a wordless shout in his throat and in two steps he was back, gripping her arms, ready to shake her like a rag doll. Instead, he kissed her with a violence that surprised him, pressing her back against the concrete, still clutching her arms, as if he could squeeze into her the things for which he had no words.

Before he could even register what he'd done, her lips parted. She kissed him back, equally desperate, equally fierce, her own hands reaching up to grasp at his shoulders.

He hadn't meant to do it. Carl had told himself so many times that he never would, long after he'd stopped telling himself he didn't really want to. Yet it was more sublime than he had ever dreamed. Her body melted towards his, her passion eager as his. He could taste her, feel her pressed against him. He slid his hands to her waist, let them slip under her top, feeling the heat and smoothness of her skin. Her own hands slithered over his arms and chest. Then he felt the shudder pass through her, the pause. Her hands stiffened against him and she pushed him gently away.

Taamarai looked up at him, wild-eyed and distraught. "I'm sorry. I'm so sorry. I can't do this. I'm sorry." She had wriggled away from him, towards the stairwell. She looked back as if she might say something else but managed only a final "I'm sorry." Then she turned and ran, disappearing down the stairs.

In the rapidly falling light, Carl leaned against the concrete, the taste of her in his mouth, the memory of her skin on his fingertips. He stayed up on the roof, hammering at the training bag until the light disappeared, asking himself why he'd done it and refusing to hear the answer.

When he came back into 502, Ali was sitting on the couch, a comforter and pillow stacked next to her and the television playing low.

"Dad?" She looked at him inquiringly. Ali had been surprised to find the beer bottle beside the couch and the television on, but since Carl's most recent disappearing act, she had tried not to wonder. Like he'd said, it was none of her business. At least he was back again.

"What's up?" he asked and frowned at the comforter and pillow.

"Taamarai." Ali nodded towards her own bedroom. "She was in the corridor when I got back from track. She looked really wrecked. She was saying she'd sleep in the stall and got weird when I said she could sleep on the couch here. So I said she could have my room. That's okay, right?" She hesitated at the look on his face.

"Sure. You did the right thing."

Ali visibly relaxed but still seemed shocked at such a dramatic change in her friend. "She didn't want anything to eat, either. I've made some soup, on the stove." Ali sounded lost and looked surprised when Carl walked over and rested a hand on her shoulder.

"It's a good thing you've done. I'm beat, too. I'll head to bed soon but I'd love some of that soup." He headed over to the kitchen, poured himself a bowl and brought it back to the table. "This is good."

Ali uncurled from the sofa. She paused, then hugged him briefly but keenly around his shoulders.

"Dad?" She paused.

"Yeah?"

For a moment, he thought she wouldn't say anything, then she muttered, "I'm glad it's good."

After Carl had eaten, an oppressed air seemed to hang over the apartment. It was broken by a knock at the door. He checked the peephole and wasn't surprised to see Darren, looking aggrieved. Carl pulled open the door and stood across the entrance.

"Have you seen Tam?" No hello, no pleasantries. Darren might almost sound like he was worried, Carl thought.

"Yeah. I've seen Taamarai," Carl replied blandly.

"Thank God! Do you know where she is?"

Carl looked him up and down. "Yeah."

"Where is she?" Darren was getting annoyed now. Carl knew he was being childish, but it was taking most of what he had not to punch the man in the face.

"She's sleeping."

"In there?" Darren was already looking past him and took a step forward to go in.

"I said she's sleeping." Carl blocked him with an arm across the doorway. For a moment, Darren looked confused.

"I want to see her. Let me in. I've been worried sick about her."

Carl squared himself off, inviting the smaller man to push him. "Well, now you know where she is and that she's okay." When Darren didn't seem to get the message he said, slowly and spitefully. "She doesn't want to talk to you. She'll come find you when she wants to."

As the door swung shut Carl heard Darren shout out, "Tam, Tam it's me!" After a few half-hearted attempts yelling at the closed door, though, Darren gave up and his footsteps retreated. Carl knew if it was him on the other side of a closed door, being told he couldn't see her and check she was okay, he would tear down the walls if he had to.

When Carl got back to the lounge, Ali was already curled up under her comforter, headphones in, watching a movie. She waved briefly to him as he headed for the bathroom.

In his bed, Carl was sharply conscious of Taamarai, only a wall away, but he was also exhausted. As he closed his eyes, he could feel her kiss again and the memory followed him into sleep.

It was dark and quiet when he woke. He fumbled for his phone to check the time – just past one. His mouth tasted sour and he needed water. He pulled on a pair of sweat pants, opened his bedroom door, and was pleased to see that Ali didn't move as he passed by. In the kitchen, he poured a glass of water and drank it gratefully. For a few moments, he stood in the dark, holding the edge of the sink, trying and failing to think about nothing at all. He sighed, then quietly turned back to his room.

As he reached the hallway, a door opened behind him and he turned sharply. Carl hadn't heard Taamarai get up. She had gone to the bathroom, long before he woke, and sat in the dark against the bath. She couldn't stop thinking and only moved when she was cold and her legs began to ache. Now, she looked across the living room at him.

She was wearing shorts and a vest and her face was a mask of shadows. She glanced across to the couch, where Ali still hadn't moved then Taamarai began to walk towards him, the rings on her toes clicking softly on the linoleum. It was the way back to her room – Ali's room – but as she got nearer, she didn't head that way.

Carl froze, and she kept her eyes on the floor until she was almost close enough to touch him. Then Taamarai looked up. She lifted her hand and reached out, placing it over the butterfly on his chest. He still didn't move. She took a step closer. She could rest her other hand on his side now. Carl didn't react as she reached up and kissed him.

He felt the strangeness of her lips on his, the tentative moment when an ambivalent gesture became undeniably something else. Then he reached for her, sliding his hands up her back and into her hair. Neither of them made a sound as he took her hand and led her to his room. Taamarai kept hold of him as he closed the door and this time waited, letting him make the choice. Carl had already made it once before and couldn't make any other. He kissed her cautiously at first, then harder.

Taamarai pressed her hands against Carl's chest, feeling the warmth, the texture of his skin. There was an urgency now that she couldn't conceal. She didn't even want to. His hands were moving, too. She felt him brush carefully at the hem of her vest and, before he could hesitate, she peeled it over her head herself. His eyes widened, then closed as he sought her lips again. She reached for the waist of his sweatpants.

They almost fell onto his bed and Carl felt embarrassed by the adolescence of it all – his messy room and unmade bed and the awkward, silent groping in the dark. She deserved better. Then everything else disappeared except the moment.

There was no finesse or complexity to their lovemaking but they both fell back trembling when it was done. Taamarai rolled over, pressing her body against him. He pulled the blankets over them both and let his mind settle into the warmth of her against him.

Chapter Twenty-Nine

Streaks of pale light woke Carl as the dawn always had. He kept his eyes closed for a moment. Maybe the night before wouldn't be real, and he wanted those recalled pleasures for a moment longer.

At last, he looked to his side. Taamarai was still there. He could see her hair, wild above the covers. She had moved away slightly in her sleep, but now he let himself pay attention, he could still feel her foot resting against his, her hand touching his side. He stretched his arm towards his phone to check the time. The moment he moved, though, she stirred and rolled over to face him, her eyes bleary but already full of uncertainty.

"Hey," he tried to say. It came out a hoarse whisper but enough to provoke a small smile.

"Hey," she murmured. Carl leaned up on his elbow so that he could reach out and brush the hair from her face. It was all he had meant to do, but his hand drifted irresistibly across her cheek and down to her shoulder. She pulled her hand out from under the covers, letting them slip away as she did, and reached out to touch his face in return. He felt her fingertips tracing his jaw.

Carl leant forward, almost dizzy with hope and fear. His lips brushed hers and Taamarai welcomed his kiss again. They moved closer together and reached for each other, slower this time, but no less urgent. Her response astonished him more than it had the night before. Then some part of him had known it might just be desperation, the same self-loathing need that had driven him to the bar and Reggie.

This time, they had both had time to think. They saw each other in the light of day. Carl's own feelings cut through him like fire, and he focused on her every reaction, her breathless, starved wonder as if she had never felt the sensations before. Just as in the night, she curled against him when they finished and Carl's eyes squeezed shut as she pressed her lips against the bare skin of his arm, a gesture somehow more intimate than anything that had gone before.

At last, Taamarai broke the silence. "I should go. Back to Ali's room, I mean. Before she wakes up." She kept her voice a low whisper and searched his face, though he couldn't tell what for. Then she got up and began to look around for her clothes, pulling them on shyly.

Carl swung his legs over the side of the bed and, as she was about to head for the door, to real life and all of its complications, he pulled her back onto his lap. He kissed her again and she held him, losing herself as deeply as him in their closeness. When she pulled away, it was with evident reluctance.

She opened the door and stepped carefully out. Then Carl heard Ali's disbelieving voice. "Taamarai? What are you doing?" Cursing under his breath, he found his own sweatpants and pulled them on. When he emerged from his room, Ali was staring at Taamarai in shock. "Dad?!"

"Ali." Taamarai stepped forward, reaching out, but Ali pulled away.

"You've been..?" She spluttered for a moment then glared at them both with accusing eyes. "How long?"

"How long what?" Taamarai whispered.

"The two of you?" Ali was heading for a scream. "You two! How long?"

"Calm down." From Carl, it was an order. Taamarai spun to look at him, begging him wordlessly not to make it worse.

"Ali...Ali, it's never happened before. Ali, I promise." Taamarai kept her hand out towards Ali. "Never. Just last night. Ali, I was upset. I'm not making excuses. Ali, I'm sorry."

"You are?"

Taamarai turned with despair towards Carl's question, desperate not to hurt anybody and knowing that she might hurt everyone.

"Dad?!" Ali was almost hysterical.

"Hush," Carl instructed. "She's telling the truth." He turned to Taamarai. "But I still want to know – are you sorry?" He thought she would run away or look back at Ali and tell her whatever she thought Ali wanted to hear.

Instead, Taamarai just continued to stare at him and, when she spoke, it was soft but unmistakable. "No." Then she looked up more firmly and the woman was back, the one he saw at times with such awe. "Ali, please come and sit down." This time she didn't wait for Ali to come to her but took her hand and led her over to the couch.

"Ali." Carefully, she stroked her hair. "I'm sorry I put you in this situation. I'm sorry you feel surprised and hurt." She took a deep breath and then looked over at Carl. "We both are." She held his stare, willing him not to say anything but also to hear her. "But Ali, I'm not sorry about what happened last night." They all knew she was talking to him. Carl felt unsteady on his feet.

"You're not?" Ali sounded lost and hurt.

"I'm not." Taamarai's voice was like the ground under his feet. "But whatever you need. Whatever you want, Ali. I'll do whatever you want. If you say we should never see each other again, if you want me to leave and never come back, that's what I'll do. I never meant to hurt you. We never meant to hurt you." Taamarai sounded on the verge of tears too now, and clung to Ali's hand. Ali didn't say anything for a long time and Carl could only stand, watching them both.

After a while, Taamarai said, "I'm going to go now. Whatever happens, Ali, you're always in my heart. I'll come back later and whatever you decide...." She got up and he thought she might look back, but she simply walked out.

For even longer, Ali continued to sit there, then at last, her eyes red from crying, she glared up at him. "Dad?"

He ran his hand over his head. "Ali." Suddenly he felt very tired. "What do you want me to say?" Everything seemed to have changed so quickly. Her body, her taste, her smile in the morning light. Now this. He knew Taamarai had meant what she said. If Ali told her never to come back, she wouldn't. And whatever he was feeling only grew stronger for that certainty.

"Are *you* sorry?" Ali wasn't shouting any longer. She had wiped a few tears from her cheeks and looked genuinely interested to know the answer.

Carl looked her squarely in the eye. "No."

Ali thought about this, then asked, "How long?"

"She told you. Last night was the first time."

"I know that. I know Taamarai wouldn't lie." Ali glowered, as if challenging him to contradict her. "How long have you wanted to?"

He rubbed his eyes and turned away towards the bathroom but didn't walk away. "Ali, what difference does that make?"

"Look at me." Another time he might have shouted at her for the tone she was taking, but he just turned back round. "How long?"

Carl tried to think about things he had carefully avoided up to now. "I don't know." He looked away again but Ali gave him time. "I don't know. When she took me to your school? When I woke up in the hospital with you both there?" He leant back against the wall. "When she gave me that damn book of poems?"

"That was," Ali spluttered, "that was, like, the first time you met her!"

"Well?" He folded his arms across his chest, not wanting to answer her questions but unable somehow to walk away. "What about you?"

"What about me?" Ali sounded angry again.

"When did you start loving her? You telling me it wasn't that first day?"

Their eyes met and Carl knew he had just crossed another line. Ali didn't draw attention to it, though. She thought about the question and eventually looked down at her hands. "That's different." She sounded defeated.

"I know it is." Before he could say any more, Ali burst into tears and ran for her room, slamming the door behind her. For a long time, he heard her crying. He poured himself a soda, thought about going out to the bar, but didn't.

The sound of Ali crying gradually wore away and became silence, then she started up one of her records, loud and fast and physically aggravating to him. Carl sat for a while longer, his own frustration bubbling up inside him. At last, he marched to the door and knocked hard on it. "Ali, turn that down!" There was no reaction from inside. "Ali, open the goddamn door!" He banged angrily on the shaking wood.

After a moment, Ali emerged looking nervous but still defiant. Carl had been fully prepared to let her have even a part of the helpless, hopeless anger inside him. He met her eye and saw that she was terrified at an overturning of some part of her world that only now looked as large in her mind as it had really become. She looked full of uncertainty, simultaneously wary of him and afraid for him. In an instant, he saw the strength Ali had needed growing up with him.

Carl felt lightheaded for the second time that day. This time it was the same wave of shame that had consumed him when he came out of the hospital. Once again, words failed him. He pulled Ali into a tight embrace, crushing her close to him as if his life depended on her. It had, for so many years that he had taken it for granted.

Ali seemed surprised for a moment, holding back, full of the pride he had taught her – that self-protecting coldness. Then it dissolved. She hugged him back, pressing her face into his chest like she had when she was too tiny for him to push away and scold for crying.

"I love you, Ali. You hear?" His voice was muffled in her shoulder but she hugged him tighter in response. "I love you." Her life flashed before him and he saw too clearly how he had made choices for her but never told her why, the times he had made the wrong choices and never admitted it to her or himself, when he had pushed her away because he told himself that being alone had made *him* strong and because he didn't know what to do with the fear he felt for her. "I'm sorry, Ali. I'm so sorry. But I love you."

For a while they just clung to one another, before he heard Ali's voice beside his ear, snuggly from tears he would not reprimand ever again. "I love you too, Dad." Carefully, she stood back a bit, recovering some of her teenage space but not pushing him away. She looked up and then asked, carefully, as if worried it might be the wrong question, "What about Taamarai?"

He looked at her with raw, hurting eyes. "What about Taamarai?"

"Do you love her, too?" Ali seemed afraid of the answer but he wasn't sure what she wanted him to say.

"Ali, like Taamarai said, we both want whatever's best for you. Whatever you want." As painful as it was, he knew he meant it too.

She looked at him stubbornly, refusing to give him a clue. So much like him. "I want to know if you love her."

He closed his eyes. Behind his eyelids, Taamarai leaned up to kiss him. She sat on his couch watching the game. She told him he was wrong, he'd done good. She looked right into him. "Yes." The word was ragged, dredged from somewhere deep. Ali hugged him again.

"I'm sorry, too." Ali murmured. "What I said...." She didn't let go of him. "I guess, I mean, I know you and Taamarai get on really well. I just never...." She squeezed him again, apologizing with touch. "Anyway. I'm sorry."

She pulled away to stare at him seriously, looking older than him in that way she'd been able to do now and again since she was about four years old. "It's okay. You two, I mean. If you want." She thought about her own feelings. "I dunno. I never thought about it. You and somebody else. Not really. But it makes sense."

In his turn, Carl looped a single arm around Ali's shoulder and pulled her to him, kissing her gently on the top of her head. She'd got big. Yet for the first time since she had been toddling around on the floor, it felt natural to hug her properly and for a minute or so they just stood that way. After a while, Ali stepped back and leant in the doorway facing him. Carl shrugged, feeling the expectation to say something, to have an answer.

"I know. It's weird," he conceded. "But I don't know what'll happen, Ali. Me and Taamarai. Last night was.... Well, things can happen and it don't mean anything. It don't mean me and her..."

Ali laughed awkwardly, looking mortified to be having this conversation with her father but much happier than not having it. "Dad, I know having sex doesn't mean you're going to get married or anything." She seemed concerned and full of confused questions, stuck between two adults she might become.

"But it doesn't mean nothing, does it?" Apparently too concerned to be embarrassed for a moment, she asked earnestly, "I mean, you and Taamarai. You, like, work together and, I mean, I've never seen you, like, hang out, like that. You know, go on trips and stuff. Laugh." She tried to form her ideas. "Can you really like somebody like that and then it still doesn't mean anything?"

Carl stared at the floor. Really, that was the question he'd been trying not to ask himself since the moment he kissed Taamarai. He didn't need to ask it to know his answer and that terrified him. And he could ask it a million times and still not know Taamarai's and that scared him even more. "I dunno, Ali. I dunno."

She reached out and hugged him again, becoming the parent. "It'll work out, Dad. I know it will." She grinned shyly. That confidence of youth but something older too, that Taamarai had immediately seen about Ali and that Carl couldn't understand how he hadn't. That care for him he had never noticed until he woke up in the hospital – his baby, always trying to protect him.

"But Dad, you can tell her. How you feel. Sometimes you gotta fight for things. You gotta know what you want. You taught me that."

Ali squeezed him one last time then disentangled herself and headed for the door. She went out without a word and he just watched her go. He *had* taught her that, and thought when he did that it was a lesson he'd learned long ago.

Chapter Thirty

At *Amma's Kitchen*, Carl could see the breakfast queue had already started. He was late but Taamarai looked surprised he was there at all, then she carried on as if everything were completely normal. He did the same, slotting into their routines and refusing to think about whether she had gone back upstairs to Darren that morning or what might happen later that day.

The rush was long. Things were going well. Everything seemed normal, yet so different. Taamarai didn't meet his eye. She chatted with the customers like she normally would, but not with him. She wasn't not talking to him, but they seemed to have nothing to say to one another. As she handed orders down to him, though, sometimes their fingertips would brush. It must have been happening since the stall opened, he decided. It had just never felt electric before.

In their quiet patches, Taamarai found reasons to rush around or bustle off – getting fresh milk from the nearby corner store, rearranging the refrigerator. In the afternoon, one of the other stallholders came by to see if Carl was okay. His absence had been noticed and they had been worried. He lied about being sick and felt the strangeness of people caring.

As the day drew to a close, Taamarai began packing down. Carl told himself he wouldn't do or say anything. Whatever happened next would be up to her. He could practically feel Ali urging him on. *Just tell her I'm sorry. That it's okay.* It was still so simple for Ali. After all the crap she'd had to watch growing up around him, it still seemed so simple.

"It's all locked up." Taamarai sounded bright and cheerful as she came back around to the front of the stall. He knew it had to be fake but he couldn't have pulled it off. He couldn't pull it off now. He couldn't pretend but didn't seem able to do anything else either, so they walked back in silence, neither of them apparently keen to get back to Gabriel Heights. Carl felt like it should be so easy to reach over and take her hand but their steps were out of sync.

Only when they got to the door of 502 did Carl realize what would happen next. He would go in and close the door behind him. She would go upstairs, and thinking about that would destroy him.

"Taamarai?"

She looked up at him.

"Don't go back to him." He almost said "please," but just took her hand instead. Her fingers remained loose in his and his heart squeezed painfully.

"Carl." She looked cornered. "I'm sorry."

Carl knew he wasn't really angry and that anger wouldn't help, but it was all he seemed able to call on when the fear came, and this time it was white cold and vicious. She had said she wasn't sorry. Given how sorry she seemed to be about everything else, how sorry Darren made her feel just for existing, he had clung to that. Now she was sorry.

"Stop saying that!" He was louder than he needed to be and not saying any of the things he meant, except that he did mean for her to stop saying those words, words that hurt and made him afraid that he could be hurt. "Stop being sorry!"

Her hand gripped his at last and she moved to stand right in front of him. "Carl, I don't know what else to say. You're hurt and angry and I did that. How can I not be sorry?" She stared up at him, that frank look that seemed to meet him somewhere deep inside. "I never want anything bad for you or Ali. I never wanted to hurt you."

"Then say you're not sorry. Say you're not sorry about last night." Speaking the words was a kind of relief. He couldn't tell her or himself it didn't matter now.

Taamarai was still looking at him, her eyes full of questions and something small and tentative. Its light flickered and grew.

"I'm not sorry for that." Her voice was firm and certain, like she sounded when it was just them – him, her and Ali. When she was home. He'd never thought of it that way before. "I'm sorry it's all so complicated, that Ali is hurting and that you are too."

He took her gently by the shoulders. That was what she thought of first? His heart ached.

"Taamarai, Ali doesn't mind. I promise. She told me. She was shocked. I guess I was too. I think she was worried. That it'd spoil things. Anyway, Taamarai." He wanted to blurt out that Ali thought it would all work out and they should be together but again, it was too easy when you were fifteen.

"She is? She's really okay?" Taamarai looked like a weight had been lifted from her as he nodded.

"She's good. She's gonna be just fine." He didn't mean just about this and she seemed to understand. Then she shook her head.

"I'm glad. I'm so glad that she's not angry. But Carl, it still isn't fair. I'm married. It isn't fair on Ali, or on you." Her face contorted in pain. "Or on Darren."

"Fuck Darren!" It was hard not to give fuller vent to his contempt.

She shook her head and smiled sadly. "He doesn't deserve this. He isn't the man I thought he was, but he hasn't changed. I have and that isn't his fault. But it doesn't change the truth, the promises. I'm married." Her face twisted in conflict. "Strange, isn't it?" When she began to speak again her voice was soft and musing. "Last night didn't feel like cheating, even though I know it was." She seemed to think about something, seeing it from some new angle, then she looked hard at him. "Carl?"

"Yeah?"

"Kiss me?"

He frowned in surprise, but didn't need asking twice. As he bent toward her, Taamarai seemed still to be thinking with her lips, testing, winding her arms slowly around his shoulders. Carl closed his eyes and pulled her to him.

"Tam!"

Both of them froze then Taamarai leapt clumsily backwards, detaching herself from Carl and spinning towards the stairs. Carl looked up straight into Darren's face. He was standing a few feet away, his eyes glowing with a weird triumph.

"Darren?" Taamarai looked horrified and full of guilt.

"I thought I heard somebody on the stairs. I was worried about you so I thought I'd see if you were back from work yet." His eyes bored into her and he sneered, "I guess now I know why you never came home last night." Then his face became sad, or a semblance of sad. Something he probably thought was appropriate to the moment.

"Is this really what you think of me? Cheating on me with," he glanced at Carl, "somebody like him?" Darren looked like he might cry. "I always knew that I loved you more than you loved me. I knew this would happen one day, but," his face became magnanimous and gentle, "that's why I decided that I'd always forgive you, Tam."

With his strange audience, Darren warmed to his theme. "I meant what I said on our wedding day. For better or worse. I'll always know that it's a little bit spoiled but I'll always want to have you in my life." He looked at her pityingly. Was that even a little victoriously, Carl wondered?

"But it's time to go home now, Tam, back to Boston, where we can be together again, just the two of us." He caught Carl's eye as he said it, looking defiant and smug at the same time.

"Darren," Taamarai opened her mouth. She knew she was about to say she was sorry. But was she? She was shocked that

Darren had appeared just now and seen what he had, but she searched her feelings. She ran up against a wall of rage. This should never have been necessary. All of this could have been different long ago if Darren had cared to make it so.

Her anger wavered against another emotion. In her fingertips, on her lips, in her brain, buzzed a blinding euphoria. She closed her mouth and was conscious that she could see Carl out of the corner of her eye, but not what he was doing or how he looked.

"Darren," she sounded stronger this time. "I'm not going anywhere. This is my home." He looked about to interrupt but she didn't give him chance. "I'm sorry you saw what you did just now, but we've been separated for months. I didn't ask you to come back." She hadn't thought about it in such clear terms until now, but it was still the truth. "But if you'd asked me, I would have told you not to. Us, this, it doesn't make me happy. I don't think it does you either, but I can't decide that for you."

For a few seconds, Darren said nothing, then his jaw dropped in total shock. "What? Tam, what are you saying? It's over?" He stared at the floor, processing this for some time, then asked, "You're really just going to throw it all away?"

Darren came towards her and Taamarai sensed Carl step up beside her. She was relieved that Darren stopped dead, but also felt a spike of anxiety. There was no reason for Carl to pretend now, not for her sake, and Taamarai had long known that that was the only reason he stayed polite around Darren. Still, she resisted the urge to take Carl's hand, trusting him and standing her own ground.

"That isn't how I see it, Darren. I haven't been happy for a long time. I tried to tell you that and to find ways to work it out." The anger rose but so did the desire to be done with this. It suddenly seemed intolerable for it to last a moment longer. "It's over."

Darren looked stuck between shock and rage. When he spoke at last, his voice was a deathly hiss. "I don't deserve this." He took in a ragged breath and laid a hand on his chest, as if afraid he might fall down dead. Taamarai flinched but held her tongue, biting back the reassurance that he had trained her to give.

For long enough that it became awkward, Darren said nothing, then he looked up with narrowed eyes. "You always said that when one person walked away from a relationship, they should leave with nothing." She had indeed said it. So had he. She supposed she had known he would turn those words back on her, though she hadn't expected it to be so soon. "So, did you mean it?" He fixed her with a stare.

Taamarai took a deep breath. In between trying to convince herself that nothing at all had happened and that everything hadn't changed, she had spent much of the day at the stall working out what she could afford to lose. The answer was anything, if it would get Darren out of her life. "I did. Whatever's in our joint account and savings is yours."

"Including the stuff in the apartment?" This was more of a surprise, given how much Darren seemed to complain about almost everything she owned. It suddenly struck Taamarai that Darren perhaps hadn't been as shocked by this turn of events as he looked. Still, she took another breath. There were things she would miss, things she loved, but her brother's letter was safe in her purse.

She nodded. "There isn't much that's worth anything but whatever you want, take it."

Darren looked disappointed. Then his eyes lit up with a smile that didn't reach his mouth. "What about the stall?" His voice was stone cold. "You keep going on about how you've built a business here."

Taamarai felt the first touch of fear, but shoved it back down. "I have. It doesn't turn much of a profit yet. Not after I've paid everyone." She clenched her fists at her sides and lifted her jaw. "But if you want any part of it, you'll have to take me to court for it."

"So you didn't mean it." Darren laughed bitterly. "I thought you didn't. Only when it suited you. Like your vows." The words stung, but Taamarai sagged with relief. She knew Darren well enough to know that his efforts to hurt her with words were also a tacit acknowledgement that he was not going to risk a court case.

Darren wrinkled his nose. "And your brother's money?" He

looked like he was trying to get a rise out of her and was surprised
when Taamarai actually smiled. He glowered as she took Carl's
hand.

"No, that's all yours, Darren. You can have every cent in that
account."

"Well, that's something." He crossed his arms over his chest and
took on another face that Taamarai realized she recognized as soon
as it appeared, like an actor playing out his different parts before
her eyes. Now, it was time for the solemn father.

"It looks like I can't change your mind. But I'll always love you,
Tam. You know that, don't you? What you're doing to me? I'll never
love anyone else." He shook his head. "I wish you could know how
hard it is seeing you letting yourself down like this. You could have
done something really great with your life, and instead you're just
throwing it away."

He turned to Carl, apparently unafraid, though Taamarai knew
he was bluffing, relying on her protection. "Did you even finish
high school?"

Taamarai bit her tongue. There was no point arguing back. It
wouldn't achieve anything, only make the conversation longer. She
felt Carl tense beside her and hoped he had worked that out too.

"Not like you'd recognize. So what?" Carl asked coldly.

Darren laughed, that childish, petulant laugh of his. "And you
think you're good enough for someone like Tam? That she'll stick
with you when she couldn't even manage to stay with somebody
like me?"

Carl took a step forward. "Least I know her name." Taamarai
held her breath while Carl continued to eye up Darren. "Your
problem is you *think* you're good enough for her. I know I'm not,
but here she is anyway. Maybe you're right. Maybe she won't be
here tomorrow." Taamarai took a step forward now, moving to
stand right beside Carl, their shoulders touching, hoping that he
understood. If he did, he didn't react, except to say, "But that's her
choice too and it's got nothing to do with you."

Taamarai hadn't really expected Darren to argue. He was scared of Carl, and she was gratified to see him turn his back, but she also knew Darren would want the last word. Sure enough, he looked over his shoulder, tears running down his face. "Goodbye, Tam. You'll realize one day that you threw away the best thing that ever happened to either of us." Then he stumped off, his shoulders down like the lead singer in an indie music video.

When he turned the corner on the stairs and vanished out of sight, the emotions came, too powerful to contain. Taamarai felt her shoulders begin to shake. There was pain, but something else too. A relief like nothing she had ever felt, a crazy, joyful lightness, and deep and confusing shame. It was unthinkable to turn and look at Carl after he'd witnessed the final, broken bargaining that she had thought of as a marriage.

That left her with nowhere to turn until she found her view of the stairs blocked by Carl's chest. He moved in front of her and wrapped his arms around her shoulders, pulling her towards him. Taamarai let her tears come for so many things: the strain of years lying to herself, shielding Darren from others' eyes and keeping her brother's secret from him. But they were also tears of relief for the possibilities of life, stretched out in front of her in glorious uncertainty.

At last she looked up, her eyes bloodshot but her smile as bright as Carl had ever seen. "I'm free." She whispered it only half to him. Carl knew that feeling, and once he might have been angry, insulted even, to see it in her eyes. There had been no bars for her. Now he shared her relief.

There was something else, too, though. Something discomforting. He tried to pin it down and say it before he could decide whether he wanted to or not. "What he said, he's right. Whatever this is, it don't have to last forever. You don't have to...stay." Carl was not sure that he had ever felt so exposed.

Taamarai looked up into Carl's eyes. "Darren isn't right. Maybe not about anything." She laughed a little, but Carl still looked frozen. "Definitely not about you." She leaned back, not pulling away but resting in the circle of his arms so that she could meet his eye comfortably.

"I can't say anything about forever. Not anymore. Maybe he's right that you'd be a fool to trust me. I can only tell you what I feel right now." Taamarai stared hard at his face. Something cautious told her to wait. Something else murmured that she had waited for so many dark years and that, since the day she met him, she had been honest with Carl even when it made her afraid. She reached up and touched his face. "And what I feel is that I love you."

Carl felt his heart stop and start up again. He couldn't say a word. Instead, he pulled her close, kissing her as he had on the roof, hard and full of feeling. Taamarai kissed him back, her arms tightening around him, and he felt himself letting something heavy slip from his shoulders. He had carried it for so long, he didn't remember picking it up.

Epilogue

Taamarai pushed open the door at the bottom of the stairs with her elbow. The shopping bags were heavy and she was tired but happy. It had been a week since the three of them had carried a surprising number of boxes up these new stairs.

Carl had worked in stoic silence while Ali and Taamarai raced each other up and down, joking about how much easier only one flight was. It had been strange leaving Gabriel Heights and laughter kept them focused on the future. Another U-Haul had been returned on time and since then, she and Ali, and Carl under their instruction, had made a decent job of turning the tired two-bedroom apartment into something homey.

The day after she left him, Darren had emptied their joint account and savings. A week later, Taamarai had moved her things, also with Ali and Carl's help, into 502 and relinquished the lease on her own apartment. In the week leading up to that move, she and Carl had not spent a night apart. It had therefore surprised Taamarai when, as they turned in, Carl had asked stiffly if he should sleep on the couch. She could have the room to herself, he had muttered. Taamarai had been confused, then laughed. Did he want to sleep on the couch, she had asked?

The directness felt unfamiliar – bold – both unlike herself and more herself than she had ever been, as she took Carl by the hand, leading him to bed as he had on their first night together. He had followed as she once followed him, but pulled her close the moment the door closed. And so, they had moved in together.

Three months after that, Darren had written to her. She hadn't read the mail for a few days. He'd send one every few weeks, explaining that she'd made a mistake or angrily demanding some new explanation that might make sense of what had happened without needing him to hear a word she had said so far. When she did open the message, it was a request for a continuing share of the profits of the stall.

Though Carl had argued with her, Taamarai had sent him three months of money, then spent a stressful week seeking legal advice. Darren would never be able to say she owed him, Taamarai had sworn to herself. And he would never take anything from her again. It had taken another two months to confirm that the stall was a registered business on which Darren could make no claim. Though he refused to sign them, Taamarai had served him with divorce papers and then determined to forget about Darren.

One night, as they sat at dinner after a long, busy day, she had pushed the business papers over to Carl and been delighted by his shock at seeing himself the named co-owner. He had tried to argue about that, too, and Taamarai had held her ground. It had nothing to do with their relationship, she insisted. The fact was that he did half the work and should have a rightful half share. Carl had been very quiet for a few days and Taamarai had begun to wonder anxiously if, underneath his obvious happiness, she had hurt him in some way.

In bed that night, he had taken the lead and when they lay together afterwards, Taamarai had been about to speak when he touched her lips. Words stumbled out of him.

"I've never had nothing that was mine. Sometimes I would, then I'd mess it up." She knew he was thinking of Ali. It was too soon to tell and she seemed to be doing great, but he was processing a lifetime's worth of repressed guilt at how much he had gotten wrong.

"Carl, you're not going to mess this up," Taamarai reassured him.

"Shh." He kissed her hand. "It's not that. It's...." She held him as his thoughts struggled into sentences. "People look at me different." He let his fingers play in her hair. "They talk to me different. I keep thinking, what do they think, seeing us? Seeing you. With me. With a business." He fell silent and wasn't finished but was clearly stuck.

"Since when have you cared what other people think?" Taamarai asked, joking gently.

He laughed shortly and shifted so that she was resting more comfortably on his arm. "That's fair. I guess I don't."

Taamarai loved the feel of his chest, the rising and falling of his ribs and the steady beat of his heart, and waited quietly.

"I care what you think." He seemed to need to contemplate this admission for some time. "I care what Ali thinks." Finally, he turned and kissed her forehead. "Thank you."

Taamarai had lain awake as he slept, hearing him breathing. She had done it for a million nights, after Darren fell asleep, and felt like she was dying. That night she felt so alive she could hardly keep still.

Then, earlier that month, Carl had asked her, cautiously, what she thought about viewing a place. It was heading for winter and the stall was still doing well – better than they could keep up with on one stove in an open market. He had looked nervous – a rare thing for Carl – when he handed her an envelope of cash. Not much, he had said with embarrassment, in comparison with what her brother had left her. But maybe a deposit?

Taamarai had hugged him, sensing that he didn't want to answer questions, but her hand drifted over his scars and he didn't correct her guess.

They opened the restaurant, a grand but thrifty affair, with paper plates and the name of the burger chain that had occupied the premises before them covered up with a sign painted on the back of old wallpaper. In the rush to open up, they had stayed on at 502 but the lease on the restaurant included the apartment above it and they couldn't afford to maintain rent on two places for long. So, a week ago had been moving day. Again.

Today had been their first day closed since then and Taamarai had spent most of it shopping, looking for the best prices on vegetables and rice. It seemed better than staying home on her own. Ali was running in a competition and Carl had wanted to go and watch her. There was only space on the bus for one parent to accompany each runner and they had insisted that Taamarai shouldn't take a public bus to meet them. She understood. They were on a budget and anyway, Carl and Ali had catching up of their own to do. Still, happy as she had been for them to go off together, Taamarai had hoped they might be home by now and was a little disappointed to see no light on under the door at the top of the stairs. She turned the key in the lock.

As the door opened, the unmistakable but surprising smell of freshly baked cake wafted out to her. She lowered the bags and reached for the light switch, fumbling still for exactly where it was. For a moment, the sight before her was too strange. Then her parents hurried towards her, her mother's arms stretched out, her father more reserved, but still wanting to be near her.

"Amma!" Taamarai rushed forward and into her mother's arms and felt her mother stroking her hair, touching her face, reassuring herself that every part of Taamarai was whole and well and as she remembered it. Taamarai just held her mother. She felt her father's hand on her shoulder, then his arms around them both.

When Taamarai eventually disentangled herself from her parents, still holding her mother's hand, she looked beyond them to where Ali grinned beside a laden table and a large cake.

"Happy birthday!" Ali mouthed it smugly, her eyes shining.

Ali looked like she didn't want to intrude but as Taamarai reached for her, she came over for a long hug.

"I'd forgotten," Taamarai laughed.

"We hoped you had," Ali responded. "Paati was worried you

might think it was weird not getting a call from her on your birthday." Taamarai wondered where Ali had learned the Tamil for grandmother. Probably from her mother. She sounded as if she had been calling Taamarai's mother that her whole life and Taamarai saw her mother beam.

Carl was leaning in the kitchen doorway. He wasn't smiling, and Taamarai knew that to most people he would look an odd member of the party – withdrawn, maybe even sullen. But to her his happiness was obvious, along with a certain radiating self-satisfaction. While Ali turned back to the table, helping Taamarai's parents set up food for everyone, Taamarai walked towards him.

"How did you pull this off?" she asked when she was close enough to be heard without raising her voice. He shrugged. Taamarai held his stare until she couldn't help laughing. "Thank you."

He took a step towards her and reached out to brush hair away from her face. His fingertips always seemed to drift over her skin as he did so with a delicacy that made Taamarai shiver, as if each time he uncovered some precious treasure.

"You happy?" he asked.

Behind them the chatter of Ali and her parents created a bubble. Inside it, between them, everything was quiet. Taamarai nodded. That made him smile, just a brief curl of the lip.

"Good." She saw him glance over her shoulder, checking that everyone else was busy and Taamarai closed her eyes as he leaned in and kissed her. He never said it aloud, though Taamarai did often.

"I love you," she whispered, and felt him squeeze her waist and touch his forehead briefly to hers and she couldn't understand why the rest of the world struggled to hear the words he left unsaid.

Hungry for More?

If you enjoyed *Better Than This* why not try out some of the dishes from the book?

Claim your free electronic copy of *Taamarai's Kitchen: recipes from* Better Than This.*

Download from
https://luciddreamerpublications.com/sales/

 This free recipe book features ten simple, tasty recipes with vegetarian/vegan options, and substitutions to suit any budget and seasonal ingredients.

To claim, simply enter your email address when prompted at the link above, then click 'confirm' in the welcome email to join my mailing list and get updates on future Rose Marzin publications (including a Christmas sequel to *Better Than This,* coming December 2023). You can unsubscribe any time.

**Taamarai's Kitchen* is also available in paperback from Amazon. All proceeds from hard-copy sales of *Taamarai's Kitchen* will be donated to Mahalir Sakthi, a charity empowering women and girls in Madurai, Tamil Nadu (India).

About the Author

Rose Marzin writes contemporary romance (at least for now!). She lives with her partner and two cats in England and writes all the time, about everything. Rose Marzin is a pen name and she writes in her other life as well.

Between writing, she loves cooking, walking in the country, the music of Leonard Cohen, travel and studying languages, especially Tamil.

A lifelong romantic, she loves happy endings, complex characters and understanding how we can get ourselves into hopeless situations, and back out of them. She believes that love comes in different shapes and sizes, in unusual moments and unexpected places, and that we all deserve to be happy, especially when we don't believe that ourselves.

Contact Me

Contact me via my newsletter or at rosemarzin@ luciddreamerpublications.com

Let me know what you thought of *Better Than This* or send me pictures of your creations from *Taamarai's Kitchen*.

I promise never to share your details with third parties.

Printed in Great Britain
by Amazon

17266212R00164